He didn't know it yet, but her trip was a thing of the past.

In a distinctly masculine scrawl, he'd written his instructions for her to come to his office the next morning.

An amused smile curved her lips. As arrogant as she remembered. Theron had only got more gorgeous over the last few years. While she'd been waiting to grow up so she could stake her claim, he'd only become more desirable. More irresistible.

It wouldn't be easy. She didn't imagine he'd fall readily into her arms. The Anetakis brothers were hard. They could have any woman they wanted. They were ruthless in business, but they were also loyal.

She'd made her decision already.

The trip to Europe was off. Her seduction of Theron was on.

THE TYCOON'S REBEL BRIDE

BY
MAYA BANKS

Dear Reader,

How often in life do we think we're on course, know exactly what we want and are taking steps to achieve that goal? There's comfort and security in knowing just where you're headed. But what if you got there and realised it wasn't where you wanted to be after all?

This is the issue that Theron Anetakis struggles with in *The Tycoon's Rebel Bride*. He's ready to settle down, start a family, have a peaceful companionship with the woman he's chosen. That is until Isabella Caplan bursts into his well-ordered existence with the force of an F5 tornado.

She manages to upend his world, but worse, she makes him question what it is he truly wants. And she teaches him the most important lesson of all: to go after what you want and never settle for less.

I hope you enjoy Bella and Theron's story as much I loved writing it. Their story is fraught with excitement and emotion, but most important, a deep and abiding love. It's my hope you'll sigh along with me as they find their path to happily ever after.

Maya Banks

Maya Banks has loved romances from a very (very) early age and, almost from the start, she dreamed of writing them as well. In her teens, she filled countless notebooks with overdramatic stories of love and passion. Today her stories are only slightly less dramatic, but no less romantic.

She lives in Texas with her husband and three children and wouldn't contemplate living anywhere other than the South. When she's not writing, she's usually hunting, fishing or playing poker. She loves to hear from readers and she can be found online at either www.mayabanks. com or www.writemindedblog.com, or you can e-mail her at maya@mayabanks.com.

To Fatin and Ali, two terrific ladies
I am very privileged to know and call friends

One

Theron Anetakis sifted through the mountain of paperwork his secretary had left on his desk for him to read, muttering expletives as he tossed letters left and right. Occasionally one would garner more than a brief glance and then he'd shove it to a separate pile of things requiring his attention. Others, he consigned to the trash can by his feet.

His takeover of the New York offices of Anetakis International hadn't been without its pitfalls. After the discovery that one of the staff members had been selling Anetakis hotel plans to a competitor, Theron and his brothers had cleaned house, hiring new staff. The culprit, Chrysander's former personal assistant, was behind bars after a plea bargain. They had been leery of replacing her and allowing another employee unfettered access to sensitive company information, but in the end, Theron had opted to bring in his secretary from the London office. She was older, stable and most importantly, loyal. Though after the debacle with Roslyn, none of the Anetakis brothers were keen to trust another employee implicitly.

Theron's arrival from London had been met by a pile of documents, contracts, messages and e-mails. Two days later, he was still trying to make sense of the mess. And to think his secretary had already weeded out the majority of the clutter.

He paused over one letter addressed to Chrysander and almost tossed it as junk mail, but yanked it back into his line of vision when he saw what it said. His brow furrowed deeper as he scanned the page, and stretched out his other hand for the phone.

Uncaring of the time difference, or that he would probably wake Chrysander, he punched in the number and waited impatiently for the call to go through. He spared a brief moment of guilt that he would also be disturbing Marley, Chrysander's wife, but hopefully he would pick up the phone before it wakened her.

"This better be damn good," Chrysander growled in a sleepy voice.

Theron didn't waste time with pleasantries. "Who the hell is Isabella?" he demanded.

"Isabella?" There was no doubt as to the confusion in Chrysander's voice. "You're calling me at this hour to ask me about a woman?"

"Tell me…" Theron shook his head. No, Chrysander wouldn't be unfaithful to Marley. Whatever this woman was to Chrysander, it must have been before he met Marley. "Just tell me what I need to know in order to get rid of her," Theron said impatiently. "I've a letter here informing you of her progress, whatever the hell that means, and that she's graduated successfully." Theron's lips thinned in disgust. "*Theos,* Chrysander. Isn't she a bit young for you to have been involved with?"

Chrysander exploded in a torrent of Greek, and Theron held the phone from his ear until the storm calmed.

"I do not like your implication, little brother," Chrysander said in an icy voice. "I am married. Of course I am not involved with this Isabella." And then Theron heard Chrysander's sharp intake of breath. "*Bella*. Of course," he murmured. "I'm not thinking clearly at this hour of the night."

"And I repeat, who is this Bella?" Theron asked, his patience running out.

"Caplan. Isabella Caplan. Surely you remember, Theron."

"Little Isabella?" Theron asked in surprise. He hadn't remembered her at all until Chrysander mentioned her last name. An image of a gangly, preteen girl with ponytails and braces shot to mind. He'd seen her a few times since, but he honestly couldn't conjure an image. He remembered her being shy and unassuming, always trying to fade into the background. She'd been at his parents' funeral, but he'd been too consumed with grief to pay attention to the young woman. How old would she have been then?

Chrysander chuckled. "She's not so little anymore. She will have just graduated. Was doing quite well. Intelligent girl."

"But why are you getting a report on her?" Theron asked. "For God's sake, I thought she might be a former mistress, and the last thing I wanted was her causing trouble for Marley."

"While your devotion to my wife is commendable, it's hardly necessary," Chrysander said dryly. Then he sighed. "Our obligation to Bella had temporarily slipped my mind. My focus of late has been on Marley and our child."

"What obligation?" Theron asked sharply. "And why haven't I heard of this before?"

"Our fathers were longtime friends and business partners. Her father extracted a promise from our father that if anything should ever happen to him that Isabella would be looked after. Our father preceded her father in death, so I assumed responsibility for her welfare when her father also passed away."

"Then you should know that, according to this letter, she's arriving in New York two days from now," Theron said.

Chrysander cursed. "I can't leave Marley right now."

"Of course you can't," Theron said impatiently. "I'll take care of it. But I need details. The last thing you need right now is to be saddled with another concern. New York is my responsibility. I'll count this as yet another problem I've inherited when we traded offices."

"Bella won't be any problem. She's a sweet girl. All you need to do is help her settle her affairs and make sure her needs are provided for. She doesn't gain full control of her inheritance until she's twenty-five or she marries, whichever happens first, so in the meantime Anetakis International acts as the trustee. As you are now the New York representative of Anetakis, that makes you her guardian of sorts."

Theron groaned. "I knew I should have bloody well made Piers take over the New York office."

Chrysander laughed. "This will be a piece of cake, little brother. It shouldn't take you long at all to make sure she's settled and has everything she needs."

Isabella Caplan had no sooner made it past the airport security checkpoint when she saw a man in a chauffeur's uniform holding a sign with her name on it.

She held up a hand in a wave and made her way over. To her surprise, two other men stepped forward to flank her. Her confusion must have showed because the chauffeur smiled and said, "Welcome to New York, Ms. Caplan. I'm Henry, your driver for today, and these gentlemen are from Mr. Anetakis's security detail."

"Uh, hi," she said.

"I've arranged for someone to collect your luggage from baggage claim," Henry said as he herded her toward the exit. "It will be delivered to the hotel shortly."

Outside, one of the security men held the limousine door open for her then got in after her, while the second climbed into the front seat with Henry. Privacy wasn't in the cards, and what she really wanted to do was wilt all over her seat.

Isabella leaned back as the limousine pulled away from the passenger pickup area en route to Imperial Park, the hotel owned by the Anetakis brothers. Chrysander had arranged a suite anytime she visited New York, not that it had occurred often.

This trip had been planned as nothing more than a brief stopover on her way to Europe, a fact she'd apprised Chrysander of in her correspondence. All of that had changed the minute she'd received a terse missive from Theron Anetakis informing her that he was now overseeing her affairs, and he would meet briefly with her in New York to make sure she had everything she needed for her trip abroad.

He didn't know it yet, but her trip was a thing of the past. She was going to stay in New York…indefinitely.

The limousine pulled up in front of the hotel and ground smoothly to a halt. Her door opened, and the security guard who'd ridden in front extended his hand to assist her out. Once inside the lobby, she was ushered immediately to her suite, bypassing the front desk altogether.

Within ten minutes, her luggage was delivered to her room along with a bouquet of flowers and a basket filled with an assortment of snacks and fruits.

If that wasn't enough, just as she settled onto the couch to kick off her shoes and catch her breath, another knock sounded. Grumbling under her breath, she went to open the door and found another hotel employee standing there. He extended a smooth, cream-colored envelope.

"A message from Mr. Anetakis."

She raised an eyebrow. "Which Mr. Anetakis?"

The young man looked discomfited. "Theron."

She smiled, thanked him and then closed the door. She turned the envelope over and lightly ran her finger over the inscription on the front. Isabella Caplan. Had he written it himself?

Experiencing a moment of silliness, she brought the paper to her nose, hoping to catch his smell. There. Light but undeniably his scent. She remembered it as though it were yesterday. He obviously still wore the same cologne.

She broke open the seal and pulled the card from the envelope. In a distinctly masculine scrawl, he'd written his instructions for her to come to his office the next morning.

An amused smile curved her lips. As arrogant as she remembered. Summoning her like a wayward child. At least Chrysander had dropped by her suite to check in on her. But then she'd been a mere eighteen, and he'd also provided a veritable nanny to chaperone her for her visit to the city.

She'd be more than happy to meet Theron on his terms. It would make it that more satisfying to rock him back on his heels. The basis for her big trip to Europe had been solely because that was where Theron lived. Or had lived. When Chrysander married, he and his wife moved to his Greek island on a permanent basis. Which meant that Theron had moved a lot closer to Isabella. Finally.

The trip to Europe was off. Her seduction of Theron was on.

She sank onto the couch and put her feet up on the coffee table. Vibrant red toenail polish flashed in front of her as she wiggled her toes. The delicate ankle bracelet flashed and shimmered with the movement of her foot.

Theron had only gotten more gorgeous over the last few years. He'd lost the youthful handsomeness and replaced it with raw masculinity. While she'd been waiting to grow up so she could stake her claim, he'd only become more desirable. More irresistible. And she'd only fallen more in love with him.

It wouldn't be easy. She didn't imagine he'd fall readily into her arms. The Anetakis brothers were hard. They could have any woman they wanted. They were ruthless in business, but they were also loyal, and honor was everything.

The phone rang, and she sighed in aggravation. The phone was across the room, and she was quite comfortable on the couch. Shoving herself up, she stumbled over to answer it.

"Hello?"

There was a brief silence.

"Ms. Caplan—Isabella."

She recognized the accented English, and a thrill skirted down her spine. It wasn't Chrysander, and given that Piers was out of the country and had never so much as had a conversation with Isabella, it could only be Theron.

"Yes," she said huskily, hoping her nervousness wasn't betrayed.

"This is Theron Anetakis. I was calling to make sure you made it in okay and are settling in with no difficulty."

"Thank you. Everything is fine."

"Is the suite to your liking?"

"Yes, of course. It was kind of you to reserve it for me."

"I didn't reserve it," he said impatiently. "It's my private suite."

She looked around with renewed interest. Knowing that she was staying where Theron spent a lot of his time gave her a decadent thrill.

"Then where are you staying?" she asked curiously. "Why would you give up your suite?"

"The hotel is undergoing renovations. The only available suite was…mine. I'm temporarily taking a different room."

She laughed. "I could have taken other accommodations. There was no need for you to move out for me."

"A few days won't make a difference," he said. "You should be comfortable before your trip to Europe."

She swallowed back the denial that she would be going to Europe. No sense in putting him on guard as soon as she arrived.

There'd be plenty of time to apprise him of her change in plans. Mainly when he had no chance of talking her out of it.

A mischievous smile curved her lips. "I received your summons."

He made a sound of startled exclamation that sounded suspiciously like an oath. "Surely I didn't sound so autocratic, Ms. Caplan."

"Please, call me Isabella. Or Bella. Surely you remember when we weren't so formal? Granted it's been a few years, but I haven't forgotten a single thing about you."

There was an uncomfortable silence. And then, "All right, Isabella."

"Bella, please."

"All right…Bella," he conceded.

He made an exasperated sound in her ear and then said, "Now what was it we were discussing again?"

He sounded distracted, and though he was unfailingly polite, she knew he wanted rid of her as soon as possible. She grinned. If he only knew…

"We were discussing your autocratic demand for me to appear at your office tomorrow."

"It was a request, Bella," he said patiently.

"And of course I will honor it. Shall we say ten in the morning then? I'm a bit tired, and I'd like to sleep in."

"Of course. Don't overtax yourself. Order in room service tonight for dinner. Your expenses are being taken care of."

Of course. She hadn't expected anything less and knew better than to argue. The Anetakis brothers were thorough if nothing else. And very serious about their perceived obligations.

"I'll see you tomorrow then," she said.

He uttered an appropriate goodbye, and she hung up the phone. A smile popped her lips upward as she hugged her midsection in delight. Oh, she'd planned to pay him a visit the next day, all right.

Two

Theron sat back in his chair and surveyed the skyline of the city from his window. After a busy morning of meetings and phone calls, he actually had a few minutes to breathe. He glanced at his watch and grimaced as he remembered that Isabella Caplan was due in a few minutes.

He felt like a revolving door. Isabella was in, and then she'd depart for Europe, while Alannis would be arriving in a week's time from Greece. Thankfully he'd be rid of his obligation to Isabella in short order. He'd make sure she was adequately provided for, arrange for someone from Anetakis International to meet her in London and have a security team see to her safety for the duration of her stay.

Alannis, on the other hand... He smiled ruefully. She was his own doing. He and Alannis had what could only be considered a close friendship. Perhaps an understanding was a better term, though he was open to the relationship growing into more. He knew he needed to settle down now that he was taking over the New York office. It was something he'd discussed candidly with Alannis a few weeks before.

They'd make a good couple. They understood each other. She was from a solid Greek family, old friends of his father's. Her own father owned a shipping company. They were well matched, and so it stood to reason that they'd gravitate toward each other.

She'd give him friendship and children. He'd give her security, protection.

Yes, it was time to settle down. His move to New York was in all likelihood permanent, as Marley had no desire to move from the island where she and Chrysander had made their home. And if he was going to be living here on a permanent basis, it seemed the best course to find a wife and start his family.

His thoughts were interrupted by a knock on his door. He frowned and looked up as he uttered the command to enter.

"Sir, Ms. Caplan is here to see you," Madeline, his secretary, said as she poked her head in the door.

"Send her in," he said brusquely.

As he waited, he straightened in his seat and drummed his fingers idly on the desk. He tried to draw on his vague memories of the girl but all he could picture was a very young Isabella with big eyes, gangly legs and braces. He wasn't even sure how old she was now, only that she'd graduated. Wouldn't that make her somewhere around twenty-two?

He summoned a gentle smile as the door swung open. No need to scare her to death. He was on his feet and walking forward to greet her when he pulled up short, all the breath knocked squarely from his chest.

Before him stood not a girl, but a stunningly beautiful woman. An invisible hand seized his throat, squeezing until he twisted his neck to alleviate the discomfort.

She smiled tentatively at him, and he felt the gesture to his toes. For a long moment, all he could do was gawk like a pimply-faced teenager experiencing his first surge of hormones.

Isabella was dressed in formfitting jeans that slung low on her hips. Her top, if you could call it an actual top, hugged her generous curves as snugly as a man's hands. The hem fell to just above her navel, and that, coupled with the low-slung jeans, bared her navel to his view.

His gaze was drawn to it and the glimmer of silver in the shallow indention. He frowned. She had a belly ring?

He looked up, embarrassed to be caught staring, but then he locked eyes with hers. Long, dark hair fell in layers beyond her shoulders. Long lashes fringed sparkling green eyes. A hint of a smile curved plump, generous lips and white teeth flashed in his vision. Two dimples appeared in her cheeks as her smile broadened.

This was not a woman who could ever escape notice. The past several years had wrought big changes. To think he'd remembered her as someone who faded into the background wherever she was. A man would have to be blind, deaf and dumb to overlook her in a room.

"What the hell are you wearing?" he demanded before he could think better of it.

She raised one dark brow, amusement twinkling in her eyes. Then she glanced down as she smoothed her hands over her hips.

"I believe they're called clothes," she said huskily.

He frowned harder at the playfulness he heard in her voice. "Is this the sort of thing Chrysander allowed you to run around in?"

She chuckled, and the sound skittered across his nape, raising hairs in its wake. It was warm and vibrant, and he derived so much pleasure from it that he wanted her to laugh again.

"Chrysander has no say in what I wear."

"He is—was your guardian," Theron said. "As I am now."

"Not legally," she countered. "You're doing a favor for my father, and you're the executor of his estate as it pertains to me until I marry, but you're hardly my guardian. I've managed quite well on my own with minimal interference from Chrysander."

Theron leaned back against his desk as he studied the young woman standing so confidently in front of him. "Marry? The terms of your father's will is that you gain control of your inheritance when you turn twenty-five."

"Or I marry," she gently corrected. "I plan to be married before then."

Alarm took hold of Theron as he contemplated all sorts of nasty scenarios.

"Who is he?" he demanded. "I'll want to have him fully investigated. You can't be too careful in your position. Your inheritance will draw a host of unwanted suitors who only want you for your money."

Another smile quirked at the corner of her mouth. "It's nice to see you again, too, Theron. My trip was fine. The suite is lovely. It's been awhile since I last saw you, but I'd recognize you anywhere."

Her reproach irritated him because she was exactly right. He was being rude. He hadn't even properly greeted her.

"My apologies, Isabella," he said as he moved forward. He grasped her shoulders and leaned in to kiss her on either cheek. "I'm glad to hear your trip was satisfactory and that the suite is to your liking. May I get you something to drink while we discuss your travel arrangements?"

She smiled and shook her head, and then moved past him toward the window. Her hips swayed, and her bottom, cupped by the too-tight denim bobbed enticingly. He sent his gaze upward so that he wasn't ogling her inappropriately.

It was then that a flash of color at her waist stopped him. He blinked and looked again, certain he had to be mistaken. As she stopped at the window, the hem of her shirt moved so that a tiny portion of what looked to be a tattoo peeked from between her jeans and her shirt.

His gaze was riveted as he strained to see what the design was. Then he scowled. A tattoo? Obviously Chrysander had failed miserably in his role as her guardian. What the hell kind of trouble had she gotten herself into? Tattoos? Talk of marriage?

He closed his eyes and pinched the bridge of his nose as he felt the beginnings of a headache.

"You have a wonderful view," she said as she turned from the window to look at him.

He cleared his throat and sent his gaze to her face. Anywhere but at the breasts hugged tight by the thin T-shirt. *Theos,* but the woman was a walking time bomb.

"Have you already made all the arrangements for your trip to Europe or would you prefer for me to see to them?" he asked politely.

She shoved her fingers into her jeans pockets, a feat he wasn't certain how she managed, and leaned against the window.

"I'm not going to Europe."

He blinked. "Pardon?"

She smiled again, the dimples deepening. "I've decided not to travel to Europe for the summer."

He put a hand to his forehead and massaged the tension. Damn Chrysander for getting a life and saddling him with Isabella Caplan.

"Does this have anything to do with your sudden desire for marriage?" he asked tiredly. "You still haven't answered my question about the intended groom."

"That's because there isn't one yet," she said mischievously. "I never said that I had a man lined out yet, just that I intended to be married before I turned twenty-five. As that gives me three more years, there certainly isn't a need to start ordering background checks."

"Then why aren't you going to Europe? It was your plan at least a week ago according to the letter you sent to Chrysander."

"I sent Chrysander no such thing," she protested lightly. "The man Chrysander hired to oversee my education and my living arrangements informed Chrysander of my trip to Europe. I simply changed my mind."

His hand slipped to the back of his neck as a full-blown migraine threatened to bloom.

"So what do you intend to do then?" He was almost afraid to hear the answer.

She smiled broadly, her entire face lighting up. "I'm getting an apartment here in the city."

Theron choked. Then he closed his eyes as he felt the cinch draw tighter around his neck. If she stayed here, then he would be stuck overseeing her affairs, checking up on her constantly.

Suddenly her impending marriage didn't strike such a chord of irritation. She was twenty-two. True, it was young to marry these days, but certainly not outside the realm of possibility. Perhaps the best thing he could do for her was to introduce her to a man well equipped to provide security and stability for her.

The thought was already turning in his head, gaining momentum, when she spoke again.

"I'm sorry?" he said when he realized he had no idea what she'd said to him.

"Oh, I only said now that we've gotten my arrangements out of the way, I need to be going. I have an apartment to find."

Alarm bells rang at the idea of Isabella traipsing around a city she wasn't intimately familiar with, alone and vulnerable. Hell, she could wind up in an entirely unsuitable neighborhood. And then there was the matter of her security. Now that she was going to be here and not in Europe, he'd have to scramble to get a team in place. The last thing he needed was for her to be abducted as Marley had been.

"I don't think this is something you should do alone," he said firmly.

Her expression brightened. "That's so sweet of you to offer to go apartment hunting with me. I admit, I wasn't looking forward to it on my own, and your knowledge of the city is so much better than mine."

He opened his mouth to refute the idea that he'd volunteered anything, but the genuine appreciation on her face made him snap his lips shut. He let out a sigh, knowing he was well and truly screwed.

"Of course I'll accompany you. I won't have you staying just anywhere. I'll have my secretary come up with a few suitable places for you to view and then we'll go. Perhaps tomorrow morning? You're welcome to stay in the suite for as long as you need it."

She frowned. "But I hate to put you out."

He shook his head. "It's no bother. Chrysander still has a penthouse here that I can use. I need to be looking for a place as well now that I've permanently relocated here."

Her eyes sparked briefly, but then her expression faded to one of neutrality.

"In that case, I appreciate the offer, and I'd love to go apartment hunting with you tomorrow. Shall we do lunch as well?" she asked innocently.

"Of course I'll feed you," he said with a grunt. Why did he feel as though he'd been run over by a steamroller? The idea that this mere slip of a girl had run so roughshod over him left him irritated and feeling like he'd been manipulated, but there was nothing but genuine appreciation and relief in her expression.

She hurried over and threw her arms around him. She landed against his chest, and he had to brace himself to keep from stumbling back.

"Thank you," she said against his ear as she squeezed him for all she was worth.

He allowed his arms to fold around her as he returned her hug. Her body melted against his, and he felt every one of those generous curves he'd noticed earlier. His hand skimmed over the small portion of flesh on her back that was bared by her shirt, and he wondered again over the tattoo he'd seen there. It was driving him crazy not to know what it was.

He shook his head and gently extricated himself from her grasp. "Let me call for the driver so he can return you to the hotel."

She kissed him on the cheek and then turned toward the door. "Thank you, Theron, and I'll see you first thing tomorrow."

He was left rubbing his cheek where her lips had brushed just seconds before. Then he cursed and strode around to the back of his desk again. He'd been so ready to condemn Chrysander for being involved with someone so young, and here he stood lusting over the same girl. Pathetic. It had obviously been way too long since he'd been with a woman.

He buzzed his secretary and quickly gave her instructions to find three or four possible apartments. If all else failed, he could give her Chrysander's penthouse to use.

After talking with Madeline, he then picked up the phone to arrange for a security detail for Isabella.

As he hung up, he remembered that Alannis would be arriving in a week, and he groaned. He'd counted on not having Isabella to contend with when his future fiancée arrived. One woman was always more than enough, and splitting attentions between more than one was a recipe for disaster.

But maybe Alannis would have ideas where Isabella was concerned. Together they could introduce Isabella to a few eligible men—men who'd passed muster with Theron, of course.

Deciding that this was another task suited for Madeline, he buzzed her and asked her to compile a list of eligible bachelors complete with background checks and a checklist of pros and cons. She sounded amused by his request but didn't question him.

Theron sat back in his chair and folded his hands behind his head. This wouldn't take long at all. He'd find her an apartment, find her a husband, and then he would turn his attentions to his own impending nuptials.

"Isabella!" Sadie cried as she threw open the door to her apartment.

Isabella found herself enveloped in her friend's arms, and she returned the hug just as fiercely.

"Come in, come in. It's so good to see you again," Sadie exclaimed as she ushered Isabella inside.

The girls sat down in the small living room, and then Sadie pounced. "So? Did you see him?"

Isabella smiled. "Just came from his office."

"And?"

Isabella shrugged. "I told him I wasn't going to Europe and that I was going to look for an apartment here. He's going to help me," she added with a small smile.

"So he took it well?"

Sadie flipped her long red hair over her shoulder, drawing attention to her pretty features. A year older than Isabella, she had graduated the term before and moved to New York to pursue a career on Broadway.

"I wouldn't say well," Isabella said in amusement. "I think it was more a matter of him wondering what on earth he was going to do with me. The Anetakis brothers take their responsibilities very seriously. They're Greek, after all. And I am one huge responsibility Theron needs to be rid of. I'm sure he was looking forward to herding me onto a plane for Europe as soon as possible."

"Okay, so spill," Sadie said eagerly. "What's your plan?"

Isabella grimaced. "I'm not altogether sure. I had planned

to go to Europe and be an all-around nuisance to him there. Now all of a sudden he's here in New York so I'm having to scramble with the change of plans. The good news is we're having lunch tomorrow when we go apartment hunting. I guess I'll see where things go from there."

"How did he react when he saw you?" Sadie asked. "It's been what, four years since he got a good look at you?"

"Ugh. Yes. Thank goodness I've finally blossomed."

"So? Did he appreciate your womanly charms?" Sadie asked with a wide grin.

"I'm sure he noticed, but I think it was a cross between interest and being appalled. You have to understand that Theron is very, uhm, traditional." She sighed and leaned back against the couch. "But if I had shown up dressed like a good, modest Greek girl, he wouldn't have given me a second glance. I would have been relegated to little sister status, just as Chrysander has done, and there would be no changing it."

"Ah, so better to throw out the challenge from the outset," Sadie acknowledged.

"Exactly," Isabella murmured. "If he never sees me as a nonthreatening entity, then it will be damn hard for him to turn a blind eye to me."

Sadie laughed and clasped Isabella's hands in hers. "I'm so glad to see you again, Bella. It has been too long and I've missed you."

"Yes, it has. Now enough about me. I want to hear all about you and your Broadway career. Tell me, have you landed any roles?"

Sadie twisted her lips into a rueful expression. "I'm afraid the parts have been few and far between, but I haven't given up. I have an audition next week as a matter of fact."

Isabella frowned. "Are you making it okay, Sadie?"

"I have a job. Not many hours. Just a couple of nights a week.

The money is fantastic and I get to look drop-dead gorgeous," Sadie said cheekily. "It'll do until I get my big break."

Isabella viewed her friend with suspicion. "What is this job?"

Sadie grinned slyly, her eyes bright with mischief. "It's a gentleman's club. Very posh and exclusive."

Isabella's mouth dropped open. "You're working as a stripper?"

"I don't always strip," Sadie said dryly. "It's not required per se. But I get better tips when I do," she added with a bigger grin.

Isabella stared for a long moment and then burst out laughing. "Maybe I should take lessons from you. Theron would have to notice me if I did a striptease in front of him."

Sadie joined in her laughter until the two of them were wiping tears. "If he didn't notice you, hon, then the man is dead."

Impulsively, Isabella leaned up and hugged Sadie. "I'm so glad I'm here. I've missed you. I have such a good feeling about being here in New York. Like maybe this will actually work and I can make Theron fall in love with me."

Sadie returned Isabella's hug and then pulled away, a gentle smile on her face. "I have every faith that Theron will fall hopelessly in love with you. But if he doesn't? You're young and beautiful, Bella. You could have your choice of men."

"I only want Theron," she said softly. "I've loved him for so long."

"Well then, we need to think of a way to catch him, don't we?" Sadie said with a grin.

Three

"Alannis," Theron greeted her smoothly. "I trust things are well with you?"

He listened as she uttered a polite greeting, somewhat distant and reserved, but then he expected nothing less. Alannis was steeped in propriety and would never offer a more effusive greeting. It simply wasn't her style.

"I've made arrangements for the Anetakis jet to fly you from Greece to New York a week from now. Will your mother be traveling with you?"

It was a senseless question, meant to be more polite than inquisitive since he knew well that Alannis's family would never allow her to travel to see an unmarried man unchaperoned.

"I'll look forward to your arrival then," he continued. "I've arranged for a night at the opera shortly after you arrive." If all went well, he'd request a moment alone to propose and then the two families could go ahead with the wedding plans.

Of course now he needed to apprise his brothers of his intentions.

He hung up the phone and stared at it for a long moment. He had no doubt Chrysander would, in his newfound loving bliss, be reluctant to encourage Theron to enter into a loveless marriage. Piers on the other hand would shrug and say it was Theron's life and if he wanted to mess it up, that was his prerogative.

In time he could grow to like Alannis very well. He liked her already and respected her, which was more than he could say for a lot of the women of his acquaintance. He knew better than to expect a woman to love him as deeply as Marley loved his brother. But he'd like to think he could be friends with his future wife and enjoy her companionship in and out of bed.

He frowned when he thought of Alannis naked and in his bed, beneath his body. He glanced down at his groin as if expecting a response. If he was, he was disappointed.

Alannis...she came across as cold and extremely stiff. He supposed he couldn't blame her for that. She was most assuredly a virgin, and it would be up to him to coax the passion from her. It was his duty as her husband.

With a sigh, he checked his watch, and to his irritation noticed that Isabella was late. He drummed his fingers impatiently on his desk. Madeline had provided three possible apartments, all in good areas and in close proximity to the Imperial Park Hotel. She hadn't as of yet provided a list of eligible men.

No matter. The first order of business was to see her settled. The sooner, the better. Then he'd worry about marrying her off.

When he heard his door open, he looked up, startled. Then he frowned when he saw Isabella stride inside. On cue, his intercom buzzed, and Madeline's voice announced somewhat dryly that Isabella was on her way in.

"Good morning," Isabella sang out as she stopped in front of his desk.

He swallowed and then his gaze narrowed as he took in her attire. It wasn't exactly immodest, and as such he couldn't offer a complaint. It covered her. Sort of.

His mouth went dry when she put her hands on his desk and leaned forward. Her breasts spilled precariously close to the neckline of her T-shirt, and he could see the lacy cups of her bra as they pushed the soft mounds upward.

He cursed under his breath and directed his gaze upward. "Good morning, Isabella."

"Bella, please, unless you have an aversion to the name?"

He didn't, though it somehow seemed more intimate, particularly when he took the meaning of the Italian form of her name. *Beautiful.* That she was. Stunningly so. Different from the usual sophisticated type of women he gravitated toward, but beautiful nonetheless. There was something wild and unrestrained about her.

He ground his teeth together and shifted his position. Where his groin had remained stoic when thinking of Alannis, it had flared to life, painfully so, as soon as Isabella had walked into his office.

He was her guardian, someone to look after her welfare, and here he sat fantasizing about her. Disgust filled him. Not only was it disrespectful to Isabella but it was disrespectful to Alannis. No woman should have to put up with her soon-to-be fiancé lusting after another woman.

"Bella," he echoed, taking her invitation to use her nickname. It suited her. Light and beautiful.

He rose from his seat and walked around the front of his desk. She eyed him curiously, and he found himself asking her why.

She laughed. "You're dressed so casually today. I'm so used to seeing you in nothing but suits and ties."

"When have you seen me?" he asked in surprise. He

thought back to the times when she would have seen him, and while he probably was wearing a suit, it was hardly a basis for her supposition.

She flushed, and he watched in fascination as color stained her cheeks. She ducked away, her hair sliding over her shoulder.

"Pictures," she mumbled. "There are always pictures of you in the papers."

"And you get these papers all the way out in California?" he asked.

"Yes. I like to keep up with the people looking after my financial well-being," she said evenly.

"As you should," he said approvingly. "Are you ready to go? I have a list of potential apartments. I took the liberty of scaling down the possibilities to a few more suitable to a young woman living alone."

And then he realized he'd made a huge assumption. There was certainly no reason to believe that a woman as beautiful and vibrant as Isabella would be living alone. He refused to retract the statement or ask her if she was currently involved with anyone. But he'd need to know because if she was involved, seriously, then he could forego the whole process of introducing her to prospective husbands.

"I'm ready if you are," she said as she smiled warmly at him.

As they walked from the building that housed the Anetakis headquarters, Theron put his hand to the small of Isabella's back. She felt the touch through her shirt. It seared her skin, and she was sure that if she could look, there would be a visible print from his fingers, burned into her flesh.

After loving him from afar for so many years, she'd been prepared for disappointment, that maybe the man he'd become wouldn't live up to the dream. She'd been so far removed from the truth that reality overwhelmed her. He was more, so much more than she could have imagined. Her feelings hadn't gone away when she'd seen him again. They'd cemented.

She sat next to him in the back of the limousine. In addition to the driver, Henry, there was one additional member of his security detail that rode up front. When they pulled up in front of the first apartment building, she noticed that another smaller car pulled in behind them, and two men got out and cautiously scanned the area.

"I don't remember the security being this tight the last time I visited," she murmured as they walked toward the entrance.

Theron stiffened. "It's a necessary evil."

She waited for him to say more but he didn't volunteer further information.

Three hours later, they'd toured the apartments on his list with him vetoing the first two before she could even offer an opinion. He was tight-lipped about the third but offered her the choice between it and the last on their list.

She stifled her laughter and solemnly informed him that she liked the fourth. He nodded his approval and set about securing it for her.

"Will you have your things shipped to the apartment?" he asked as they walked back to the limousine.

She shook her head. "I plan to shop for everything I need here and have it delivered. It will be quite fun!"

He growled something under his breath but when she turned to him in question, he pressed his lips together.

"I'll arrange for someone to take you shopping," he said grudgingly.

She raised an eyebrow. "I assure you, I have no need of a babysitter, Theron. Chrysander saddled me with one four years ago, and I had no more need of it then than I do now."

"You will not roam all over the city by yourself," he said resolutely.

She shrugged and offered a faint smile. "You could always go with me."

He gave her a startled look.

"No? You seem the logical choice given I don't know anyone else here." She purposely kept silent about Sadie. There was no reason for Theron to know about her, and he wouldn't approve if he knew she worked in a strip club. And find out he would, because the instant she let him know of someone she was spending time with, he'd perform an extensive background check and then forbid her to associate with Sadie any longer.

Not that she'd listen, but she intended for their relationship to get off to the best possible start. Lust was fine for now, but she wanted to make him fall in love with her. She wanted him to need her.

"You're right, of course," he said with a grimace. "I forget you've lived in California and have only been here to visit."

She slid into the limousine and smiled over at him as he got in on the other side. "Does that mean you'll go shopping with me?"

He grunted, and she couldn't hold the laughter in any longer. His eyes widened, and he stared openly at her as though he found the sound of her laughter enchanting.

All the breath left her as she saw for just one moment a look of wanting in his eyes. Just as soon as it flashed, he blinked and recovered.

"I'll see if my schedule permits such a trip," he said tightly.

"Where are you taking me for lunch?" she asked, more to remind him of their date than any real curiosity over their destination. She didn't care where or what they ate. She just wanted the time with him.

"We have an excellent restaurant at the hotel," he said. "My table is always available to me. I thought we could eat there and then you could retire to your suite to rest."

She resisted the urge to roll her eyes. He was smooth. Plotting the easiest way to get rid of her. She couldn't blame him. She was an unexpected burden, and he was a busy man.

She chewed her bottom lip and looked out the window at the passing traffic as she contemplated how to get him to see beyond the inconvenience to the woman who loved him and wanted him so badly.

"Is something the matter, Bella?"

She turned to see him staring at her in concern. She smiled and shook her head. "Just a little tired. And excited."

He frowned. "Maybe you should allow me to see to the furnishing of your apartment. If you would mark down your preferences, I could have a designer work with you so that you didn't have to go out shopping for all the things you need."

"Oh, no, that wouldn't be near as much fun. I can't wait to pick out everything for the apartment. It's such a gorgeous place."

"What are your plans, Bella?" he asked.

She blinked in surprise. "Plans?"

"Yes. Plans. Now that you've graduated, what are your career plans?"

"Oh. Well, I planned to take the summer off," she hedged. "I'll focus on the future this fall."

He didn't say anything, but she could tell such an approach bothered him. She smiled to herself. It probably gave him hives. He and his brothers all were intensely driven with a *take no prisoners* approach when it came to business. They weren't the world's wealthiest hotel family for nothing.

When they arrived at the hotel, Theron ushered her inside as his security team flanked them on all sides. It was odd and a bit surreal, almost like they were royalty.

A few minutes later, they were escorted to Theron's table at the restaurant. It was situated in a quiet corner, almost completely cutoff from the rest of the diners.

He settled her into her chair and then circled around to sit across from her. He dropped his long, lean body into his seat and stared lazily at her.

"What would you like to eat, *pethi mou?*"

Isabella cringed at the endearment. He'd called her the same thing when she was thirteen. *Little one.* It set her teeth on edge. Hardly something that evoked images of the two of them in bed, limbs entwined.

"What do you suggest?" she asked.

She studied his lips, the hard, sensual curve to his mouth and the dark shadow already forming on his jaw. She was tempted, so very tempted to reach across and run the tip of her finger along the roughness and then to the softness of his lips.

What would it be like to kiss him? She'd kissed several boys in college. She said *boys* because next to Theron, that's all they were. Some were very good, others awkward and "pleasant."

But Theron. Kissing him would be like chasing a storm. Hot, exciting and breathless. Her pulse jumped wildly as she imagined the warm brush of his tongue.

"Bella?"

She blinked and shook her head as she realized Theron had been calling her name for a few seconds.

"Sorry," she murmured. "Lost in my thoughts."

"I was suggesting you try the salmon," he said dryly.

She nodded jerkily and tilted her head toward the waiter who was standing beside the table waiting for their order.

"I'll have what he suggests," she said huskily.

Theron placed their order in succinct tones, and the waiter hurried away shortly afterward.

"Now, Bella," Theron said, as he sat back in his chair. He looked comfortable, at ease as he raked his gaze over her features, setting fire to every nerve receptor. "Perhaps we should talk about your future."

A nervous scuttle began in her stomach. "My future?" She laughed lightly to allay the pounding of her heart. If she had any say, her future would be inexorably linked to his.

"Indeed. Your future. Surely you've given it *some* thought?"

He sounded slightly scornful, impatient with someone who didn't have an airtight plan. If he only knew. She'd done nothing else for the past years but plan for her future. With him.

"I've given it a lot of thought," she said evenly.

"You mentioned marriage. Are you truly considering being married before you turn twenty-five."

"I count on it."

He nodded as if he approved. She almost laughed. Would he be so approving if he knew he was her intended groom? A sigh escaped her. She felt so evil, like she was plotting an assassination rather than a seduction.

"This is good," he said almost to himself. "I've taken the liberty of forming a list of possible candidates."

Her brow crinkled as she stared at him in puzzlement. "Candidates? For what?"

"Marriage, Bella. I intend to help you find a husband."

Four

Isabella eyed Theron suspiciously, wondering if he'd suddenly developed a sense of humor.

"You intend to do *what?*" she asked.

"You want a husband. After my initial misgivings, I've decided it's a sound idea. A woman in your position can't be too careful," he continued, obviously warming to his subject. "So I've taken the liberty of drawing up a list of suitable candidates."

She burst out laughing. She couldn't help herself. As absurdities went, this might well take the cake.

He blinked in surprise then frowned as she continued to chuckle. "What do you find so amusing?"

She shook her head, the smile not dropping from her lips. "I'm in the city all of two days, and already you're planning to marry me off. And tell me, what do you mean by *a woman in my position can't be too careful?*"

"You're wealthy, young and beautiful," he said bluntly.

"You'll have every man between the ages of twenty and eighty plotting to wed and bed you, not necessarily in that order."

She sat back in mock surprise. "Wow. And not a word about my intelligence, wit or charm. I'm glad to know I don't plan to wed for superficial reasons."

Theron sobered then reached over and took her hand. Warmth spread up her arm as his fingers stroked her palm. "This is precisely why I felt I should be involved in your search for a husband. Men will try to take advantage of you by pretending they're something they're not. Fortune hunters will pretend they know nothing of your wealth. They'll be swept away by your *kindness* and *generosity.* It's important that any man we allow close to you be carefully vetted by myself."

Her lips twitched, but she dare not laugh. He was utterly serious, and she had to admit that his concern was endearing. It would be quite sweet if he weren't so intent on marrying her off to another man.

"Don't be disheartened, *pethi mou,*" he soothed. "There are many men who would give you the world. It's a matter of finding the right one."

It was all she could do not to cringe. If that wasn't a painful lecture, she'd never heard one.

"You're right, of course," she murmured.

Because what else was she going to say? What she really wanted to do was lean over and ask him if he could be that man. But she already knew the answer to that. He couldn't be that man. At least not yet. Not until he had time to get used to the idea.

Theron smiled his approval and slipped his fingers from hers as he leaned back in his chair. She glanced down at her open hand, regretting the loss of his touch.

"So tell me, what are your requirements in a husband?" he asked indulgently.

She gazed thoughtfully at him, her mind assembling all the

things she loved most about him. Then she started ticking items off on her fingers.

"Let's see. I'd like him to be tall, dark and handsome."

Theron rolled his eyes. "You've described the wishes of half the female population."

"I also want him to be kind and have a sense of responsibility. As I'd prefer not to have children right away, his agreement on that matter would also be important."

"You don't want children?" he asked. He seemed surprised, but then he likely thought all women aspired to pop out a veritable brood as soon as they got a ring on their finger.

"I didn't say I didn't want them," she replied calmly. "Let me guess, you'd want them immediately?"

He arched one brow. "We aren't discussing me, but yes, I see no reason to wait."

"That's because you aren't the one having them," she said dryly.

For a moment it looked as though he would laugh, but then he waved his hand and urged her to continue with her wish list.

She pretended to consider for a moment. "I want him to be wealthier than I am so that my money is a nonissue."

Theron nodded his agreement.

Then she let her voice drop, and she leaned forward. "I want him to burn for me, to not be able to go a day without touching me, holding me, caressing me. He'll be an excellent lover. I want a man who knows how to please me," she finished in a husky, longing-filled voice.

He stared at her, his eyes sharp. For a moment she imagined that there was answering passion in his eyes as they flickered over her exposed skin.

"Do you not agree that these are things I should expect?" she asked softly as she studied him.

He cleared his throat and looked briefly away. Was she affecting him at all or was he completely immune? No, there was something in his eyes. His entire body emanated sexual awareness. She might be young, but she wasn't naive, and she certainly wasn't stupid when it came to men. She'd had her share of interested parties. She could read harmless, flirty interest, and then there was the dark, brooding intensity of a man whose passions ran deep and powerful.

Never before had she felt the intense magnetism that existed between her and Theron. She'd spent years searching for something that even came close to the budding awareness that had begun in her teenage years.

She'd experimented with dates. Kisses, the clumsy groping that had inevitably led to her showing the guy the door. There was only one who ever came close to coaxing her to give him everything. In the end, it had been him who'd called a stop to their lovemaking. At the time, she'd been embarrassed and certain that she'd made some mistake. He'd kissed her gently, told her that he was greatly honored by the fact that he would be her first, but that perhaps she should save her gift for a man who held a special place in her heart.

Then, she'd seen it as a cop-out, a man running hard and fast from a woman who obviously equated sex with commitment or at least a deeper relationship. Now, she was just grateful that she hadn't blithely given away her innocence. Travis was right. Her virginity was special, and she'd only give it to a special man.

She blinked again when she realized Theron was talking to her.

"I think you are wise to place emphasis on…these qualities," he said uncomfortably. "You wouldn't want a man who'd mistreat you in any way, and of course you'll want someone who shares your vision of marriage and a family."

"But you don't think I should want a good lover?" she asked with one raised eyebrow.

His eyes gleamed in the flickering lamp situated in the

middle of the table. Her breath caught and hung in her chest, painful as her throat tightened. She swallowed at the raw power radiating from him in a low, sensual hum.

"It would indeed be a shame if a man had no idea what to do with a woman such as yourself, Bella."

He looked up in relief when the waiter came bearing the tray with their food. Isabella, on the other hand, cursed the timing.

Theron surprised her, however, when after the waiter retreated, he caught her eye and murmured in his sexy, accented voice, "Your mother died early in your childhood, did she not? Has there been no one else to speak to you about…men?"

She gaped at him in astonishment. Did he honestly think she'd reached the ripe old age of twenty-two without ever hearing the birds and the bees talk? She wasn't sure who was more horrified, her or Theron. He looked uncomfortable, and hell, so was she.

Picking up her fork, she cut into her fish and speared a perfectly cooked piece. It hit her tongue, and she nearly sighed in appreciation. It was good, and she was starving.

Theron was clearly waiting on her to answer his question. His really ridiculous question aimed more at a fourteen-year-old, pimply faced girl than a twenty-two-year-old woman.

"If I say no, are you volunteering to head my education?" she asked with a flash of a grin.

He shot an exasperated grimace in her direction. "I'll take that as a yes that someone has spoken to you of such matters."

"Next you'll be offering to buy my feminine products," she muttered.

He choked on the sip of wine he'd just taken and hurriedly set the glass back down on the table. "You imp. It's not polite to make someone laugh as they're taking a drink."

"I'll remind you that you started this conversation," she said dryly.

She watched him take a bite and then wipe his mouth with his napkin. He had really gorgeous lips. Perfect for kissing.

"So I did," he said with a shrug. "I merely wondered if you'd spoken to another woman about men and husbands and of course which men make the best husbands."

"And lovers," she added.

"Yes, of course," he said in resignation.

She sat back in her seat and stared at him in challenge. "You don't want the woman you marry to be a good lover?"

He gave her what she could only classify as a look of horror. "No, I damn well do not expect my wife to be a good lover. It's my duty to…" He broke off in a strangled voice. "We're not discussing my future wife," he said gruffly.

But her curiosity had been well and truly piqued. She sat forward, and placed her chin in one palm, her food forgotten. "It's your duty to what?"

"This is not a conversation that is appropriate for us to have," he said stiffly.

She sighed and nearly rolled her eyes. He sure didn't mind playing the guardian card when it suited him, and the last thing she wanted was to plant any sort of parent role into his brain. But she desperately wanted to hear just what he considered his duty to be to the woman who'd share his bed.

"You're my guardian, Theron. Who else can I talk to about such matters?"

He let out a long-suffering sigh and took another sip of his wine. "I don't expect my wife to be sexually experienced when she comes to my bed. It's my duty to awaken her passion and teach her everything she needs to know about…lovemaking."

Isabella wrinkled her nose. "That sounds so medieval. Have you ever considered that she might teach you a thing or two?"

He set the glass down again, a look of astonished outrage on his face. Clearly the thought had never occurred to him that any woman could teach him anything when it came to sex. So he fancied himself a good lover then. She had to fight off a full-body shiver. She wanted his hands on her body so badly. She'd be more than willing to be an eager pupil under his tutelage.

"I assure you, there is little a woman could teach me that I am not already well acquainted with," he said with a thread of arrogance.

"That experienced, huh?"

He grimaced. "I don't know how our conversation deteriorated to this, but it's hardly an appropriate conversation between a guardian and his ward."

And up went the cement wall again. At least he was struggling to put her back on a non threatening level which meant he considered her just that. A threat.

She dug cheerfully into the remainder of her meal, content to let silence settle over the table. Theron watched her, and she let him, making sure not to look up and catch his stare. There was curiosity in his gaze but there was also interest, and not the platonic kind. He might fight it tooth and nail, but his eyes didn't lie.

When they were finished eating, Theron queried her on her next course of action.

"I'll need furniture, of course. Not to mention food and staple items."

"Make a list of food items and any other household things you need. I'll have it delivered so that you don't have to go out shopping," Theron said. "If you can stand a few more days in the hotel suite, I'll see if I can fit in a furniture shopping trip later in the week."

"Oh, I need everything," she said cheerfully. "Towels, curtains, dishes, bed linens—"

He held up his hand and smiled. "Make a detailed list. I'll see that it is taken care of."

He tossed his table napkin down and motioned for the

waiter. Then he glanced at Isabella. "Are you ready to return to your suite?"

Isabella wasn't, but she also knew that she'd monopolized Theron's entire morning, and he was a busy man. She nodded and rose from her seat. They met around the table, and he put his hand to the small of her back as they headed for the exit.

"I'll see you up," Theron said when they walked into the lobby.

The elevator slid open and the two stepped inside. Even before it fully closed, Isabella turned to Theron. He was so close. His warmth radiated from him, enveloping her. She could smell the crispness of his cologne.

"Thank you for today," she murmured.

She reached automatically for his hands and knew that he was going to lean in to kiss her on either cheek. The elevator neared the top floor.

"You're quite welcome, *pethi mou*. I'll have my secretary call you about your apartment and also about our shopping trip."

As she thought, when the elevator stopped, he leaned down, his intention to kiss her quickly. She stepped into his arms, her body molding to his chest. Before he could react, she circled her arms around his neck and as his lips brushed against her cheek, she turned her face so that their lips met.

The air exploded around them. Their mouths fused and electricity whipped between them like bolts of lightning. At first he went completely still as she boldly kissed him. And then a low growl worked from his throat and he took control.

He yanked her to him until there was no space between them. His arms wrapped around her body, and his hand slid down her spine, to the small of her back and then to cup her behind through her tight jeans.

She was intensely aware of his every touch. His fingers felt like branding irons against her skin, burning through the denim of her pants. His other hand tangled roughly in her hair, glancing over her scalp before twisting and catching in the thick strands.

It wasn't a simple kiss, no loving caress between two people acquainting themselves. It was the kiss of two lovers who were starved for each other.

No hesitancy or permission seeking. It was like they'd been separated for a long period and were coming back together, two people who knew each other intimately.

The warm brush of his tongue coaxed her mouth further open and then he was inside, licking at the edge of her teeth and then laving over her tongue, inviting her to respond equally.

She went willingly, tasting him and testing the contours of his lips.

His hand moved from the curve of her bottom up underneath her shirt and to the small of her back where his large hand splayed out possessively as he crushed her to his hard body.

Her breath caught, and she gasped when his hand made that first contact with her bare skin. Her breasts swelled and throbbed against his chest.

She dare not say a word or make a sound, because if she did, the moment would be lost. He would remember who he was kissing. Instead she focused her energy on making it last as long as she could.

When his lips left hers and stuttered across her jaw and to her neck, she moaned, unable to remain silent. She shivered and quaked, her senses awakening after a long winter.

Never had she felt anything like his lips, whisper soft, across the delicate skin beneath her ear.

Her knees buckled, and she clutched frantically at him. Suddenly his mouth left her, and he cursed. She closed her eyes, knowing the moment was over.

He yanked her away, his hands tight around her arms. His eyes blazed, equal parts anger, self-condemnation and...hunger. She stared helplessly back at him, unable to say anything.

He cursed again in Greek and then shook his head before shoving her out of the elevator. He ushered her to the door where he jammed the card into the lock.

He held the door open with one hand, and she slowly entered. When she turned around to say something, he was already letting the door close. Before it clicked shut, she heard his footsteps hurrying away.

Turning until her back rested against the door, she closed her eyes and hugged her body as she relived those precious moments in Theron's arms.

Their passion had been immediate. The chemistry between them was positively combustible. The last unknown was unveiled. In every other aspect, Theron had proved himself to be her perfect match. All she hadn't known is if they were sexually compatible, not that she'd harbored any doubts, and now in the space of a few heated moments in the elevator, the last piece had fallen neatly into place.

Now all she had to do was make him see it.

Five

Theron pinched the bridge of his nose between his fingers and cursed long and hard. His head felt like someone had taken a hammer to it, he was tired, and he hadn't slept more than an hour the entire night.

Madeline kept staring at him throughout the morning as though he'd lost his mind, and maybe he had. He'd forgotten two meetings and had waved off three phone calls, one of which was from his brother Piers.

All that occupied his thoughts was a dark-haired minx with sultry green eyes. *Theos mou,* but he couldn't forget her kiss, the feel of her mouth on his, her body molded to his as though she were made for him.

He was her guardian. He was responsible for her well-being, and yet he'd damn near hauled her into the bedroom of her suite and made love to her. His body still ached to do just that.

He shook his head for what seemed like the hundredth time since he'd gotten to his office this morning. No matter what he did, though, he couldn't rid himself of her image. Her scent. She was destined to drive him crazy.

Impatient and more than a little agitated, he slapped the intercom. Madeline's calm voice filtered through as she asked what he needed.

"Do you have that list drawn up for me yet?"

"Which list would that be?"

"The list of eligible men I asked for. The men I intend to introduce Bella to."

"Ah, that one. Yes, I have it."

"Bring it in then," he demanded.

A few moments later, Madeline walked through his door holding a piece of paper.

He motioned for her to sit down in front of his desk. "Read them off to me," he said as he leaned back in his chair.

"Did you sleep at all last night?" Madeline asked, her eyes narrowing perceptively.

He grunted and closed his eyes as he waited for her to give up and do as he asked.

"Reginald Hollister."

Theron shook his head immediately. "He's an immature little twerp. Spoiled endlessly by his parents. Bella needs someone…more independent."

Madeline made a show of scratching him off. "Okay then, what about Charles McFadden?"

Theron scowled. "There's rumor that he abused his first wife."

"Bradley Covington?"

"He's an ass," Theron said.

Madeline sighed and quickly crossed him off.

"Tad Whitley."

"Not wealthy enough."

"Garth Moser?"

"I don't like him."

"Paul Hedgeworth."

Theron frowned as he tried to think of a reason why he shouldn't consider Paul.

"Aha," Madeline said when nothing was forthcoming. She drew a large circle around his name. "Shall I invite him to your cocktail party Thursday night?"

"He's too handsome and charming," Theron muttered.

Madeline smiled. "Good, then Isabella should be well pleased."

She glanced down her list then looked back up at Theron. "I think we should include Marcus Atwater and Colby Danforth, as well. They're both single, very good-looking and aren't currently in a relationship."

Theron waved his hand in a gesture of surrender. This was probably best left to Madeline anyway. She'd know better what Isabella would like than he would.

They were interrupted when the door burst open and Isabella hurried in, a bright smile on her face.

"Sorry to just barge in," she said in an out-of-breath voice. "I didn't see Madeline…oh, there you are," she said when she caught sight of his secretary.

Madeline rose and smiled in Isabella's direction. "Quite all right, my dear. I was just on my way out. I'm sure Mr. Anetakis has time for you. He appears to have canceled all his morning meetings."

He scowled at Madeline, not that she seemed particularly intimidated. She patted Isabella on the arm as she passed and then she turned as she reached the door. "I'll hold your calls and take messages."

"That won't be—"

But Madeline was gone, and he was left with Isabella. His gaze drifted over her to see that she was wearing shorts. Really short shorts that bared her long, tan legs.

A dainty ankle bracelet hung loosely at her foot. She wore sandals that showed off bright pink toenails. As his gaze drifted upward again, he saw that the T-shirt she wore was cut off so as to bare her midriff, and the belly ring she wore, and it molded to her breasts like she was planning to enter a wet T-shirt contest.

He wasn't going to survive this.

He cleared his throat and gestured toward the seat that Madeline had vacated. "I'm glad you're here, Bella. We need to talk."

She turned for a moment, and he caught a glimpse of the tattoo on her back. It sparkled almost. It was either a fairy or a butterfly. He couldn't tell and it was making him nuts. He wanted to go over and shove her shorts down so that he could see it.

A tattoo. He caught himself just short of shaking his head again. What had she been thinking? If she was his, she would have never done something so foolish. There was no reason to take such a risk with her body.

Theos, now he was sitting here considering what he would and wouldn't allow her to do if she was his. She wasn't his. Would never be his. He mustn't even entertain such a thought.

She settled into the seat in front of him which put her breasts right in his line of vision. He certainly couldn't accuse her of baring too much cleavage. The shirt covered her very well, but the shirt clung to the globes, outlining every curve and swell. It was far more enticing than the lowest cut neckline.

"What did you want to talk about?" she asked.

By now he was hanging onto his temper and control by a thread. And yet she stared calmly at him as though they were about to discuss the weather. He wanted to beat his head on the desk.

He rubbed his hand tiredly over his face and then focused his attention on the matter at hand.

"About last night…" he began.

She held up her hand, startling him into silence.

"Don't ruin it, Theron," she said huskily.

He blinked in surprise. "Ruin what?"

"The kiss. Don't ruin it by apologizing."

"It shouldn't have happened," he said tightly.

She sighed. "You're ruining it. I asked you not to."

He stared at her open-mouthed. How the hell was he supposed to hand her the lecture he'd carefully planned when she looked positively disgruntled over the fact that he'd brought it up?

"If you positively must regret it, I'd appreciate it if you did so quietly," she said before he could offer anything further. "You're allowed to forget it ever happened, you're allowed to regret it, you're allowed to swear on all that's holy that it'll never happen again. Just don't expect me to do the same, and I'd appreciate it if you didn't patronize me by making light of it. As kisses go, I thought it was damn near perfect. You saying differently doesn't make it any less in my mind."

He was speechless. A first for him. He who always had something to say. He was the diplomat in the family, always the level-headed one, and yet he'd been reduced to a mindless, gaping idiot by this infuriating woman.

She crossed one leg over the other and pressed her hands together in her lap. "Now, if that's all you had on your mind, I thought we could finalize the arrangements for the apartment and plan our shopping trip? I arranged for the papers I need to sign for the apartment to be faxed here since I was sure you'd want to look over everything first."

That was it? She could so easily shove what happened the night before out of her mind when he'd been consumed the entire morning? The memory didn't just consume him, it tortured him endlessly.

Even now he looked at her lips and remembered the lush fullness against his mouth. He could remember her taste and scent. The throb in his groin intensified as he imagined how she'd look, spread naked on the bed as he moved over her.

He cursed again and ripped his mind to present matters.

"Check with Madeline and see if she has the agreement. I'll have my lawyer look it over if you like. As for shopping, Madeline will know my appointments for the week. Stop on your way out and have her schedule a few hours for us to pick out your furniture."

She flashed him a smile that warmed parts of his body that didn't bear mentioning. With a toss of her long hair, she rose gracefully from the chair. She gave him a small wave bye then turned and walked to the door.

A fairy. Her tattoo was a fairy with a sprinkling of glittery dust and sparkles radiating from the design.

It suited her.

But it brought up another very intriguing thought. Did she have any other tattoos? Maybe one or two that could only be seen when she wore no clothing? It made him twitchy as he imagined going on a hunt with her body as the map.

Isabella left Theron's office, biting her lip to keep from smiling. He'd certainly been prepared to give her an endless lecture on how they could never again do what they'd done the night before. It wasn't anything she hadn't expected which was why she'd been prepared to head it off before he ever got started.

She mentally patted herself on the back at the expert way she'd diffused the situation. He was probably still off balance and trying to figure out just what had happened.

She approached Madeline's desk and politely asked if Madeline had received a fax for her.

Madeline tapped a stack of papers at the edge of her desk and then smiled up at Isabella.

"Did he tell you about the party?" Madeline asked.

Isabella picked up the rental agreement and frowned. "No, he didn't mention it."

Just then Theron stuck his head out the door. "Bella, I forgot to tell you that I have a cocktail party planned this Thursday that I'd like you to attend. Seven p.m. at my penthouse. Madeline will arrange for a car to pick you up at the hotel."

Before she could respond, he withdrew into his office again and closed the door.

"Well, there you have it," Madeline said in amusement. "I don't suppose he's also told you the occasion?"

Isabella turned back to the older woman, her frown deepening. "Why do I get the idea that I'm being royally set up?"

"Because you are?" Madeline said cheerfully.

Isabella flopped down in the chair beside Madeline's desk. "Tell me."

Madeline pulled out a sheet of paper and thrust it toward Isabella. "I wasn't told to keep this secret so I'm not violating anyone's confidence, and I figure if I was invited to a party where my future husband was in attendance, I'd at least want the opportunity to buy a gorgeous dress for the occasion."

Isabella snatched the paper and stared back at Madeline in astonishment. "Husband?"

Madeline's eyebrows went up. "He didn't tell you that he was searching for a husband for you? I'd have to think that came up in conversation at least once."

"Well it did, briefly I mean. Just yesterday. He's already found someone?"

Isabella tried to keep the horror from her voice, but she wasn't entirely certain she'd been successful judging by the sympathy she saw in Madeline's eyes. She'd gone along with it because she hadn't really thought that Theron was serious, and even if he was, she figured she had plenty of time.

"Maybe he's in a hurry so that he can concentrate on his own upcoming wedding," Madeline said in a soothing voice.

"What?" Isabella croaked.

"He didn't tell you that, either?" Madeline asked cautiously. "Well then, you didn't hear that from me."

Isabella leaned forward. "Tell me," she said fiercely. "Is he really getting married? Is he engaged?"

Madeline looked stunned for a moment and then understanding softened her expression. "Oh dear," she breathed.

She got up and walked around to where Isabella sat stiffly, her hands gripped tightly in her lap. "Why don't we go into the conference room," Madeline said quietly.

Isabella let Madeline lead her into the other room where Madeline shut and locked the door. "Have a seat," she directed Isabella.

Numbly Isabella complied and Madeline took the seat next to her.

"Now, how long have you had this crush on Theron?"

"Crush?" Isabella asked in a mixture of amusement and devastation. "A crush is a passing fancy. I've been in love with Theron ever since I was a young girl. Back then it might have been considered a crush, but now?"

Madeline shook her head and patted Isabella's hand. "He has the right idea to introduce you to potential husbands then. He has an arrangement with the Gianopolous family to marry their daughter Alannis. She and her mother arrive in New York in less than a week's time. I'd hate to see you…hurt. Perhaps the best thing to do would be to focus on the men Theron has in mind for you. This fascination with Theron can only end in disappointment."

Isabella knew that Madeline was nothing but well-intentioned, but she also had no idea of the depth of Isabella's feelings and her determination.

Still, the thought of Theron already being engaged, of having a commitment to another woman… She closed her eyes against the sudden stab of pain. No wonder he was so put off by the kiss they'd shared the night before.

"When do they marry?" she asked in a soft voice.

"Well, he has to propose first, but from what I understand

that's a mere formality. He didn't want a long engagement, so I imagine it will be this fall sometime."

"So he hasn't even proposed yet?"

Relief filled Isabella. If he hadn't asked, then there was time to make sure he didn't.

Madeline frowned. "I don't like the look you're giving me."

Isabella leaned forward and grabbed Madeline's hands. "You have to help me, Madeline. He's making a huge mistake. I need to make him see that."

Madeline shook her head vehemently. "Oh, no. I'm not getting involved in this. Theron has made his choice, and I make it a point never to get involved in my employer's personal life. You're on your own."

Isabella dropped Madeline's hands with a sigh. "You'll thank me for this when he's a much happier man."

Madeline stood and regarded Isabella with reservation. "Don't make a fool of yourself, Isabella. No man is worth losing your self-respect over. If your mother was alive, she'd probably tell you the same thing."

"My mother loved my father very much," Isabella said softly. "He loved her, too. They'd both want me to be happy. They'd want me to marry the man I loved."

"Then I'll wish you luck."

Isabella smiled, though it was completely forced. "Thank you, Madeline."

They left the conference room, and Isabella quickly signed the rental agreement before handing it over to Madeline. "Let him read over it and if he has no objections, fax it back for me, please."

"And your shopping trip? When would you like to schedule that?"

Isabella shook her head. "I'll go by myself. When is the cocktail party again?"

"Thursday night. Seven."

Isabella slowly nodded. "Okay, I'll be there."

She turned to walk out of the office, her mind reeling from the unexpected shock of Theron's upcoming proposal. She flipped open her cell phone and dialed Sadie's number.

"Sadie? It's me, Isabella," she said when Sadie answered the phone. "Are you busy? I need to come over. It's urgent."

Six

"This is a disaster," Isabella groaned as she flopped onto Sadie's couch.

Sadie sat next to her, concern creasing her pretty features. "Surely you aren't giving up. He hasn't even proposed to her yet."

"*Yet*. That's the problem," Isabella said glumly. "*Yet* means he fully intends to, so for all practical purposes, he's engaged."

"She might not say yes," Sadie pointed out.

Isabella gazed balefully at her. "Would you say no to Theron Anetakis?"

"Well, no…."

"Neither will she," Isabella said with a sigh. She stared up at the ceiling as she raced to come up with a plan. "She's no doubt a good Greek girl from a good Greek family. She'll have impeccable breeding, of course. Her father probably has loads of money, and she would probably drink battery acid before ever going against her parents' wishes."

"That exciting of a girl, huh?"

Isabella laughed as she looked back at Sadie. "I'm not being very charitable. I'm sure she's lovely."

"Now you make her sound like a poodle," Sadie said in amusement.

Isabella covered her face with her hands and tried not to let panic overtake her. Or despair.

"Oh, honey," Sadie said as she wrapped her arms around Isabella. "This doesn't change anything. Truly. You still have to do the same thing as always. Get him to see you. The real you. He won't be able to resist you once he spends time with you."

Isabella let herself be embraced by her friend. At the moment she'd take what comfort she could get. Being alone had never really bothered her, but now she was faced with the possibility of not being with the one person she wanted.

"We kissed last night," she said when Sadie finally drew away.

"See? I told you," Sadie exclaimed.

"Don't celebrate yet," Isabella said glumly. "He gave me the lecture this morning, or at least he tried."

Sadie's eyebrow went up. "The lecture?"

"Oh, you know, the whole *this can never happen again, it was a mistake* lecture."

"Ah, that one."

"At least now I know why."

"Okay, so it won't be as easy as you thought it might be," Sadie said. "That doesn't mean you won't be successful. From what you've said, it hardly sounds like a love match."

Isabella sighed again. "So what do I do, Sadie?"

Sadie squeezed her hand and smiled. "You make him fall in love with *you.*"

"Which requires me to make him see past this whole guardian-ward thing. The kiss was…" She took a deep breath and smiled dreamily. "It was hot. I need him to see me like he did in that moment."

"If I can make this all about me for a moment, I might have a somewhat devious method for getting him to see you sorta naked."

Isabella reared her head back in surprise. "You certainly have my attention now."

Sadie grimaced. "I'd planned to ask you this anyway, and it sounds awfully self-serving, but it *could* work. Maybe."

"So, tell me," Isabella said impatiently.

"I have an audition Saturday night. Well, it's not exactly an audition but it could turn into one if I play my cards right."

"Will you just get on with it?" Isabella said. "The suspense is killing me."

Sadie grinned. "I have to work this Saturday. It's a pretty big deal. A group of rich out-of-towners who only come through once a year. Well this weekend is it and they've rented out the entire club for the night. All of the dancers are expected to be there, no excuses. Only I have this party I was invited to. Howard Griffin is going to be there and Leslie is going to introduce me."

"Who is Howard? And who is Leslie?" Isabella asked.

"Howard is producing a new Broadway musical. And, he's opening auditions next week. They're by invitation only. People would kill to get an invite from him. Including me. Leslie has an invite but then she's all over Broadway right now. Everyone wants her. I met her a couple of weeks ago, and we became friendly. She's doing me such a huge favor by basically recommending me to Howard. I can't miss that party."

"Okay, so what does that have to do with me?"

Sadie gave her an imploring look. "If I don't show up for work, I'll lose my job, and until I land enough steady roles—big roles—I can't afford to lose the kind of money I make at the club. So I thought you could fill in for me just for a few hours Saturday night."

Isabella burst into laughter. "You want me to pose as you in a strip club? Sadie, we look nothing alike. I'm a terrible dancer. I'd get you fired in two seconds."

Sadie shook her head vigorously. "First of all, I wear a blond wig. We're of similar height and with the right makeup, no one would be able to tell the difference if you wear the same clothes. No one looks at your face in that place anyway," she added dryly.

"And how does this have anything to do with Theron? He'd have heart failure if he knew I even went into a strip club, much less worked there for a night."

Sadie's eyes twinkled in amusement. "Just think about it. If he knew where you were, he'd blow a gasket, and he'd no doubt go haul you out by your hair which would of course force him to see you half naked."

"How does this not get you fired?" Isabella asked pointedly.

A frown creased Sadie's forehead. "Damn," she muttered. "I hadn't thought of that."

Isabella instantly took pity on her friend. "How about I cover for you without Theron knowing, and I'll figure out another way to get his attention."

"Are you sure?" Sadie asked anxiously.

"I'll give his security team the slip. Apparently he's hired a team to follow me around New York. If you ask me, he's taking this guardian thing a bit far."

Sadie's mouth gaped open. "You have a security team?"

"Yeah, I know, ridiculous isn't it? I'm to report to his office bright and early in the morning to meet them, and then, according to Theron, I'm to go nowhere without them."

A mischievous smile curved Isabella's lips.

"Why do I get the impression you'll see this security as a challenge?" Sadie asked.

Isabella's grin broadened. "It'll make Theron crazy. See, I can give them the slip to cover for you at the club. Word will get back to Theron. He'll never know where I went, but it'll give him another chance to lecture me. I'll think of some way to get his attention. If the lecture gets too bad, I'll just kiss him again."

"You know, I hope he's worth all this trouble you're going to," Sadie said. "My first thought is that no man is worth all this effort."

"He's worth it," Isabella said softly.

Isabella climbed out of the taxi in front of Theron's office building and walked briskly toward the entrance. She took the elevator up to his floor, and when she entered his suite of offices, she saw a pile of luggage in the hallway.

She walked into Madeline's office to ask what was going on, but saw that the area was full of people. She approached Madeline's desk and leaned over to whisper.

"What's going on?"

Madeline cleared her throat. "Alannis and her mother arrived early. That is your security team," she said, pointing in the direction of three intimidating-looking men. "And the others are this morning's appointments which are waiting because Alannis and company are in his office."

Frowning, Isabella straightened and glanced toward Theron's closed door. Without another word, she headed for his office, ignoring Madeline's calls.

Part of her wanted to run as fast and as far away as she could, but another part of her wanted to see for herself the woman that Theron wanted to marry.

She threw open the door and walked in. Theron who was standing in front of his desk looked up and frowned when he saw her. Not good. An older woman also turned, and her frown was much larger. The last, who had to be Alannis, picked up her head and stared curiously at Isabella.

Of course she wouldn't be homely, because that would be

asking far too much. Alannis and her mother both were extremely beautiful in a classy, elegant way. While her mother wore her hair upswept in a neat chignon, Alannis's hair fell to her shoulders in a dark wave. Her brown eyes were warm and friendly, and she smiled tentatively in Isabella's direction.

"Bella," Theron said gruffly. "Did Madeline not tell you I was occupied?"

The reproach was clear in his voice, but Isabella ignored it. She was too busy trying to find fault with Alannis. Unfortunately for her, unless Alannis's voice was grating, the woman was darn near perfect. She and Theron even looked fabulous together.

"She might have mentioned that you were busy," Isabella murmured.

"Who is this?" Alannis's mother asked imperiously.

Theron turned and smiled reassuringly. "This is the girl I told you about, Sophia." Then he looked back at Isabella. "Isabella, I'd like you to meet Alannis Gianopolous and her mother, Sophia. Ladies, this is Isabella Caplan, my ward."

Sophia immediately lost her guarded look and smiled warmly at Isabella. To Isabella's further surprise, the older woman approached her, holding her hands out.

"It's a pleasure to meet you, Isabella. Theron has told us so much about you. I think it's wonderful that he's taking the time to introduce you to potential husbands."

Sophia kissed her on either cheek while Isabella murmured her stunned thanks.

"I'm very happy to meet you, Isabella," Alannis offered with a shy smile.

"Likewise," Isabella said weakly. Her gaze found Theron's again. She looked for any sign that he was miserable, but his expression was unreadable.

"Was there something you needed?" Theron prompted.

She made a show of checking her watch. "You told me to be here this morning. Well, here I am."

He frowned for a moment and then remembrance sparked in his eyes. "Ah, yes, of course. You'll have to forgive me." He flashed a smile in Alannis's direction. "In the excitement of Alannis's arrival, I completely forgot about your security team. They're waiting out front. I've briefed them on my expectations. Madeline can go over the rest with you."

He walked over to his intercom and proceeded to tell Madeline that he was sending Isabella out to meet her security force.

And just like that, she was dismissed.

Sophia hugged her warmly while Alannis gave her a friendly smile. A moment later, Isabella found herself all but shoved from the office.

Numbly she made her way back to Madeline's desk. Madeline gave her a quick look of sympathy before getting up and circling her desk.

"Come with me," she directed as she all but dragged Isabella after her.

Isabella allowed herself to be led into the same conference room as the day before. Madeline shut the doors behind them and then turned on Isabella.

"I've changed my mind. I've decided to help you."

Isabella looked at her in surprise. "What do you mean?"

Madeline sighed. "Alannis is a lovely girl."

"Now you're making her sound like a poodle," Isabella pointed out, remembering that Sadie had told her the same.

"She's truly lovely, but she's all wrong for Theron. I knew it the moment I met her and her forceful mama. Alannis is a mouse while Theron is more of a lion."

"Maybe he wants a mouse," Isabella murmured.

"Have you given up then?" Madeline asked as she tapped her foot impatiently.

Isabella gave her an unhappy frown.

Madeline shook her head in exasperation. "This marriage

would be a disaster. You know it and I know it. Theron has to know it somewhere behind that thick skull of his."

"I thought you had a strict policy against interfering in your employer's personal life?" Isabella said.

Madeline snorted. "I'm not going to interfere. You are."

Isabella raised her eyebrows.

"He plans to propose this Friday night after the opera. He has the tickets, the ring, the entire evening planned. I've given you the information. What you do with it is up to you," she said with a shrug.

"So soon?" Isabella whispered.

"Yep, which means you have to move fast," Madeline said cheerfully.

Isabella slowly nodded. Her mind was already racing a mile a minute.

"While you're pondering, let me introduce you to your security team," Madeline said as she herded Isabella back toward the office where the men waited. "They have strict instructions to accompany you wherever you go." She turned to Isabella and grinned. "Should make things interesting for you."

Isabella only half heard the introductions. She had to crane her neck to look up to the three really large men. They certainly fit the part of security, though she couldn't imagine that subtlety was their strong point. But then subtlety wasn't one of Theron's strong points, either.

As Madeline introduced the last man, Theron's door opened and he and Alannis and her mother came out. Alannis's arm was linked with Theron's, and his head was bent low as he listened to something she said.

Isabella stared unhappily at them until Madeline elbowed her in the ribs.

"You're being far too obvious, my girl," Madeline whispered. "Smile. You don't want mama bear to be suspicious. I get the impression she can be a barracuda when it comes to her daughter."

Isabella forced a smile to her lips just as the three approached.

"I trust you found your security team to your liking?" Theron asked politely.

Isabella nodded and smiled more broadly. Then in an even bigger effort to kill them all with kindness, she turned her attention to Alannis. "How was your trip? Everything went well, I hope."

Alannis's smile lit up her entire face. "It did," she said in only slightly accented English. "I'm very happy to be here." She glanced up at Theron, and Isabella flinched at the open adoration in her expression.

"We look forward to seeing you again Thursday evening," Sophia said.

"Thursday?" Isabella parroted. She glanced at Theron in confusion.

"The cocktail party," Theron said smoothly. "I, of course, extended an invitation to them, as well."

"Of course," Isabella said faintly.

Though his almost fiancée stood at his side, clinging to his arm like seaweed, Theron's gaze was on Isabella, his dark eyes probing. His eyes traveled a path of awareness over her skin.

Did he love Alannis? Did he feel a certain affection for her? She was older than Isabella, but not by much. Maybe a few years? There was youthful innocence in Alannis's eyes that made Isabella feel older and more jaded.

Isabella swallowed the rising knot in her throat and she turned brightly to Sophia. "I too look forward to seeing you again. Perhaps you can tell me all about Greece. I've heard it's such a lovely place to visit. Maybe I can honeymoon there after I marry."

Sophia beamed at her while Theron's face darkened.

"We should go now," Theron said to Sophia. "You and

Alannis have had a long trip. I'll have your luggage delivered to the hotel at once."

He nodded in Isabella's direction as he and the other women walked past. "Let me know if you have any problems, Bella."

She nodded, unable to speak past the lump in her throat that she couldn't quite make go away.

Seven

He couldn't stop thinking about her. Theron rubbed his face in annoyance as he focused on what Alannis and Sophia were talking about. He'd taken them to lunch after they'd settled into their suite, but he was only reminded of having eaten with Isabella at this same table just before kissing her senseless in the elevator.

Sophia was overjoyed with his plan to propose to Alannis after the opera. He'd planned the evening meticulously, buying tickets for Alannis's favorite performance with a plan to end the evening with an after-party at his hotel.

So why wasn't *he* more enthused?

Alannis was obviously excited. Theron was sure Sophia had hinted broadly of his plan to ask Alannis to marry him, although he'd asked Sophia to keep the details secret.

It seemed everyone was thrilled except him.

"Have you found suitable candidates for Isabella?" Sophia asked.

"Pardon?" Theron asked as he shook himself from his thoughts.

"You mentioned that you were trying to find her a husband," Sophia said patiently. "I wondered if you'd found a suitable match yet."

"Oh. Yes, of course. I plan to introduce her to a few carefully screened men at the cocktail party Thursday night."

Sophia nodded approvingly. "She's a beautiful young girl. She seems lonely, though. I doubt she'll have any problem in finding a husband."

Theron frowned. No, she wouldn't have any trouble in that area. Men would line up for a chance to be her husband.

Sophia leaned forward, excitement lighting her eyes. "You know, Theron, I'd love to sponsor Isabella myself. She could return to Greece with me. Myron would be more than happy to introduce her to any number of fine young men from good families."

"That's a wonderful idea, Mama," Alannis said.

"I'll bring it up to her when I speak to her next," Theron said. He wasn't sure why, but the idea of her leaving the country and marrying someone so far away left a very bad taste in his mouth.

Not that her marrying closer made him feel any better.

He listened as Alannis recounted the details of her trip and her excitement over visiting New York for the first time. But his mind simply wasn't on the present. His thoughts were occupied by a vibrant, dark-haired temptress with a smile that would melt a man at twenty feet.

As if he'd conjured her, he glanced up and saw her across the room. She was walking beside the host as he directed her to a table by the window.

Remembering Sophia's assertion that she seemed lonely, he took the opportunity to study her. Sophia was right. Isabella did look lonely. Even a little sad.

She was dressed in jeans and a plain T-shirt. Her hair was drawn into a ponytail, and the smile that he'd just pondered over was absent.

She was seated by herself, and then she smiled up at the waiter as he attended her. But her smile didn't quite reach her eyes.

For the first time he reflected on her circumstances. How difficult it must be for her to be alone in an unfamiliar city. No family, and if she had friends, he hadn't been made aware of them. Guilt crept over him as he remembered his eagerness to rid himself of her.

Now he was glad he'd planned the cocktail party for Thursday night. Maybe instead of making it a bland gathering at his penthouse with polite conversation, he could turn it into a party at the hotel welcoming Isabella to New York. He could still introduce her to the men on Madeline's list, but at least she would have some fun if he livened things up a bit. A girl her age would be bored silly at the kind of gathering he'd first envisioned.

Feeling marginally better, he refocused his attention on Alannis and reminded himself that in a few days' time, he'd be asking her to be his wife. She'd be his lover and the mother of his children. She was the woman he'd spend the rest of his life with.

Cold panic swept over him until sweat beaded his forehead. Instead of infusing comfort and contentment, the idea of making such a commitment filled him with dread.

Why was he reacting so badly now when a week ago he looked forward to a life with Alannis? It didn't make any sense.

Again his gaze wandered to where Isabella sat. She stared out the window, a pensive expression on her face. Her fingers twined in a strand of her hair as she twirled it absently. She sipped at a glass of water, her gaze never breaking.

Theron reached into his pocket and pulled out his Black-

Berry. He thumbed a quick message to Madeline asking her when his shopping trip was scheduled with Isabella. After all, he didn't want to commit to an appointment with Alannis at the same time.

After a moment, Madeline returned his message. He frowned when he read it and then glanced up at Isabella again. She was going alone? She didn't want him to go with her?

Still frowning, he keyed in his response to Madeline.

Find out when she's going. Clear my schedule.

As soon as Isabella left her suite, a man fell into step beside her. She still hadn't gotten used to this whole security team thing, and it made her nervous to have men dogging her heels everywhere she went.

He got onto the elevator with her and stood in the back as they rode down. When they got to the lobby, they were joined by the other members. Trying to pay them no mind, she headed out the front where the taxis waited.

Before she got two steps toward the first in line, one of the men stepped in front of her, barring her path. She drew up short and sighed in exasperation.

"Look…what is your name?" They had been introduced to her yesterday, but she'd been reeling from the news of Theron's upcoming engagement. "Or should I just call you Huey, Louie and Dewey?"

The man in front of her flashed white teeth as he grinned. So they did have another expression besides the stone statue look.

"You can call me Reynolds." He gestured to the two men on either side of her. How had they gotten there anyway? "The one on your left is Davison and the other guy is Maxwell."

"Okay, Reynolds," she said patiently. She addressed him because he seemed to be in charge, and he was the one blocking her way to the taxi. "I need to get into that taxi. I'm going shopping. There isn't any need for you guys to follow me on a girly trip. You could wait here at the restaurant."

He smiled again. "I'm afraid I can't do that, Ms. Caplan. Our orders are to go everywhere you go."

She muttered an expletive under her breath and watched as amusement crossed his face again. "Even to the bathroom?" she asked sweetly.

"If necessary," he said, wiping the smile right off her face.

"Well, hell," she grumbled. And then she pointed out the obvious. "There's no way we'll all fit in that cab." She smiled as she waited for him to agree.

He looked sternly at her. "We have strict instructions that when you go anywhere, you're to take the car that Mr. Anetakis provided for you. This morning, however, you're to wait here for Mr. Anetakis to arrive."

She frowned and then stared at Davison and Maxwell. If she expected confirmation or denial from them, she was sorely disappointed. They simply stood, their gazes constantly moving around and beyond her as though looking for potential danger.

"You must be mistaken," she said to Reynolds. "I'm not meeting Theron today. I'm going shopping for my apartment."

Reynolds checked his watch and then looked up as a sleek, silver Mercedes vehicle pulled up and stopped just a few feet from where they stood.

To her never-ending surprise, Theron stepped from the car and strode in her direction. As he drew abreast of her, he pulled his sunglasses off and slipped them into the pocket of his polo shirt.

He reached for her hand, his fingers curling firmly around hers. Then he turned to Reynolds. "Is there a problem?" he asked with a frown.

Reynolds gave a quick shake of his head. "Ms. Caplan was about to leave in a cab. I was in the process of explaining to her why she couldn't."

Theron nodded his approval and then turned back to look

at Isabella. "It's important that you heed my instructions, *pethi mou*. The arrangements I have made are for your well-being and safety."

"Of course," she murmured. "I won't keep you. I'm sure you're here to see Alannis." She glanced over at Reynolds. "Will you call for the car since I'm not allowed in a taxi?"

Theron raised one eyebrow. "A few days ago, you wanted me to accompany you. Have you changed your mind?"

Confusion crowded her mind, and she scrunched up her brow as she stared up at him. "I assumed that since you have guests here, that you wouldn't have time to go with me."

"Ah, but you're my guest, too," he said as he pulled her hand. He guided her toward the still waiting Mercedes and gestured for her to get into the back. Then he spoke to Reynolds over the door. "You're excused until we return. My team will handle her security."

Isabella scooted over and settled into the comfortable leather seat. Theron ducked in and sat down next to her. As the driver pulled away, Isabella shook her head and smiled ruefully.

"When was the last time you didn't get your way about something?"

He gave her a puzzled look.

"And why all the security?" she asked in exasperation. "It seems a little pretentious."

His face immediately darkened. "Before they were married, Chrysander's wife was abducted and held for ransom. She was pregnant at the time. Her kidnappers have never been apprehended. I take no chances with the safety of those under my care."

"How are Chrysander and his wife?" she asked softly.

"They are well. Marley prefers the island so they stay there. Chrysander occasionally leaves for business purposes but he doesn't leave Marley or their son very often."

"I can't imagine Chrysander so in love," she said with a laugh. "He seems so intimidating."

"You obviously don't feel the same around me," Theron said dryly.

She let her gaze wander slowly up his body until she stared into his eyes. "The way I feel about you in no way compares to how I feel around Chrysander."

There was a surge in his expression, an awareness that he fought. Such conflicting emotions shooting across his face. Before he could respond to her enigmatic statement, she turned to look out the window.

"So what made you come along this morning?" she asked cheerfully.

Though she was no longer facing him, she could feel his every move. She could feel him breathe so tuned into his body was she.

"I would have thought you'd be far too busy with work and entertaining your…guests."

"I'm not too busy to renege on a promise I made," he said. "I told you I'd go shopping with you and here I am."

She turned then and smiled. "I'm glad. Thank you."

They spent the morning going down the list of items she wanted for her apartment. Theron seemed appreciative of the fact that she didn't take forever making her selections. But the fact was, she didn't really labor over furniture styles because if things went the way she wanted, then she wouldn't be staying in the apartment long term. And if they didn't go her way, she wasn't going to stick around New York City only to watch Theron with another woman.

By two in the afternoon, she was tired and hungry and told Theron so. He suggested they eat at the hotel again. She was thrilled that he didn't seem intent on rushing back to Alannis as soon as the shopping was done.

When they got back to the hotel, they were met by

Reynolds who told Theron he and the others would stand by in the restaurant while they ate. Already, she was growing used to the small entourage of people who followed Theron wherever he went.

If he was this protective over someone he deemed "under his care," then how much more so would he be when it came to someone he loved?

She smiled dreamily as they were escorted to Theron's table. She could handle his overprotective tendencies if it meant he loved her.

"You look well pleased with yourself, *pethi mou*."

Theron's voice broke through her thoughts.

"Are you happy with your purchases?"

She nodded and smiled. "Thank you for going with me."

"It was my pleasure. You shouldn't be alone in such an unfamiliar place."

After placing their orders, Theron sat back in his seat, glass of wine in hand and stared over the table at her.

"So tell me, Bella. Why New York? Did you not have friends in California you preferred to stay close to? And have you given more thought to what you will do now that you've graduated from university?"

She smiled patiently. "My indecision must drive someone such as yourself insane, but I really do have a well-thought-out plan for my future."

"*Such as myself?*" he asked. "Dare I ask what that's supposed to mean?"

"Just that I imagine your life is planned out to the nth degree and that you have no patience for people who aren't as organized as you. Am I right?" she asked mischievously.

He struggled with a scowl before finally relaxing into a smile. "There's nothing wrong with having one's path planned out in advance."

"No, there isn't," she agreed. "I have mine quite mapped

out, however, things don't always go according to plan. The real test is how you manage when your plans fall apart."

"Very wise words coming from someone so young."

She wrinkled her nose and rolled her eyes. "Do you keep reminding yourself of my age so that you aren't tempted to do something outrageous like kiss me again?"

He blinked at her, his mouth falling open. Then he snapped it closed and his jaw tightened. "I thought we agreed to forget that ever happened."

"I agreed to do no such thing," she said lightly. "You can do as you like, however."

He was saved from making his response when the waiter returned bearing their food. Isabella watched Theron all through the meal. His agitation was evident in his short, jerky motions as he dug into his food and ate. Several times he looked up and their gazes connected. There was such fire in his eyes. He wasn't immune to her. Not by a long shot. If she had to guess, he was very affected.

She'd already shoved her plate aside when she heard Theron's name called from a few tables away. She glanced over to see a handsome man approach their table. He was well dressed, he screamed wealth and refinement, and he looked at her with undisguised interest even though it was Theron's name he spoke.

Theron looked less than pleased by the interruption, but it didn't seem to bother the man who now stood at their table.

"Theron, it's good to see you. I was happy to receive your invitation for Thursday night."

He glanced over at Isabella as he spoke and she stared back, wondering if this was one of the men on Theron's infamous potential husband list. She cocked her eyebrow in question but Theron ignored her.

"Are you coming?" Isabella spoke up, offering the man a bright smile. "I have it on good authority that Theron is using Thursday's little soiree to find me a husband."

She grinned at the man's look of surprise. Then he laughed while Theron scowled even harder.

"You must be Isabella Caplan. I'm Marcus Atwater, and yes, I'll be attending. Now that I know my attendance puts me in the running, I wouldn't miss it for the world."

Isabella smiled and extended her hand. "Please, call me Bella."

Marcus took her hand but instead of shaking it, he raised it to his lips and kissed it.

"All right, Bella. A beautiful name for an equally beautiful woman."

"Is there something you wanted, Marcus?" Theron asked pointedly.

His glare could melt steel, but Marcus didn't seem to be too bothered—or intimidated.

Isabella sat back. Maybe Theron seeing another man openly flirt with her would bring out those protective instincts. Maybe, just maybe if he suddenly had a little competition…

"Nothing at all," Marcus said congenially. "I saw you with a beautiful woman, and I merely wanted to make her acquaintance and see for myself if this was the mysterious Isabella Caplan, the same woman you were throwing the party for. I'm glad now that I came over." He glanced back at Isabella again. "Save me a dance Thursday night?"

She smiled and nodded. "Of course."

She watched him walk away before turning back to Theron. "So tell me, how did he rate among the other men you considered for my husband?"

Theron gave her a disgruntled look. "He's toward the top," he mumbled.

"Oh good, then you won't mind if we spend time together at your cocktail party."

"No," he said through gritted teeth. "He would be a good

choice. He's successful, doesn't have any debt, he's never been married before, and he's healthy."

"Good God, tell me you didn't hack into his medical records," she said in disbelief.

"Of course I did. I wouldn't suggest you marry a man who was in ill health or had defects that could be passed on to your children."

He seemed affronted that she'd ask such a question.

She stifled her laughter and tried to look serious and appreciative. "So can I assume that any man at your party has been carefully screened and has your stamp of approval then?"

He nodded slowly but he didn't look happy about the fact.

"Well then, this should be fun," she said brightly. "A room full of wealthy, good-looking men to choose from." She leaned forward and pretended to whisper conspiratorially. "Did you also find out if they were good in bed?"

Theron choked on his drink. He set it down and growled in a low voice, "Of course I didn't question their sexual prowess."

"Pity. I suppose I'll have to find out myself before settling on one man in particular."

"You'll do no such thing," Theron snarled.

Her eyes widened innocently as she viewed his obvious irritation. He looked near to bursting a blood vessel.

His phone rang, and he looked relieved as he fumbled for it. After a few clipped sentences, he rang off and looked over at her.

"You'll have to excuse me, but I have to go. I have an important meeting I can't miss."

She shrugged nonchalantly. "Don't mind me. I was going up to my suite anyway."

Theron motioned for Reynolds and then rose from his chair.

"Your security detail will see you up to your suite. And Bella, don't try to go anywhere without them."

Eight

Theron's admonishment still rang in Isabella's ears the next morning as she plotted her path past her security team. It wasn't that she minded them going shopping with her. They might even be able to offer a male perspective on which dress looked best on her. She wanted to look good for the cocktail party, and not because of the men Theron had invited with her in mind.

As soon as she stepped out of her room, Reynolds fell into step behind her.

"Good morning," she offered sweetly.

"Good morning," he offered in return. "Where would you like to go this morning?" He pulled out his cell phone to call for the car.

"I want to do a little sightseeing," she said. "I don't know my way around the city very well, so I'll have to rely on you."

"What interests you?" he asked politely.

She pretended to think. "Museums, art galleries, oh, and I'd like to see the Statue of Liberty."

He nodded even as he relayed her wishes to the driver.

The elevator opened into the lobby where they were joined by Davison and Maxwell. She halted in front of them, took one look and shook her head.

"Is there a problem?" Reynolds asked.

"Look, if you guys are going to shadow me, I'd prefer you didn't look like something out of a mafia movie. Not to mention, I'd rather not broadcast the fact that I'm going around with three bodyguards. That will only make me more conspicuous."

"What do you suggest then?" Maxwell muttered. He didn't look entirely pleased with her assessment.

"Well, you could lose the shades. They make you look like secret service wannabes."

Maxwell and Davison both removed the sunglasses, and Davison glared at her. She grinned in return.

"Now get rid of the tie and the jacket."

All three men shook their heads. "The jackets stay." Davison spoke up for the first time. To get his point across, he pulled the lapel, opening the jacket enough that she could see the pistol secured by a shoulder holster.

Her mouth fell open. She wasn't a screaming ninny about guns. She well understood the need for them. She just hadn't realized that Theron was that concerned over her safety. For a moment she wavered. Maybe breaking away wasn't such a great idea. But then in her mind, having three hulking men made her much more noticeable than if she zipped to the department store and back for her dress.

"Okay, definitely leave the jackets," she muttered.

They walked outside where the car had pulled around. Davison got into the front while Maxwell walked around to the opposite passenger door and climbed in. Reynolds opened the passenger door closest to her and waited for her to get in.

She faked exasperation and slapped her forehead with her open palm. "Wait right here. I forgot my purse," she said.

"I'll get it for you. You get in," Reynolds said.

But she was already striding toward the hotel entrance. She turned back holding up a finger. "I won't be a minute."

Reynolds started after her, but she quickly rounded the corner and ducked into the men's bathroom. He'd most definitely search the women's room when he figured out she'd disappeared, but hopefully he wouldn't think to look in the men's.

She cracked the door just enough that she could look out. Reynolds hurried by and then he barked into a small receiver that hung from his shirt.

Seconds later, Maxwell and Davison ran by the bathroom, their faces grim. She slipped out with no hesitation and ran for the hotel entrance, hoping they didn't look back in the time it took her to get to a taxi.

She slid into the cab at the front of the line and offered the driver double his fee if he got the hell out fast. Only too happy to comply, he peeled out of the entryway and rocketed in front of two other cars. Horns sounded and angry shouts filled the air but the driver shook his fist and then grinned.

"Where you going, miss?"

She glanced up to see him staring at her in the rearview mirror.

"I'm not completely sure," she admitted. "I need a dress. A really gorgeous dress that'll make a man drool at a hundred yards."

"I know just the place," he said, nodding his head.

Not completely willing to forego any precautionary measures, she asked if he'd wait while she shopped, meter running of course.

He dropped her off in front of the upscale department store then gave her his cell number.

"Give me a ring when you're checking out, and I'll pull up and pick you up here," he said.

"Thank you," she said as she climbed out.

Making sure to keep in a clump of people, she entered the store. She wasn't a complete idiot when it came to safety. She avoided corners, anything off the beaten path and stayed in plain sight of the security cameras. When it was time for her to try on her dresses, she had the extremely helpful saleslady accompany her to the dressing room. After all she needed an opinion.

After trying on six dresses, she found the one. It slipped over her body, hugging every curve like a second skin. The genius of the dress was in its simplicity. There weren't any ruffles or frills, nothing to take away from the shape of her body. It was sheer with spaghetti straps, and it fell two inches above her knee. With a pair of killer heels, she'd have the men eating out of her hand.

She frowned as she realized it didn't really matter what the other men did. Theron was the only one who mattered, and it was anyone's guess how he would react.

She stepped out of the dressing room to show the saleslady. Her entire face lit up.

"It's perfect, Ms. Caplan. Just perfect. With the right shoes, you'll be a knockout."

Isabella smiled. "Would you happen to have a pair of black shoes in a three-inch heel that would go well with this dress?"

The saleslady smiled. "I'll be right back."

A few minutes later, Isabella twirled and glanced down her legs at the shoes. The heels were basically toothpicks, but they did look gorgeous on her.

Not content to sell her an outrageously expensive dress—the shoes were nearly as expensive—the saleslady also insisted she accessorize with just the right jewelry—and handbag of course.

Two hours after she'd ditched her security team, Isabella settled into her cab and headed back to the hotel. When they pulled up, she collected her bags and leaned up to pay the driver.

"Thank you so much. I truly appreciate you waiting for me."

"It was no problem, miss. Good luck at your party tonight. I'm sure you'll knock their socks off."

She smiled and got out then waved as he drove away. With a smile, she entered the hotel and headed for the elevator. The absence of her security team gave her pause, and then guilt crept in. She'd been so caught up in her shopping that she hadn't even considered phoning Reynolds to assure him that she was okay, and she hadn't ever provided him or Theron *her* cell number, so it wasn't as if they could have called her.

With a sigh, she pulled out her cell as she inserted the key to her hotel room. She entered, punching Reynold's number. Then she looked up and saw four very angry men staring at her from inside her room.

Theron rose from where he was sitting on the couch, his eyes sparking. He motioned to the other three men. "Leave us," he said shortly.

Isabella let the bags slide from her fingertips as the three men filed by. Reynolds shot her a disapproving look, and she smiled tentatively.

When they were gone, she glanced over at Theron who had closed the distance between them. He glowered menacingly, his face a veritable storm cloud.

"You didn't fire them, did you?" she asked uneasily.

"Rest assured I know exactly where the blame lies," he gritted out.

She bent down to collect her bags and walked around him toward the couch.

"Taking off from your security team was a foolish thing to do, Bella. Did I not impress upon you the need for them? What were you thinking?"

She turned and regarded him thoughtfully. "I had my reasons," she said simply.

He threw up his hands in exasperation. "What reasons?" he demanded.

She smiled. "Nothing you would approve of. I didn't stay long, and I took precautions. The very nice cabdriver looked out for me quite well, and the saleslady never left my side. Well, except when she went to get me shoes."

Theron's face went gray. "Cabdriver? You entrusted your well-being to a cabdriver?"

"Relax," she said with a grin. "He was a perfect gentleman. He drove me to the department store and waited for me until I was through."

Theron swallowed and looked as though he was fighting to keep his temper in check. Hmm. Theron losing his cool. That might be worth the price of admission.

"Why did you leave without your security team? What was so important that you would risk yourself in this manner?"

She held up her shopping bag. "I needed a dress for the party tonight."

He drew in a deep breath, closed his eyes and then reopened them. He strode over to where she stood and gripped her shoulders. "A dress? You gave me the fright of my life for a dress?"

He shook her as he spoke and she gripped his waist to keep her balance.

"It wasn't just any dress," she murmured as she tried to keep the smile from her face. She probably shouldn't bait him as she was, but making him lose his composure had suddenly become her mission. "I could hardly meet my future husband in anything but a truly spectacular dress."

"You are the most infuriating, frustrating woman I've ever had the misfortune to meet," he growled.

And then he crushed her to him, slanting his lips over hers in a forceful kiss that took her breath away. She moaned as his hands gripped her arms then slid over her back like bands of steel.

He tasted her hungrily, like a man starving, as though he couldn't get enough. Tingling awareness snaked up her spine.

Her breasts throbbed, and her nipples became taut points, pushing at his chest.

The sounds of their kiss, hot and breathless filled the room. One of his hands slipped to the waist of her jeans, and he yanked at her shirt until it came free. Then he slid his fingers over the bare skin of her lower back, right where her tattoo rested. He traced patterns over the small of her back as though he was aware of what was there.

Eager to taste him, she traced his lip with her tongue until he reached out to duel delicately with his own. Warm. So masculine, he tasted of strength, of heady power.

She lost herself in his arms, melted against his mouth. Her pulse sped up and bounced erratically. How she craved him.

His hand crept higher until it collided with her bra strap. He fumbled over the clasp and then he froze.

With a muffled curse, he broke away, his breaths coming hard and ragged. His eyes blazed like an out-of-control fire, and then he dropped his hands from her body like she'd burned him.

He swore again, a mixture of Greek and English and then ran a hand through his hair.

"*Theos mou!* We can't…not again. This mustn't happen again. I'm sorry, Bella."

He held up his hands and then backed away. He paused at the door, his motions haphazard, like he was drunk. Then he turned to stare at her, his eyes still burning with unresolved desire.

"Your security team goes *everywhere* with you. Are we understood? From now on, they even go to the bathroom with you."

She nodded, unable to do anything more. She was shaking too badly. As he left her hotel room, she gripped her arms and rubbed up and down to make the chill bumps go away.

"You can deny it all you want," she whispered to the empty room. "You want me every bit as much as I want you."

Nine

Theron rubbed the back of his neck in an effort to relieve the enormous tension that gripped him. Isabella still hadn't arrived, and he felt equal parts relief and disappointment.

He glanced around the ballroom of the Imperial Park Hotel, taking in the guests milling around, talking and laughing as a jazz band played softly from an elevated platform.

Alannis stood at his side, her hand resting on his arm. Sophia stood on Alannis's other side, her pride in her daughter evident.

He ducked his head to hear what Alannis was trying to tell him and nodded appropriately though his concentration was shot. When he stood to his full height again, his gaze went to the doorway, and his breath caught in his throat.

She was here.

Isabella stood as she gazed nervously over the room. Theron swallowed when he took in her attire. The term *little black dress* could have been coined for this occasion.

The material molded to her every curve and settled a few

inches above her knees. She wore her hair up, drawing attention to the shape of her neck. Stray tendrils escaped the elegant knot and whispered against her skin.

His fingers itched to let her hair down and watch it fall to her shoulders. He wanted to run his hands through the silken mass, feel it twine around his knuckles.

"Oh, look, there's Isabella," Sophia exclaimed.

As if he wouldn't be aware the moment she stepped into the room.

"Excuse me," he murmured to Alannis.

She let him go with a smile, and he made his way to where Isabella stood.

There wasn't an easy way to address the awareness between them, so he chose to ignore it—and the fact that he'd kissed her just hours before.

"Bella," he greeted as he stopped in front of her.

She gazed up at him with wide green eyes, her mouth curving into a smile of welcome.

"Sorry I'm late," she said in a breathy voice. "I don't suppose you saved me a dance?"

He nearly groaned. The thought of having her pressed that close to his body was torture.

"The dancing hasn't begun yet," he said as he turned to look at the band. "Perhaps we can kick it off together, and then I'll introduce you around."

He motioned to the pianist who nodded in return. A slow, sultry melody started, and Theron offered his hand to Isabella. Her fingers trembled slightly in his grip, and he squeezed to reassure her.

When they reached the middle of the area that was the designated dance floor, he turned, and she went willingly into his arms. The moment she melted against him, he went completely rigid.

Her scent surrounded him as the warmth from her touch

invaded his body. There wasn't a single inch that wasn't aware of her feminine form. He glanced down as they made a slow turn and swallowed hard. She wasn't wearing a bra and the lush mounds were pressed tightly against his chest, thrusting upward, straining against the neckline of her dress.

It was all he could do not to haul her out of the room so that no one else could see her.

He blew out his breath as inconspicuously as possible and reminded himself that she wasn't his, and he had no right to be possessive.

It still didn't help the rise of irritation when he saw how many men were staring avidly at Isabella. No, she wouldn't have any shortage of suitors after tonight. He should have been relieved, but he was anything but.

It was all he could do to keep the scowl from his face.

"The party is lovely," Isabella said with a smile as she gazed over his shoulder. "Thank you for putting it on."

"You're quite welcome, *pethi mou*. I want you to enjoy yourself."

"How are your guests settling in?" she asked innocently.

His eyes narrowed. Did she know of his plans for Alannis? It wasn't as if she wouldn't know in a short time, but for some reason he was reluctant to tell her of his impending engagement. Or maybe he was a first-class slimeball who'd kissed another woman within days of asking another woman to marry him.

"They're settling in quite well," he muttered as he swung her around so that she wasn't facing Alannis and her mother.

Guilt filled him. What kind of a man took advantage of a young woman when he had an agreement with another? Even Piers, who was never without a woman, would frown on seducing his ward when he had a soon-to-be fiancée waiting in the wings.

Chrysander wouldn't hesitate to kick his ass all the way back to Greece for pulling this kind of stunt with Isabella.

"So which ones are my potential husbands?" she asked as she craned to see around him.

She wore a mischievous smile that only made her sparkle all the brighter.

"I'll introduce you as soon as our dance is over," he said.

For this moment, she was his, in his arms, and he wasn't in any hurry to relinquish her to her waiting suitors. They'd gathered around the perimeter of the dance area like a bunch of vultures.

For the first time, he regretted his hasty decision to assist Isabella in her search for a husband. She was too young to think of marriage. She should be out having fun, not thinking of making a lifelong commitment.

And yet he was poised to do just that. Panic scuttled up his spine. Then he firmly tamped it down. Before Isabella came bursting into his life, he was more than content over the idea of marrying Alannis and settling down to have children. Isabella was a temporary distraction, nothing more. As soon as things were settled between him and Alannis, and he had Isabella on her path to security and stability, he was confident that he'd embrace his future without hesitation.

When the song died, Theron dropped his hands and then enfolded Isabella's in his. "Come, *pethi mou.* Your party awaits."

Isabella donned her best smile and allowed Theron to lead her through the assembled guests to where the band was set up. Theron held a hand out, and the music stopped. Then he turned to face the guests.

"I appreciate you coming for the occasion to welcome Isabella Caplan to our city," Theron said in a congenial tone.

A waiter approached and handed Isabella a glass of champagne then turned to offer Theron one. He held it at waist level as he continued to address the crowd.

"We're here to enjoy an evening of entertainment, dancing

and conversation. You're welcome to stay as long as you want, or until the booze runs out," he added with a smile.

Laughter rang out.

He turned to Isabella and held out his glass. "A toast to Isabella."

"To Isabella," the guests echoed.

Theron touched his glass to hers and their gazes locked. For a long moment they simply stared. And then Theron broke away and took a long swallow.

Though she had no desire to wade through the eligible men assembled at Theron's request—it reminded her of choosing steaks at a butcher shop—she knew she'd have to play the part, particularly if she had any hope of making Theron jealous. It was a long shot, because he'd have to feel more for her than simple lust, but at the moment, it was her only hope.

The toast seemed to have signaled a return to normal activities. The band struck up a song, and people swirled onto the dance floor.

"Come with me, Bella. It's time to introduce you around."

"You mean it's time for me to meet the men you've assembled for me," she said dryly.

He glanced questioningly at her. "Would you prefer not to meet them? There's nothing to say you have to."

He sounded almost hopeful, a little too eager, which was strange considering the time he had to have spent putting together his group of bachelors. The background checks alone would have been an enormous undertaking. And he wouldn't have left a single stone unturned.

She nearly grinned at the thought.

"No, let's do it. My future awaits and all that," she said lightly.

She curled her hand around his arm and allowed him to lead her into the crowd. Unsure of what she could expect, and maybe she'd thought there would be a stampede, she was pleasantly surprised by how civilized the whole process was.

Theron took her around from group to group, introducing her to business acquaintances and friends. It was easy to immerse herself in the fantasy that she and Theron were together, and he was acting as her escort and not a man bent on marrying her off. It was also easy to forget that just a few feet away, Alannis and her mother stood, observing the goings-on.

Still, Isabella wasn't ready to let reality intrude, and she clung to Theron's arm all the while offering a smile or a laugh as she engaged in conversation. After awhile she found herself relaxing and genuinely enjoying the festive gathering.

She glanced up as an attractive man made his way in her direction, a determined look on his face. She recognized him as Marcus Atwater, the man who'd introduced himself in the restaurant the day before.

"Isabella, my apologies for my late arrival," he said as he approached. He flashed her a charming smile that she couldn't help but respond to. "I was unexpectedly tied up with a client."

He took her hand, and as he'd done in the restaurant, he lifted it to his lips. Then he cast a questioning look in Theron's direction—Theron who stood there looking as though a black cloud had parked itself right over his head.

"I'd like to borrow Isabella. I promise to keep her safe, and you can return to your own date, who, if you don't mind me saying, looks very much like she'd like to dance."

Theron scowled, and Isabella glanced over to see Alannis eyeing the dancing couples with what could only be construed as a wistful glance. Isabella didn't want to feel pity. She wanted to dislike Alannis. If she was a complete ogre it would be so much simpler, but the fact was that both mother and daughter had been extremely nice to her.

"Are you borrowing me for a dance or for some other purpose?" she asked teasingly as she slipped her hand into Marcus's.

"How about we dance first and we can discuss other purposes later," he said with a teasing glint in his eye.

Theron's expression was glacial. She released his arm to go with Marcus, but he caught her free hand, pulling her between the two men.

She stared at him for a moment, waiting for him to speak, but he seemed to be at a loss for words, or maybe he hadn't intended to pull her back.

"Was there something you wanted?" she asked.

He released her hand and shook his head even as he glanced in Alannis's direction. "No. Have fun, *pethi mou*. This is your night."

With one last look in his direction, she turned and let Marcus lead her back to the dance floor. He spun her in an expert move, and she landed against his chest. Laughing blue eyes shone down at her, and she smiled in return.

"Are you still husband hunting or have I arrived too late for consideration?" he asked with mock seriousness.

"Aren't men supposed to run in the other direction when marriage is mentioned?"

"Not if he doesn't mind being caught by the woman in question."

"You're a total flirt," she said with a laugh. "I can't possibly take such a charming man seriously."

He grinned but didn't refute her claim. They danced among the crowd of couples, and every chance she got, she snuck a peek Theron's way.

He and Alannis were dancing on the far side. She stared laughing up into his eyes, and it didn't take a genius to see how starstruck she was by Theron. Isabella knew that feeling well.

"So," Marcus said casually as he spun her around. "Are you going to let him get away?"

She yanked her gaze guiltily away from Theron to meet

Marcus's amused smile. When she realized she hadn't a hope of playing ignorant, she sighed.

"Am I that obvious?" she asked in resignation.

"Only to another man who's scouting the territory for competition."

Her shoulders slumped downward. "I knew I shouldn't have agreed to this farce. This was Theron's idea in case you haven't guessed. He's decided that it's his duty to marry me off with all possible haste."

Marcus touched her chin and gently tugged upward until she looked him in the eye. "Have you told him how you feel?"

She glanced back over at Theron then shook her head. "It's complicated."

"Tell you what. Why don't we head to that corner over there. I'll get us a drink and you can tell me all about it."

Theron's gaze found Isabella again as he listened politely to Alannis and Sophia and the small group of people who stood in the loosely formed circle to the side of the dance floor. He ground his teeth together as Marcus leaned in close to Isabella, his lips hovering precariously close to her ear as he murmured to her.

She laughed and the seductive sound rose over the clink of glasses and the murmur of conversation. Marcus's fingers drifted over her bare shoulder, lingering there much longer than Theron thought appropriate.

He had to swallow the sound of anger that bubbled up in his throat when Marcus trailed one finger down her cheek and then seductively down the side of her neck and around to the hollow of her throat.

Isabella leaned toward Marcus as if seeking his touch, and then he angled in and pressed his lips very softly to the expanse of skin just below her ear.

"*Theos mou,*" Theron growled. "Enough is enough."

"Theron, is something wrong?" Alannis asked.

She touched his arm and he turned to see concern reflected in her eyes.

"It's nothing," he said shortly.

Alannis glanced at Isabella and then back to him. "She seems to be having a good time."

"Yes." His gaze drifted back, his annoyance growing as Marcus grew bolder in his advances. "Excuse me a moment, will you, Alannis?"

He nodded to Sophia and walked as calmly as he was able over to where Marcus was standing with Isabella. He all but had her trapped in the corner, his body moving in like a predator closing in on a kill.

Just as Theron started to speak up, Marcus lowered his head to nuzzle Isabella's neck. Rage exploded over Theron. He closed the remaining distance and grabbed the other man by the shoulder, tearing him away from Isabella.

"What the…" Marcus began but broke off mid sentence. "Theron, is there a problem?"

"Come here, Isabella," Theron bit out. He held his hand out as Isabella stared at him agape.

"What on earth is wrong?" she asked even as she slid her hand into his.

He pulled until she was against his side then he focused the full force of his glare at Marcus.

"Keep your hands off her," he snarled. "You aren't to touch her. You aren't to so much as think about her. Understand?"

Marcus surprised him by grinning and then backing away, hands up. "Whatever you say." Then he winked at Isabella. "I guess I'll go. Something tells me I've overstayed my welcome."

"Oh, no, Marcus, stay." She glanced back up at Theron with a puzzled expression. "I'm sure Theron has no objections."

"I have plenty of objections. He was mauling you in plain view of a roomful of people." Then he turned again to Marcus, as he pulled Isabella even closer. He dropped his voice low enough not to be overheard. "If I find you near her again, I'll take you apart. Are we clear?"

He ignored Isabella's stunned gasp. Marcus merely smiled and continued to back away, his expression smug.

"I'll see you another time, Bella."

"Goodbye," she said softly.

"Come on," Theron said, half dragging her along with him. "You're not to leave my side for the rest of the night."

To his surprise, she didn't offer any argument. Halfway back to where Alannis and her mother still stood, Isabella stumbled, and he turned back quickly to catch her.

"Slow down," she said. "I can't walk that fast in these shoes."

"Sorry," he said gruffly as he righted her. He held her arms until he was sure she had her footing. "Better?"

She nodded and they started back again.

"Isabella, are you all right?" Sophia asked in concern when they walked up.

Isabella offered a smile. "Yes, Mrs. Gianopolous. I'm fine. Thank you for asking."

"Please, do call me Sophia." Sophia reached out and took Isabella's hand from Theron's. "Can I get you something to drink? Have you had anything to eat since you arrived?" She turned to Alannis. "Will you excuse us for a minute, dear? You stay here with Theron while I take Isabella over to grab a bite to eat."

Theron held up his hand to stop the endless stream of chatter. His head was pounding, and what he really wanted was to go pound on Marcus for touching Isabella, for putting his lips on her.

"Just stay here. I'll have a waiter bring around a tray. I'd prefer that Isabella remain with me for the remainder of the evening," he said brusquely.

The older woman's eyes widened in surprise. Alannis

moved closer to Isabella and touched her arm. "Are you sure you're all right, Isabella?" she asked softly.

Isabella's smile seemed strained when she looked back at Alannis. "I'm absolutely fine. Theron overreacted." She shot him a challenging look. "I'm not sure how he expects me to find a husband when he flips his lid the moment a man pays attention to me."

Theron took a deep breath. "I don't think what he was doing could be classified as paying attention to you. *Theos!* He was making love to you for all to see."

She raised her eyebrows and a slow smile formed on her lips. "Is that what they call kissing these days?" she taunted.

His nostrils flared at the reminder of the kisses they'd shared. He was well and truly caught in a trap of his own making.

"His actions were inappropriate," he gritted out. "You are under my protection. You'll heed my instructions."

She turned cheekily to Sophia and Alannis. "I suppose he'll mark that one off the list of potential husbands now." Then she sighed dramatically and dropped her hands helplessly to her side. "I didn't even get to dance again."

"Theron will dance with you," Alannis urged. "He's a marvelous dancer as I'm sure you determined earlier."

"Yes, do go on," Sophia said. "I'll make sure there is food when you return."

Theron's mouth went dry. He wouldn't survive another dance with her lush body molded to his. One torture session was enough for the night.

But then the alternative was letting her dance with the circling pack of men. Men he'd hand-selected.

Over his dead body.

Without another word, he snared Isabella's hand and dragged her toward the dance floor.

"You're hell on these shoes," she murmured as he pulled her into his arms.

For the first time since Marcus had arrived, Theron relaxed as Isabella's soft body molded so sweetly to his. There was an innate sense of rightness. He loved touching her. It was difficult to keep his hands from roaming up and down her soft curves.

"You feel it, too," she said softly as she gazed up at him. "You don't want to. You fight it, but you feel it every bit as much as I do. It's why you've kissed me." She laughed softly. "You can't help but kiss me, just as I'm unable to resist. I don't want to resist."

He shook his head even as his body hummed agreement.

She smiled and put a finger over his lips as they swayed with the music. Then turning, so that his back was to Alannis, she let her hands run down his chest. Her eyes narrowed to half slits, and she parted her lips in a hungry gesture.

He groaned. "We mustn't, Bella. You make me so crazy. You have to stop with the teasing."

"Who says I'm teasing," she asked as she arched one eyebrow.

He took her hands and pulled them away from his body before turning her around again so that they were sideways to Alannis.

"You see her? Alannis. I'm going to ask her to marry me, Isabella."

She greeted his announcement with calm. No visible reaction. Had she already known?

"This must stop between us," he pressed on. "We're going to marry different people."

"And yet you keep kissing me," she said with a slight smile.

"I won't do so again," he vowed.

Instead of deterring her, a sparkle lit her eyes. "If I have anything to say about it you will."

Before he could respond, she pulled away. "I'm starving." Then suddenly she leaned close and murmured so only he could hear. "You say you don't want me, yet you don't want another man to have me. Pretty strange wouldn't you say?"

She turned and walked away, her hips swaying gently as she navigated her way back to where Sophia waited with a plate of food.

Ten

"He still plans to propose tonight?" Isabella asked in dismay. She held the phone tightly to her ear as she listened to Madeline.

Somehow she'd hoped that after last night Theron would have realized he felt *something* for her. Maybe not love. Not yet, but she'd thought he'd wake up to the attraction between them.

Okay, maybe he wasn't completely unaware, but he certainly seemed determined to ignore it.

She closed her eyes as she listened to Madeline confirm that according to Theron, the proposal was still on.

"Thanks, Madeline," she said slowly.

She hung up the phone and sunk lower into the bed. Theron with Alannis. She just couldn't imagine it. Theron needed… someone to shake him up, someone who wouldn't let him get too serious and organized.

He needed someone like her.

Alannis wouldn't challenge him. There was no spark of

chemistry between them. Alannis may as well be his daughter for all the attraction that existed.

Maybe Theron wanted a comfortable, dull marriage.

She shook her head. No, she wouldn't believe that, because if she did, then she'd have to give up, and she wasn't ready to do that yet.

Reaching for the phone again, she dialed the number that Marcus had given her the night before.

"Marcus, hi, it's Isabella," she said when he answered.

"Isabella, how are you?" he greeted.

She sighed. "Word is the proposal is still on."

"Sorry to hear that. I was certain he was ready to beat me into a pulp after our little act last night."

"He frustrates me," she said glumly. "I can't figure the man out. He's so controlled in all things except when he's alone with me."

Marcus laughed. "I can't say I blame the man. I have a feeling you'd try the patience of a saint and the vows of a priest."

"I don't suppose you could get tickets to the opera tonight? I hate to ask, but I'm desperate. He and Alannis are going to the opera and then to an after-party at the hotel where he plans to pop the question."

"I'm sure I could arrange it, but how do you plan to stop him from proposing?"

Isabella sucked in a deep breath. "I'm not sure," she said softly. "But I'll think of something."

"I don't suppose now would be a good time to admit that I hate the opera," Marcus said with a laugh.

She smiled faintly. "I'm not much of a fan myself, but apparently, it's Alannis's favorite performance."

"Then might I suggest an alternative?"

Her brow puckered, and she sat up in bed, the covers gathering at her waist. "What did you have in mind?"

"How about a date? You inform that security team of yours

of your plans for the evening, that you'll be out with me. I have no doubt that they report to Theron regularly." Amusement threaded through Marcus's voice. "It'll drive him crazy that he's stuck at the opera with Alannis, and he'll have no idea what we're up to, whereas if we're both at the opera, he'll be able to see us."

"But what about the party and his plans to propose?"

"I'll have you to the party before Theron arrives. Maybe by then you'll have come up with a plan."

"I don't know," she said slowly.

"Come on," he cajoled. "We'll have a nice dinner. It'll drive Theron crazy. Then you show up at the party. He'll be putty in your hands."

"All right," she conceded.

"Great. I'll pick you up at seven then. I'll call right before I arrive so you can come down."

They rang off, and Isabella swung her legs over the edge of the bed. Once again, she was in need of the perfect dress. Something gorgeous. She wasn't sure they sold dresses for the occasion of preventing a marriage proposal.

She had a sudden, alarming thought. Did this make her the other woman? Was she a femme fatale breaking up a relationship? The thought was an uncomfortable one, and it didn't give her a good feeling. But on the other hand, she knew that she and Theron were right for each other. Even if he didn't know it yet.

Besides, nothing was settled yet. Alannis wasn't wearing a ring, and no commitment had been made. Until that happened, all was fair in love and war.

She almost groaned at the cheesy cliché. Clearly she needed to come up with something more worthy.

Pushing herself up, she headed for the shower. She only had until tonight to figure out how she was going to prevent Theron from making a huge mistake. And to prevent her own heartbreak.

* * *

Theron picked up the phone as Madeline called back to say that Reynolds was on the phone to give his daily report. He listened as Isabella's head of security listed the morning's activities which consisted of shopping and lunch alone at the hotel.

His hand tightened around the receiver when Reynolds got to her plans for the evening. An outing with Marcus Atwater.

He swore in Greek and then quickly recovered. What was she thinking? Surely she couldn't be attracted to a man such as Marcus. He was smooth, too smooth, and he'd been all over her at the party.

Not to mention he had a different woman on his arm every week.

"You are to keep a close watch on her," Theron ordered. "I don't trust this man she's going out with. Under no circumstances are they to be left alone."

"Yes, sir," Reynolds replied.

Theron hung up the phone, his lips compressed into a tight line. Was she just trying to drive him insane? She had to know he wouldn't approve of her spending time with Marcus after what had happened the previous night.

And maybe she could care less what he approved of. She hadn't exactly paid him any heed in any other area.

He leaned back in his chair and opened his desk drawer, reaching for the small black box that nestled in the corner. His fingers touched it, and then he picked it up and opened it.

The diamond ring sparkled in the light as he studied it. Tonight he'd put it on Alannis's finger. So why wasn't he more enthused? Why wasn't he looking forward to his future?

This time next year he could even have a child, a family. He'd be settled. And yet he felt decidedly unsettled about her—about everything.

His intercom buzzed again, and Madeline announced that

he had another important call. She cut the connection before he could ask who. Shaking his head, he picked up the phone.

"Have you lost your damn mind?" Piers's demand made Theron frown.

"Give him a chance," Chrysander said dryly. "Then we'll ascertain whether he's lost his sanity."

"You told Madeline not to tell me it was you two calling, didn't you?" Theron accused.

"Damn right," Piers said. "You wouldn't have answered if you'd known. Coward."

"There's nothing to say I won't hang up," Theron said idly.

"Your sister-in-law wants to know why you didn't tell her you were thinking of getting married," Chrysander said.

Theron winced. "It's not fair of you to use Marley to make me feel guilty, and you know it."

"What are you doing?" Piers asked impatiently, cutting through the banter. "What could you possibly be thinking?"

"What our brother is trying to say is that we were caught by surprise, and we'd like to offer you our congratulations, just as soon as we understand why we're only just now finding out," Chrysander said diplomatically.

Piers made a rude noise. "Not me. If he tells me he's really doing this, I can only offer my condolences."

"What's wrong with me getting married?" Theron asked, surprised by Piers's reaction.

"Besides the fact that I think anyone willingly entering the institution of matrimony has a few screws loose, there is the fact that you're marrying Alannis Gianopolous. She's so wrong for you," Piers said bluntly.

Theron frowned. "Alannis is a perfectly acceptable choice."

There was a long silence, and then Chrysander cleared his throat. "*Acceptable choice?* That's an odd way of putting it."

"I'm more interested as to why you believe she's so wrong for me," Theron said, ignoring Chrysander's remark.

"Hell, Theron, apart from the fact that her father has been angling for her to marry one of us for years, she's…she's…"

"She's what?" Theron cut in.

"Just tell us why the sudden urge to get married," Chrysander said calmly. "And why you felt the need to include such momentous news in an e-mail."

"Probably because of the reaction I'm getting now," Theron said pointedly.

"Since when did you become so worried about what we thought?" Piers asked.

"Does anyone find it ironic that not so long ago, it was me and Piers having this talk with Chrysander about Marley? We were wrong about her, and you two are wrong about Alannis."

Chrysander sighed, and Theron knew he had him. What could he say when it was the truth? Theron and Piers had been quite vocal in their opposition of Marley. They'd also been dead wrong.

"Just be sure this is what you want," Chrysander said in resignation. "And keep us apprised of your plans. Marley will want to make it for the wedding."

Piers wasn't quite so ready to throw in the towel. "Think about what you're doing, Theron. This is the rest of your life you're talking about here."

"I appreciate your concern," Theron said dryly. "I am capable of making my own decisions."

"Tell me how things are going with Isabella," Chrysander broke in, an obvious attempt to change the subject. "Did you get her off to Europe?"

Again, there was a long silence. Theron wiped a hand through his hair wishing he'd pressed Madeline harder about who was on the phone.

"She didn't go to Europe," he said.

"Who is Isabella?" Piers demanded. "Are we talking about little Isabella Caplan?"

"I'll fill you in later," Chrysander said. "Why didn't she go to Europe? Where is she then?"

"She's here. She's decided to stay in New York," Theron said. "And she's not so little anymore," he added, though he was unsure why he felt the need to make that point.

Chrysander chuckled. "Poor Theron. Saddled with women on all sides. I imagine you're cursing me about now."

If he only knew.

"I've seen to Isabella's needs, and gotten her settled in. Everything is fine. *I'm* fine. You two can get off my back now."

"He sounds a little defensive, does he not?" Piers said smugly. "I smell something here. Something rotten. I only wish I was in New York to see for myself."

"You just stay the hell where you are," Theron muttered. "You have a hotel to build."

Piers's laughter flooded the line.

"I'm hanging up now," Theron said before lowering the receiver.

Now he knew how Chrysander had felt when he and Piers had given him such a hard time about Marley. Well-meaning relatives were always the worst.

Eleven

"Have any idea what you're going to say yet?" Marcus asked Isabella as he picked up his wineglass and brought it to his lips.

Reluctantly she shook her head and stared down at her barely eaten entrée. "I don't want to make an ass of myself, but at the same time I have to make him see that I'm not teasing. I'm not playing some silly game nor is he a passing infatuation."

When she looked up, she saw sympathy in Marcus's dark eyes.

"Put yourself in his shoes," she murmured. "You're about to ask a woman to marry you. You've kissed another woman twice, and you're fighting the attraction hard. What could this other woman say to you to convince you not to marry someone else?"

Marcus set his glass down, leaned back and blew out his breath. "Boy, you don't ask the hard ones, do you? I guess it would depend on whether I truly loved the woman I was about to marry, but then I wouldn't propose unless I was certain of that. And if I was certain, and I intended to propose, then nothing would sway me."

"I was afraid you'd say that," Isabella muttered.

"All you can do is try," he said gently. "Nothing ventured, nothing gained, and all that jazz."

A smile cracked through her lips. "Between you and me, we have all the trite clichés wrapped up."

He reached over and took her hand. "Are you sure this is what you truly want, Bella? I hate to see you hurt or disappointed."

"You're sweet," she began.

"Lord, but a man hates to hear those words from a woman's lips," he said with a groan. "It's as bad as hearing *you're just like a brother to me*."

She laughed and relaxed her shoulders. Tension had crept into her muscles until her entire body had gone stiff with it. Marcus was right about one thing. All she could do was try. Whatever happened afterward was out of her control.

"You look fantastic tonight," he said as he relinquished her hands.

"Thank you. You really *are* too sweet."

She glanced down at the royal blue evening gown she'd chosen on her whirlwind shopping trip she'd dragged her bodyguards on earlier that day. She was dressed to kill, or to do battle at the very least. Without false modesty, she knew she looked her best.

High-class, posh, a far cry from her preferred jeans and flip-flops and brightly polished toes. Tonight, she fit into Theron's world. Her world too, for that matter, just one that she'd never fully embraced. She had the money and pedigree, just not the desire to fit in.

"What time should we leave?" she asked anxiously.

She couldn't help the surge in her pulse when she imagined

making it to the party too late. It made her want to break into a cold sweat that she'd arrive only to see the happy couple already engaged.

Marcus smiled reassuringly. "The opera has only just begun. We have quite awhile yet. Not to worry, I'll have you there in plenty of time. Try to relax and enjoy your dinner. It would be a terrible thing if you got to the party and promptly fainted at Theron's feet from hunger."

"Then again, it might be just the thing to stop the show," she said mischievously.

He chuckled and shook his head. "I'm almost sorry I agreed to help you, Bella. I would have rather pursued you myself."

"And if my heart weren't already lost to Theron, I would most gladly lead you on a very merry chase," she said with a grin.

"Then let me say this, and I won't broach the subject again," he said. "Should things not go the way you'd like…I ask only that you remember me."

She reached over to take his hand this time. "Thank you, Marcus. You've been a wonderful friend in the short time of our acquaintance. I hope you'll remain my friend no matter what. This is a lonely city when you know no one."

"I'd be honored. Now eat. I insist. They have the most wonderful desserts here."

Theron sat broodingly in his chair as the performance yawned on before him. Beside him, Alannis watched the stage with rapt attention, her face aglow with delight. Sophia was less enthused, but she still focused her attention forward.

Just before the performance had begun, Reynolds had reported that Isabella was meeting Marcus Atwater for dinner after a day of shopping. There wasn't a whole lot Theron could do at that point given that he was firmly entrenched in his evening. In the end, he gave Reynolds strict instructions to stick to Isabella like glue and make damn sure that Atwater didn't take advantage of her.

He was tempted to send a message to Reynolds from his BlackBerry, but he wasn't sure that Alannis was so ensconced in the performance that she wouldn't notice, and he'd promised that no business would interfere tonight.

Still, he'd requested periodic updates from Isabella's security team, and he'd find a way to check his messages even if it meant a trip to the bathroom.

For the entire next hour, he fidgeted, ready to be done. It irritated him that on a night he should be relaxed, that he was forced to think about Isabella's well-being. She was seeping into his life in a manner that didn't sit well with him. What did it say when he couldn't enjoy an evening with his future wife for thinking about Isabella Caplan?

Alannis touched his arm, and he was jerked from his thoughts.

"Theron, it's over," she whispered.

He glanced quickly to see the curtain drawn. Had he missed the encore entirely? Another nudge from Alannis had him rising to his feet. He offered her his arm and filed out of his box, Sophia and two of his security team following behind.

"And how did you enjoy the show?" he asked as they made their way to the waiting limousine.

"It was wonderful," Alannis gushed. "I do so love the opera. There was a time…"

She ducked her head, but not before he saw a bright blush form on her cheeks.

"There was a time, what?" he prompted.

"Oh, there was a time that I wanted to be an opera singer," she said self-consciously.

"And why didn't you pursue it?"

She smiled and shook her head. "I wasn't good enough. Besides, father wouldn't have had it. He thinks it's a vulgar career."

Theron raised an eyebrow. "I wouldn't have thought such talent could be considered vulgar."

"Oh, he thinks any career that lands you on stage is inappropriate for a young girl. He'd much prefer that I marry well and give him grandbabies."

Something flashed in her eyes before it quickly vanished into blandness.

"And what do you want?" Theron asked curiously.

"I like children," she said simply before turning to her mother.

Theron ushered them into the car and settled in himself as they started for the hotel. His hands were clammy, and he shook his head in disgust over his apparent nervousness. He prided himself on his control and his calm. Nothing about this situation should cause him any anxiety. He had his future mapped out, and everything was proceeding exactly as planned.

After that reminder, he relaxed in his seat. He felt in his pocket for the ring then let his hand fall when he reassured himself that it was there.

Traffic moved quickly, and a half hour later, they arrived at the hotel. Alannis yawned as Theron helped her out of the car.

He smiled and took her hand. "I hope you aren't too tired for the party."

"What party?" she asked in surprise.

Sophia smiled and tucked her arm in Alannis's. "He's planned a party in your honor, dear. It's a very special night." She winked at Theron behind Alannis's back, and Theron felt his unease increase.

"A party for me? It sounds so exciting," Alannis said, her eyes sparkling in delight.

She really was quite lovely, in a quiet, understated way. For some reason, however, he couldn't chase the image of another woman from his mind when he looked at her.

He glanced away, his jaw tight as they walked through the

lobby toward the ballroom. When they entered, the band struck up and confetti fell from the ceiling.

Alannis looked up, her eyes rapt. She held her fingers up to catch the flurries as they spiraled down like crazy, neon snow.

"Oh, it's wonderful, Theron," she breathed.

He nudged her forward again, his heart pounding with each step they took. His hand drifted into his pocket as they neared the center of the room. The edges of the box scraped against his fingers, and he fumbled with it, coaxing the velvet box inside free.

Would she be as excited when he asked her to be his wife? Would he? Or was he about to make the biggest mistake of his life?

"Alannis…" he began, cursing the fact that his voice was so shaky.

She turned and looked up at him, eyes shining and a smile curving her lips. Lips that he had no desire to kiss. "Yes, Theron?"

Isabella sat forward in her seat, straining to see out the front window. "What's the hold up?" she asked desperately. "Why aren't we moving?"

Marcus took hold of her shoulder. "It's a wreck, Bella. Calm down, sit back. We'll get there. He won't propose as soon as the party starts."

She stared out the window at the sea of cars all at a dead stop. They'd never get out of this in time.

In a burst of frustration, she reached for the door handle and yanked the door open.

"Bella, what are you doing? Get back in the car. You can't go running through the streets of New York City," Marcus exclaimed as she clambered out.

She turned and bent to stare back into the car where he sat. "I have to go, Marcus. We'll never make it in time and you know it. I have to get there before he proposes. I can't…" She swallowed and looked away for a moment. When she looked back, tears clouded her vision. "I have to go. Thank you for everything."

She closed the door, picked up the long skirt of her dress in her hands and ran through the traffic, ignoring the honks as she cut in front of cars trying to inch forward. She heard the shouts of Reynolds and glanced back to see that he was hotfooting it down the street after her. Turning, she kept on running. She didn't have time to stop and explain.

Unsure of where she was going, she kept to the sidewalk, paralleling the traffic. When she saw an unoccupied taxi, she ran to the window and tapped.

The cabbie gave her a disgruntled look and rolled down his window. "Look lady, no one's going anywhere in this mess."

She held up a hand. "Please, can you tell me how to get to Imperial Park Hotel? How far am I?"

His eyes narrowed as he stared back at her. "As the crow flies, not far. If you cut over from this street a block then up two, you'll be six or so blocks from the hotel. Just head straight for five blocks, turn left and you'll see it as soon as you round the corner."

With a murmured thanks, she gathered her dress, shed her shoes and took off running as fast as she could go.

"Hey, lady, you left your shoes!" the man shouted from behind her.

By the time she'd gone three blocks, it had started to rain lightly. Not that it mattered. She already looked a fright, and her hopes of looking like a million dollars when she burst into Theron's engagement party were doomed.

When she rounded the corner of the last block, the heavens opened and it began to pour. Blinking the water from her eyes, she dashed toward the hotel, avoiding the puddles that were already forming beneath her feet.

Please, oh please, let me be on time.

Her hair was plastered to her face by the time she made it under the awning. Water dripped from her body and from the sodden mass of her ruined dress. Her feet ached, and she was sure she'd cut her right foot on something.

Ignoring the inquisitive looks thrown her way, she rushed past several people who were trying to hurry inside. Skidding on the polished floor, she righted herself and ran as fast as she could with a wet dress wrapped around her legs.

As she neared the ballroom, she heard cheers from inside and then mad clapping. *No.* She couldn't be too late, she couldn't.

She thrust herself inside the door, her gaze wildly searching the crowd gathered. There, in the middle, stood Theron and Alannis. Alannis was beaming from head to toe as she gazed lovingly up at Theron who was smiling down at her. Around them people clapped and then they brought their glasses up in a toast.

The words were lost to Isabella. She heard nothing except the buzz in her ears. She saw nothing but how radiant Alannis looked. It was a stark contrast to how dead Isabella felt in that moment.

Slowly, every part of her aching, she turned, tears swimming in her eyes, and walked slowly back out of the ballroom. She nearly ran into Reynolds as he hurried up to her. Keeping her head down, she continued on, ignoring his demands to know if she was all right.

All right? Nothing would ever be all right again.

Gradually the sounds of laughter and happiness diminished, and she was left with only the murmur of the people milling about the lobby.

A tear slipped down her cheek, and she made no move to wipe it. Who would notice? It would look like she was caught in the rain as she had been.

As she neared the entrance, Marcus ran in and stopped abruptly in front of her.

"Isabella, are you all right?" he demanded. "That was a foolish thing you did."

He caught her shoulders and spun her so that she looked at him. And then he must have seen the misery in her eyes because his tirade ceased, and gentle understanding shone in his eyes.

"You were too late?" he asked needlessly.

She nodded and squeezed her eyes shut as more hot tears escaped.

He gathered her in his arms. "I'm so sorry, Bella. I promised I would have you here on time."

"It wasn't your fault," she whispered.

"Come on, let me get you up to your room," he urged as he turned her toward the elevator. "You're soaked through." He nodded tersely at Reynolds. "I'll take her up."

Numbly, she let him escort her into the elevator. As they rode up, images of Alannis and Theron filtered through her mind. They'd looked so happy.

Happy.

Almost like…they were in love.

She closed her eyes again. Why couldn't he love her?

Marcus took the key from her shaking fingers and unlocked her door. Cool air immediately washed over her, eliciting a chill.

"You're soaked, too," she said as she became aware of his wet shirt and slacks.

He gave her a wry smile. "I took off after you and got caught in the downpour."

She tried to smile and failed miserably. "Sorry."

He sighed. "Why don't you go take a hot bath? I'll order up room service and see if they can't also get me some dry clothing brought up from the boutique."

She nodded and shuffled toward the bathroom.

* * *

Theron slipped his hand in the inside pocket of his suit and pulled out his BlackBerry. He frowned when he saw his last message had gone unanswered.

Excusing himself from Alannis with a smile, he nodded to the other guests assembled around them and backed away. He walked out of the ballroom and headed to the men's room just two doors down. As he was about to enter, he looked down the hallway and saw Reynolds standing next to his men. He was soaking wet.

With a frown, Theron stalked toward the three men. Reynolds glanced up as he heard Theron approach.

"Where's Isabella?" Theron demanded.

"In her room with Atwater," Reynolds replied.

Sure he had heard wrong, Theron's eyes narrowed. "With who?"

"She went up a few minutes ago with Atwater," Reynolds said calmly. "They were both soaked."

Theron's pulse pounded against his temple. It was all he could do not to charge up to her room and drag Marcus out. Then he'd beat the hell out of him.

With a muttered curse, he spun around and headed for the elevator. Anger rushed like lava through his veins. What the hell was Marcus thinking? Theron knew damn well what he was thinking, and what he was thinking with.

When he finally reached Isabella's door, he rapped sharply. A few seconds later, the door opened to a smiling Marcus who wore just a bathrobe.

He looked startled to see Theron standing there, and then his eyes narrowed to slits. "Sorry, I thought you were room service," Marcus said. Then he turned his head toward the bathroom. "Stay in the tub a little longer, sweetheart. Food's not here yet."

Turning back to Theron, Marcus did a slow up and down

perusal, and then he asked in a bored voice, "Now, what can I do for you?"

"You arrogant…" Theron said in a menacing voice.

"You broke away from your engagement party to come up here and call me names?" Marcus asked in amusement.

A sound down the hallway had Theron looking to see the room service cart being wheeled toward Isabella's door. Marcus pressed forward and stared as well.

"Ah, there's the food now. If you'll excuse me. Or was there something you wanted?" Marcus asked pointedly.

Theron backed away, unsettled and feeling like he'd just gone a round in the boxing ring. Without a word, he turned and stalked away, his fists clenched into balls at his sides.

His gut churned as he got back onto the elevator. Why did it matter? He'd set Marcus up to be a choice in Isabella's hunt for a husband. Why then did he feel absolutely sickened by the prospect that Isabella had made her choice?

Twelve

Isabella was wakened by a loud knock at her door. She opened her eyes, wincing at how scratchy and dry they felt. Her hands went to wipe the swollen lids, and she remembered that she'd cried herself to sleep the night before.

Theron had proposed to Alannis. She'd been too late. And they'd looked so *happy*.

Fitting that she was completely miserable.

A knock sounded again, prompting her to slide her legs from the covers and push herself from the bed. Gathering her robe that lay over the chair a few feet away, she pulled it on and tied it as she walked to the door.

When she stared through the peephole, she saw Sadie standing outside, or at least someone who resembled Sadie. It was hard to tell with the platinum blond wig adorning her head. She opened the door, and Sadie brushed by talking a mile a minute.

"Thank goodness you're here," Sadie said. "For a minute I thought you'd forgotten about tonight."

Isabella closed the door and turned to look at Sadie.

"I've got everything in my bag, and we have plenty of time to prepare," Sadie chattered on. "It'll be a snap."

Then Sadie stopped as she got a good look at Isabella. Her brow creased in confusion, and her lips parted.

"Bella, what's wrong? Have you been crying?"

To Isabella's dismay, she felt the sting of more tears. Irritated, she blinked them away, determined not to shed a single one.

Sadie closed the distance between them and slung an arm around her friend, guiding her toward the couch. Isabella found herself seated, and then Sadie plopped down beside her.

"What happened?" she asked. "Is it Theron?"

Isabella closed her eyes and nodded.

"Oh, honey, I'm sorry." Sadie enfolded her in her arms. "Did he propose to Alannis? Is that it?"

Isabella nodded against Sadie's shoulder. Sadie pulled away and brushed the hair from Isabella's face.

"Let's forget all about tonight. We'll order in some really good takeout and binge on desserts that have a gazillion calories."

Isabella smiled. "You can't miss your party, Sadie. It's too important. Just because my life is in shambles isn't a reason for you to lose your job and your chance at Broadway."

Sadie looked doubtfully at her. "I'm not sure you're up for this, Bella."

Bella forced a broader smile to her lips. "How bad can it be? I'll dress like you, dance some and attract male attention. It won't last long, and you'll keep your job."

"Are you sure?"

Isabella nodded. "Let's order something to eat. I'm starved. Then you can teach me the moves I need to know." She glanced at the bright wig Sadie was wearing. "Is that what I'm wearing out of here tonight?"

Sadie grinned. "It's the perfect way past your security guys. I made sure they saw me come in, and honestly, who could miss this?" she said as she slid her hands suggestively down the curves of her body.

Isabella cracked up. "No false modesty for you."

Sadie winked at her then continued on. "We'll dress you like me and you'll sashay out of here. No one will know that I'm still up here. I'll give you a good head start and then I'll get ready for the party and leave, looking nothing like the blond bombshell who arrived earlier."

"Well, what's the worst that can happen?" Isabella asked with a shrug. "We get caught and Reynolds throws another fit. I'm sure Theron is too busy with his new fiancée to give a damn about my whereabouts."

"That's the spirit," Sadie crowed. "Let's do it!"

She was certifiably insane to have agreed to this. Isabella took a deep breath as the elevator stopped at the lobby level, flipped a long lock of the blond hair over her shoulder and waited for the doors to open.

The getup that Sadie had poured her into was many things. Modest wasn't one of them. And while Isabella didn't mind displaying her assets to her best advantage, this bordered on obscene.

The heels of her thigh-high boots clicked on the marble floor as she hurried for the exit. Her shorts were a slightly more expensive version of a denim Daisy Duke style, and they dipped low in front, showing her navel and more skin.

And her top. Not even a Dallas Cowboy cheerleader showed more cleavage.

But as Sadie said, no one would bother looking at her face. Not when so much else of her was on display.

She wobbled her way toward a waiting taxi and got in. As he pulled away, she supplied the address that Sadie had provided her. He didn't even blink an eye, and who could blame him with the way she was dressed? It amused her to think he might have assumed she was at the hotel for "business" purposes.

Nervousness tickled her stomach as they maneuvered through traffic. By the time the cab pulled up to the back entrance of the club, sweat beaded her forehead.

She sat for a moment staring out her window until the driver cleared his throat.

"Sorry," she muttered. She shoved the appropriate money over the seat and then got out. "Well, here we go," she said, as she tentatively walked to the door.

The hallway just inside the door was cloaked in darkness. A good thing. Even though Sadie had assured her that no one would notice the slight differences in the girls, this charade still made Isabella extremely nervous.

She was wearing so much makeup, that even her overbearing security team hadn't been able to tell it was her.

When she got to the door simply marked "girls," she eased inside. There was a flurry of activity, and no one paid her any mind. Another girl bumped into her as she walked past, and Isabella shied away, afraid of getting too close.

"Hey, Sadie," another girl called. "We weren't sure you were coming. You're up after Angel, so you better hurry and get ready."

Isabella's stomach dropped, and she swallowed back her panic. She could do this. No one knew it was her. While she wasn't the expert that Sadie was, she could still move well, and Sadie had spent the afternoon teaching her the necessary act.

She smiled and nodded in the girl's direction and took a spot at Sadie's dressing station to check her makeup and to make sure her wig was securely in place.

When she caught her reflection in the mirror, all that she could think was how sad her eyes looked. No matter how made-up her face was, how perfect the hair, the eyes told the story. And the story was that she'd lost the one man she'd hoped to spend the rest of her life with.

More to have something to do than any real need to repair her makeup, she slowly applied more lipstick, watching as her lips glistened blood red. Mechanically she brushed the mascara wand over her eyelashes, elongating her already dark lashes.

But still, her green eyes stared lifelessly back at her.

"Sadie, you're up in five," a male voice barked from the door. "Get a move on."

Isabella pushed herself jerkily from her chair and spared one last glance in the mirror. She looked scared to death.

Sucking in a deep, steadying breath, she adjusted her clothing, plumped up her breasts and headed for the door.

Theron stared out the window of Chrysander's penthouse, his mostly forgotten drink still in hand. Dusk was falling, and the lights of the city were coming alive, popping on the horizon.

He still wasn't sure his decision had been the correct one. He'd questioned himself repeatedly through the day, and yet, he could find no fault with the path he'd taken.

But now he had no idea what to do about Isabella.

He turned in irritation when his BlackBerry rang. It was sitting on the coffee table several feet away where he'd tossed it earlier. With a resigned sigh he walked over to pick it up.

Seeing Reynolds's name on the LCD immediately put him on edge. He hit the answer button and put the phone to his ear.

"Anetakis," he said shortly.

"Mr. Anetakis, this is Reynolds. We have a situation, sir."

Theron put his drink down with a thud. "What situation?" he demanded.

"Earlier this evening, Ms. Caplan gave us the slip. Again."

"What? And you allowed her to do this again?"

"I'm afraid it's worse, sir. I'll be happy to fill you in on the details later, but at the moment we're on our way to La Belle Femmes." He paused for a moment. "Are you familiar with it, sir?"

Theron's brow furrowed in concentration as he absorbed the information. "Isn't that a gentlemen's club? And why the hell are you going there?"

"Because that's where Ms. Caplan went," Reynolds said calmly. "I assumed you'd want to know."

"Damn right I want to know!" Theron exploded. "I'm on my way now, and don't think I won't want to know exactly how this went down."

He hurried toward the door, his finger on the button to call for his driver. By the time he made it to the lobby, the car was waiting in front of the building.

What in God's name was Isabella doing in a gentleman's club? What was she thinking? Was Marcus somehow responsible for this? Theron was going to kill him.

When his driver screeched up to the club entrance, Theron got out and saw Reynolds along with his two men hurrying toward him.

"Is she here?" Theron demanded.

"We just arrived," Reynolds explained. "We were about to go in to see."

Theron strode ahead of them to the door and was stopped by a large man wearing dark glasses.

"Your name, sir?" the man politely inquired.

"Theron Anetakis," he said impatiently. "Someone I know is in there. Someone who shouldn't be here."

"Unless you have a membership, I can't allow you inside."

Theron seethed with impatience and then he turned to Reynolds. "Take care of this. Pay the man whatever is necessary for membership and then rejoin me inside. I'm going in after Isabella."

"But sir, membership is not instant...."

Theron heard no more as he pushed by the man and went inside. He trusted that Reynolds and the others would be able to overcome whatever objections the club's security guard had to his presence.

The club was different than Theron was expecting. From the moment a gentlemen's club was mentioned, it conjured images of a seedy, back-alley environment where prostitution and drug use ran rampant. Here, though, it seemed the establishment catered to an upscale clientele.

The interior was clean, lavish even, reminding Theron of many high-roller areas of casinos. The waitresses, through scantily clad, weren't cheap-looking-tart material. The patrons were well-dressed, smoking expensive imported cigars and sipping only the finest brandy.

It was a place Isabella shouldn't even know existed.

Theron weaved around the tables, sharp-eyed, his brow creased in concentration as he took in every single woman. Toward the front of the room, more men were assembled in front of a curtained platform. Evidently a show was imminent.

He dismissed the men when he saw no women among them. Where the hell was Isabella and had Reynolds gotten his information correct?

He glanced toward the entrance and saw Reynolds and the two other security men rush in. Theron gestured curtly at them, and Reynolds wove his way through the tables to where Theron stood.

"Why do you think Isabella is here?" he demanded.

"I have it on good authority she is," Reynolds said grimly. "You're looking in the wrong—"

He was cut off when music began blaring behind Theron. He winced and turned around only to see the curtain rise and stage smoke slither sensuously up the long legs of a woman.

She wore thigh-high boots that only accentuated her slim legs and drew attention to her shapely behind. She began rocking in rhythm to the music, her hips swaying as her arms fell gracefully to her sides.

As the smoke cleared, she raised her arms and gripped the pole in front of her. But Theron's gaze was drawn to the tattoo in the small of her back.

He knew that tattoo. Knew it damn well. He should; he'd spent plenty of time fantasizing about it.

And then she turned, whirling around in a mass of blond hair—fake blond hair. He saw her eyes before she saw him. He saw the fear in her gaze, the wild panic as she surveyed the room full of men all eyeing her like a tasty treat.

Theron's blood boiled.

She looked up and locked gazes with him, her fear turning to utter shock as recognition flickered in her eyes.

Thirteen

Isabella blanched when she saw Theron who was clearly furious standing beyond the group of men all crowding the stage. He vibrated with rage, and his eyes flashed as he stared her down.

She had the sudden urge to cross her arms over her breasts and run for cover.

Before she could seriously contemplate doing just that, Theron stalked forward, closing in on the stage like a predator on the hunt.

He didn't stop at the edge, didn't call out to her to come down. He jumped onto the platform, and in one swift motion hauled her into his arms and threw her over his shoulder.

She gave a startled cry just as the music stopped and the place erupted in chaos. She raised her head to see Reynolds, Maxwell and Davison fend off the security guards trying to come to her aid.

Customers rose from their seats and viewed Theron with gaping mouths, but were too civilized to embroil themselves in the situation. It would probably ruin their thousand-dollar suits anyway.

The floor spun crazily as Theron leaped down. The force drove the breath from her, and she wiggled trying to get him to ease his grip.

He merely tightened his arm over the back of her legs as he strode for the exit. Then she heard him snarl, "Back off, she's mine."

And surprisingly, he walked through the door and into the night.

Still stunned, Isabella made no effort to free herself from his grasp, not that it would have done any good. His arm was like a steel band around her body, and he walked effortlessly, bearing her weight as if it were nothing.

He stopped at his car, and leaned down to thrust her through the opening into the interior. Immediately, he climbed in beside her and slammed the door.

"Imperial Park," he said curtly.

Laying at an odd angle on the seat, she attempted to straighten herself, but her legs bumped into him, and she pulled them hastily away which only made her position more precarious.

Damn the boots. She felt gawky and ungainly. A glance down made her gasp in dismay when she saw that her cleavage was precariously close to spilling from the suggestive top. She folded her arms over her chest and scooted back until her back hit the other door.

She opened her mouth to speak, but he silenced her with a glare.

"Not a word, Bella. Not one damn word," he said menacingly. Anger vibrated off him in waves. "I'll have a full explanation when we return to the hotel. Until then I don't want you to say anything."

She swallowed then gulped as she stared wordlessly at him.

Never had she seen him so…angry! He was usually so unbothered. Cool and collected. He was the epitome of order and calm.

The Theron she knew would never haul someone out of a public place nor would he snarl at a security guard twice his size.

She looked away, wrapping her arms a little tighter around herself.

"Here," he said gruffly as he shrugged out of his suit coat.

He held it out with one hand and pulled her forward as he settled it around her shoulders. She tugged at the lapels to bring it tighter around her, grateful that it at least covered her.

Several long minutes later, they pulled up to the hotel. Theron gave her a look that suggested she stay put, and she complied. He got out and walked around to her side and opened the door.

To her surprise, he reached in, drew his coat together so that not an inch of her flesh was displayed and then he simply plucked her out of the seat.

"Theron, I can walk," she protested.

"Silence," he ordered as he strode in the doors, ignoring the curious stares of passersby.

She frowned but settled wearily against his chest. He got into the elevator and stabbed at the button for her floor. Okay, she got that he was mad. Furious even. But he seemed to be taking it personally. Why wasn't he off somewhere with his new fiancée?

A fresh stab of pain soared through, taking her breath with it. She closed her eyes against the single truth that prevented her from having the man she loved. He belonged to someone else.

"Bella?"

His voice had changed, softened, and it reflected uncertainty. She pried open her eyes to see him regarding her with concern.

"Are you all right? Did something happen?" he demanded. "Did someone hurt you or threaten you?"

She shook her head, unable to speak past the lump in her throat. For a moment she could immerse herself in the fantasy that she did belong to him, that he cared about her in a deeper capacity than as a guardian, someone tasked to see to her welfare.

But it was a lie. It was all a lie.

"Then why?" he muttered.

The elevator opened, and with a shake of his head, he strode off and down to her room. Neither of them had a key, but then he didn't waste time trying to find one. He simply kicked loudly, instead of putting her down to knock. But who would open it? No one was there.

To her eternal surprise, and there had been many tonight, the door opened and a man who had security detail written all over him opened the door to admit Theron.

The surprises didn't end there. As soon as Theron walked in, a cry sounded from across the room.

"Bella! Are you all right?"

Isabella yanked her head left to see Sadie running across the room. Finally Theron let her down, and Sadie threw her arms around her.

"What are you doing here?" Isabella whispered. "Your party, Sadie. You weren't supposed to miss your party."

Sadie flushed guiltily. "The party doesn't matter. I should have never let you do this for me, Bella."

"In this we agree," Theron said stiffly. "It was irresponsible and dangerous. It's not a place that either of you should ever go into."

"But you missed your chance," Isabella said softly, ignoring Theron's outburst.

Sadie smiled sadly. "There'll be others. Besides, it wasn't worth the risk you took. I'm sorry."

"What happened?" Isabella asked in confusion. "Why are you still here and," she said, turning to face Theron, "how did he know where to find me?"

"Your security detail phoned me, as they should have," Theron said darkly.

Isabella turned back to Sadie. "How did they know?"

Sadie looked down and sighed. "When I left your room for the party, one of your guys immediately stopped me. They'd obviously seen you, posing as me, leave earlier and as we planned, never assumed it was you. However, they knew the real me hadn't entered your room, so they were suspicious. I had to tell them everything," she said uncomfortably. "They made me remain here while they went to get you." She glanced angrily at the man who was still standing by the door. "I had to endure a lecture from him the entire time you were gone."

"It's good that someone tried to talk sense into you," Theron bit out. He nodded toward the security man. "See that she gets home safely, and remain on watch to see that she doesn't go back to that club."

"But I work there!" Sadie exclaimed.

"Not any longer," Theron said with a growl. "I won't have Bella traipsing through some strip club because her friend works there."

"But—" Sadie sputtered even as she was escorted away by the security detail.

When the door closed behind them, Theron turned to glare at Isabella. He stepped forward, and she stepped back uneasily. His scowl became more ferocious as he reached to detain her.

"Now, Bella, I'll deal with you," he said in a soft, dangerous voice.

Theron's hands curled around her shoulders as he yanked Isabella to him. The coat she'd held so tightly around her fell to the floor, and her breasts thrust obscenely into his chest.

She couldn't bring herself to meet his gaze. If she did, he'd know. He'd immediately see everything she now wanted to hide. Things he hadn't been able to see before.

"Go get cleaned up," he said in a gruff voice. "I'll wait for you here."

Only too grateful to flee, she turned and headed for the bathroom. She grimaced when she caught a glimpse of herself in the mirror. Tawdry was a word that came to mind. Garish.

Sad.

She washed the heavy makeup from her face and tore the wig from her head. Then she unpinned her own hair and ran her fingers through it to tame it. A long, hot bath was extremely tempting, but not when Theron waited outside, likely growing more impatient by the moment.

She stripped out of the boots and clothes, tossing them aside. Then she realized she hadn't brought in something to change into. With a shrug, she made a grab for the bathrobe hanging on the back of the door and wrapped it securely around her.

Then she padded back out to the sitting room in bare feet, hands thrust into the pockets of the robe. Theron waited, standing by the window that overlooked the avenue below.

When he heard her, he turned, his eyes still flashing with unsettled intensity.

"Why are you here, Theron?" she asked, finally regaining her composure.

He closed the distance between them, once again curling his fingers over her shoulders. "You dare to ask that as if I have no right? As if you didn't just do something incredibly stupid? Do you have any idea what I thought when I heard where you'd gone? The fear I felt? Or the shock upon seeing you on that stage, half naked for all those men to leer at? Tell me, Bella, what would you have done if someone other than me had rushed that stage? What if he had put his hands on you? Forced you to go with him?"

She blinked at his ferocity and the absolute anger tightening his features. Any number of explanations circled her frazzled mind, but she didn't think he'd be interested in any of them. So she kept quiet.

Theron ran a hand through his hair in a gesture of frustration before locking gazes with her once more.

"Did Marcus know you were doing this?"

Isabella bobbed her head backward in surprise. "Marcus? Why would he need to know anything I was doing?"

"I would hope he was more protective of what was his—or what he had staked claim on anyway," Theron growled.

She blinked in confusion. "You're not making any sense. Marcus has nothing to do with anything. He's a friend. I don't feel the need to apprise him of my comings and goings."

Theron snorted. "*A friend?* Is that what they're calling them these days?" he asked, throwing her mocking words about kissing back at her.

"What are you insinuating, Theron?" she asked as she folded her arms over her chest.

"I was here, Bella. Last night. I came up…to see about you," he added uncomfortably.

"So?"

"And Marcus answered your door in only a bathrobe," he snapped.

Isabella's mouth fell open. "And from this, you assume I'm sleeping with him?"

"Are you saying you did not?" Theron challenged.

"I'm saying it's none of your damn business," she huffed.

A long silence fell between them as they stared at one another. Oh, she would have loved to have told him yes, that she'd slept with Marcus, but really, what was the point? He was engaged to Alannis, and she had no desire to make herself look promiscuous. He did still have control over her inheritance until she married someone else.

"I didn't sleep with him," she said tightly. "We were caught in the rain and he came up so that dry clothing could be brought to him. He changed into a robe, and I stayed in the tub until he was dressed. We ate room service and then he left."

There was a flicker of relief in Theron's eyes. Why? What could it possibly matter to him? And then he shook his head.

"Why do you insist on driving me utterly crazy?" he murmured. "Is it not enough that I spend my time thinking of you? Remembering the feel of your mouth beneath mine?"

He moved in closer, his breath hot against her face. Unconsciously, she licked her lips nervously as he moved and tilted his head in a dance around her mouth.

"You shouldn't…kiss me," she whispered.

"You've never had an objection before," he muttered just before his mouth closed hot over hers.

Fourteen

Isabella's knees wobbled, and she clutched frantically at Theron's shoulders to keep from sliding down his body. He caught her tightly against him as his lips plundered hers.

This kiss…was different. She moaned softly, a sound of surrender? Honestly, she didn't care. Maybe it was a sound of need. Or want.

He took her. There was no other word for it. He took possession of her mouth as if he owned it, as if he had exclusive rights to her mouth and refused to share it. Ever.

Her body melted against his, and she loved the hardness of his chest, his thighs, shivered as his hands roamed up her body to her neck. He cupped her nape, holding her so that she couldn't escape him. As if she wanted to.

She was a willing captive. This…this was what she'd dreamed about. Fantasized. Wanted so much. So desperately.

"I want to make love to you, Bella," he said with breathless urgency, his lips barely separating from hers. "I've fought it. *Theos,* but I've fought, but if I don't have you, I'm going to go mad."

"Yes," she whispered. "I want you so much, Theron."

His hands fumbled with the tie at her robe, his lips never leaving her mouth. It was as though he couldn't bear to stop kissing her. He devoured her even as he yanked her robe open.

And then his hands pressed against her naked skin, and she moaned and trembled, going completely weak against him.

"Soft, so soft and beautiful. Like silk," he murmured as his palms caressed her sides, moving up until he cupped her breasts.

Finally, he moved from her mouth, his lips brushing over her jaw and to her ear and then lower, down her neck. He nipped then sucked at the tender skin, eliciting shiver after shiver.

His mouth continued downward, and she caught her breath as he sank to his knees in front of her. He snaked his arms inside her robe and wrapped them around her waist, pulling her downward so that her knees bent.

His mouth was precariously close to her breasts, so much so that his breath beaded and puckered her nipples into tight knots. And then he slid his mouth over one, rolling his tongue gently over the peak.

Her robe fell to the floor at her feet, and she was naked in his arms. He sucked at her breast, his dark head flush against her body. How erotic it looked, this proud, strong man, on his knees, his arms wrapped tight around her—as though he'd never let go.

Before she allowed herself to become too entrenched in *that* fantasy, he released her nipple, and she groaned her protest.

He glanced up, his eyes glowing in the lamplight. "You're beautiful, Bella," he said in a low husky voice that was passion-laced.

His grip loosened just enough that he could rise to his feet, his shirt scraping along her bare skin. She reached out with her fingers to snag at his buttons, wanting them gone and to feel his bare skin against hers.

But he collected her hands in his and held them tightly together. "Oh, no, Bella *mou*. This is my seduction. And I intend to seduce you thoroughly."

He swung her into his arms and walked slowly to the bedroom, his gaze locked with hers. She was afraid to speak. Afraid that he would hastily back away if the spell was broken.

He laid her on the bed then straightened to his full height over her. She felt strangely vulnerable beneath his intense gaze. Shy and a little uncertain.

Her hands crept upward in an attempt to shield herself.

"Do not hide such beauty from me," he whispered.

Emboldened by the obvious approval in his eyes, she let her hands fall away. Lust flared over his face as his hands went to the buttons of his shirt. Halfway down, he lost patience and ripped the remaining buttons. He shrugged out of the sleeves and then tore impatiently at his pants.

She sucked in her breath and held it when his boxers, with his pants, slipped down and his turgid manhood came into view. Then it stuttered out, a silent staccato in the quiet as he moved closer.

He spread her knees and fit his body to hers, settling between her thighs as he came down onto the bed. Hot, silken and yet rough in a heady, masculine way, his skin clung to hers, burning her, making her move restlessly underneath him.

They kissed again, and she wrapped her arms around his neck, prolonging the mating of their tongues. Soft and wet, clinging and dueling, a precursor to the dance their bodies would yet perform.

"I've never felt so out of control," he admitted. "So restless and out of my skin. You make me crazy, Bella. I have to have you."

"Yes."

The softly whispered surrender slid from swollen lips. His

mouth skated downward to her neck and then over the slope of her shoulder.

He moved, lowering his body so that his lips found her breasts. She stared up at the ceiling, the intricate painting blurring as pleasure overtook her. For several long seconds, he lazily tongued the rigid peaks, and then he blazed a wet trail with his tongue down her midline to her belly.

He toyed with her belly ring for the briefest of seconds before traveling even lower.

She tensed when his mouth found her soft femininity, the very essence and core of her womanhood. Helplessly she arched into him, seeking more of his bold tongue. He chuckled and gave her another soft nuzzle.

"Please, Theron," she begged. "Take me."

"I want you to be ready for me, Bella *mou*," he said as he trailed one finger over her damp flesh.

"Take me," she said again as she looked down and met his gaze. "I'm yours."

Her words seemed to push him beyond his control. He slid up her body, spreading her legs and fitting himself to her in one deft movement. One moment he was probing, the next he slid inside her, breaking through the slight resistance as though it were nothing.

For a moment she went rigid with shock, only a twinge of pain, but more than that a sense of such fullness that it overwhelmed her. Her eyes flew open, and her hands went reflexively to his shoulders to push him away.

Theron stared at her in confusion even as his hips moved, and he thrust forward again. She relaxed beneath him, letting her hands glide over his shoulders and to his neck. Pleasure, sweet and yearning, bloomed, spreading like fire in the wind.

His lips found hers again in a gesture of reassurance, molding sweetly to hers, suddenly gentle and tender.

"Move with me, *agape mou*," he urged. "Wrap your legs around me. Yes, that's it."

Her skin came alive, crawling and edgy with need. Theron planted his elbows on either side of her head and held his body off her enough that she didn't bear the full brunt of his weight as he moved between her legs.

Breathing became hard. She panted against his lips as their mouths met again.

"Come with me," he whispered.

Helpless to do anything but follow the winding pleasure building so earnestly, she cried out as he stiffened above her. He gathered her softly against him, crushing her to his hardness. Murmured words fell against her ears, some she understood, some slipping away.

And then he collapsed, pressing his warm body to hers. For several long seconds, their ragged breathing was the only sound that filled the room.

Then he raised his head to stare down at her. He kissed her lightly then shifted, easing his body from hers. "I'll be right back."

She watched lazily from the bed while he strode nude to the bathroom and returned a moment later with a washcloth.

"Did I hurt you?" he asked in a low voice.

She sat up and reached for the cloth, but he held it out of her reach and then brushed it gently over her skin to clean her.

"No, you didn't hurt me," she returned quietly.

"Why didn't you tell me?"

There was no recrimination, no accusation in his voice.

"I wasn't entirely certain you'd believe me."

"And so you let me ravage you when you should have been handled gently? Made love to and cherished?"

There was genuine regret on his face. Not that he'd made love to her, if she had to guess, but for what he considered his rough treatment of her.

She reached out and touched his face, enjoying the feel of the slight stubble on his jaw. "You didn't hurt me, Theron. It was perfect."

He dropped the cloth on the floor and then framed her face in his hands. "No, it wasn't perfect, but I can make it that way."

He lowered his mouth to hers, kissing her with a tenderness that made her chest ache. Desire fluttered deep within, awakening and unfolding, reaching out.

He took his time, lavishing kisses and caresses over every inch of her body. He murmured endearments and praise, each one landing in a distant region of her heart that she'd reserved only for him.

She soaked up each touch, each word like parched earth starved for water.

And when he cupped her to him, sliding carefully into her wanting body, she knew she'd never loved him more than she did at this moment. For so long she'd waited to have him like this. Focused on her, seeing her, touching her and loving her as she loved him.

This time he urged her to completion before taking his own, and only when she quivered with the last vestiges of her orgasm did he sink deeply within her and hold himself so tightly that she could feel the tension rippling through his body.

He dropped his forehead to hers, their lips just an inch apart as he dragged in deep breaths. She tilted her chin upward so that her nose brushed against his, and then their lips met in a sweet kiss that she felt to her soul.

"Better?" he murmured.

She smiled. "Better."

Theron woke to a sweet female form wrapped tightly around his body. As he opened his eyes and blew a tendril of dark hair from across his lips, he realized that Isabella was more draped across him than wrapped exactly.

Her breasts were pressed to his chest, and one arm was thrown across his body possessively. Her limbs were tangled with his, and she slept soundly, her soft even breathing filling his ears.

Reality was swift to come, and with it, the weight of what he'd done. It wasn't unexpected, this guilt and resignation. He could blame it on passion, lust—a whole host of things—but he knew the truth.

He'd wanted her and he'd taken her, and he'd certainly known what he was about in the heat of the moment. Not once in his thirty-two years had he ever lost all conscious thought when making love, and he wasn't likely to start now.

He hadn't even used a condom, and for the life of him he couldn't dredge up a plausible excuse for his stupidity. It wasn't even that he didn't have one on him at the time. He lived his life in a state of preparedness, and he always had not one, but two condoms in his wallet.

And yet he hadn't stopped to get one, hadn't protected her, and worse, it had been a conscious decision. There was no one to blame in this whole mess but himself, and he damn well knew it.

Carefully, he extricated himself from her warm body. He tensed when she gave a soft little sigh, but then she snuggled back into the covers and settled down once more.

He strode to the bathroom to shower, aware that there would be consequences for his choices. Already he was mentally preparing and making plans. Through it all, there was an odd sense of peace instead of pained resignation.

Still, he dreaded all he had to do. And say.

Wrapping a towel around his waist, he walked out of the bathroom and recovered the clothing he'd worn yesterday. Thankfully he always kept several changes of clothing at his office. That would be his first stop.

As he was pulling on his pants, Isabella stirred, her long hair sliding over her body as she turned and reached out her hand as though seeking him. His body tightened, and arousal hummed through his veins, a soft whisper that grew louder as he stared down at her.

She opened her eyes sleepily, blinking when she saw him. He reached down and touched her cheek, smoothing a stray strand of her hair from her skin.

"There are things I have to take care of, Bella. Important things."

He bent and kissed her softly on the hair, and then without another word, turned and walked out of the bedroom.

Isabella stood beside the bed, wrapped in just the sheet, the ends clutched tightly in her hands. She glanced down at the discarded washcloth, at the evidence of her lost virginity, and felt an odd stirring deep in her chest.

Where had Theron gone? And would he be back? Or was she just the temptation that finally became too much, and he was rushing back to Alannis to make amends?

She closed her eyes and let her chin fall to her chest. She didn't want to be the other woman. She didn't like how it felt, didn't want to be responsible for someone else's sorrow. But why should she place another's over her own?

Feeling quiet sadness settle into her heart, she went into the bathroom to draw a hot bath. Part of her ached—a delicious ache—and she couldn't help but close her eyes and remember every touch, every kiss and caress, the feel of his body sliding over hers.

She soaked until the water grew tepid, and finally, shivering, she rose from the tub and wrapped herself in a towel.

There was a listlessness to her she was unused to. There was too much unknown, unresolved, and she worried that it would remain so.

Growing disgusted with her lethargy, she forced herself to dress. She refused to sit in her hotel room holding her breath like a lovesick fool, waiting for a man who might never return.

First she'd eat and then she'd head to her apartment. Her new furniture had been delivered, and Theron had arranged someone to stock all the necessities. She would go over and make a list of anything else she needed, and then maybe it was time to start thinking about what she was going to do with the rest of her life.

When she opened the door, she immediately came face-to-face with an unsmiling Reynolds. She tried to smile, but failed miserably. Then she sighed. "You might as well come in so I can apologize properly. Then you can accompany me to the hotel restaurant, and then we can go to my new apartment."

Reynolds actually smiled in return as he stepped inside. "*Now,* Ms. Caplan, you're getting the hang of how things are supposed to be done. You make my job a lot easier when I know where you're going and you aren't running off at every turn."

She made a face. "I truly am sorry I've been so much trouble. I think you'll find me a lot more accommodating from now on."

His amusement vanished, and he sobered as he studied her with questioning eyes. "I hope nothing has happened to upset you."

For a moment she said nothing. And then with a halfhearted smile, she gestured toward the door. "Let's go eat. I'm starving."

Theron settled wearily into the chair behind his desk and picked up the phone. Yet again, it would be the middle of the night in Greece, but he needed to have this conversation with Chrysander now so that he could go forward with his plans.

"*Nai,*" Chrysander barked in a sleepy tone.

"I've done a terrible thing," Theron said.

"Theron?" Chrysander asked in a more alert tone. "What the devil are you doing calling at this hour. Again. And what terrible thing are you talking about? Are you in jail?"

Theron had to laugh at that. "No, I'm not in jail."

"Then what is wrong?"

Theron rubbed his hand across his face. "I seduced Isabella."

There was a long pause. "I'm not sure I heard that correctly," Chrysander finally said. Then Theron heard him speak to Marley. "No, *agape mou,* nothing is wrong. Go back to sleep. It's just Theron." Then he came back to Theron. "Give me a moment to take this call in my office. Marley has been up all night with the baby."

Theron waited patiently as he heard shuffling in the background and even a sound like Chrysander kissing Marley. A few moments later, Chrysander's voice bled back over the line.

"Now tell me you didn't do what I think you said you did," Chrysander said dryly.

"I can't do that. It's worse, though."

"Worse than you seducing a young woman under your care? I fail to see how it can get any worse."

"She was a virgin, and I didn't use protection."

Theron cringed even as he said it. It was a conversation that made him sound sixteen years old confessing his sins to his father.

Chrysander cursed and blew out his breath. "Damn it, Theron, what in the world were you thinking? Okay, scratch that. You obviously weren't thinking. That much is established. But what about Alannis? Were you not just telling me and Piers that you were marrying her? What were you doing in bed with Isabella? And *Theos,* without protection. Are you stupid?"

"And you were so careful with Marley?" Theron said defensively.

"I was in a relationship with Marley," Chrysander growled. "I was not engaged to another woman, nor was she someone under my direct care. Theron, this goes beyond stupid."

"I'm not engaged to another woman," Theron said quietly. "I didn't ask her to marry me."

Another stunned silence ensued.

"You better back up and tell me the entire story," Chrysander said wearily. "It's obvious that you've got a huge mess on your hands. Start with the part where you didn't ask Alannis to marry you."

"I couldn't do it," Theron said with a sigh. "I arranged the night, had a party, the ring, the confetti—"

"Confetti? Who the hell has confetti for a marriage proposal?" Chrysander demanded, a thread of amusement in his voice.

"It added to the festive mood," Theron defended. "Everything was there. The moment was there...and I couldn't do it. I had my hand on the ring, the woman staring up at me, and then I let go of the box, and asked her to dance instead. We spent the evening celebrating her visit to New York instead of our impending nuptials."

"So how did this lead to you taking Isabella's virginity? Without protection," he added dryly.

"I've admitted my stupidity. There's no reason to keep beating me over the head with it," Theron said irritably. "It happened after I hauled her out of the strip club."

"You *what?*" Chrysander broke into laughter. "Theron, this is sounding more absurd all the time. Do I even want to know why someone you were supposed to be watching over was in a strip club?"

"It's not important. What's important is that afterward, I seduced Isabella. We slept together. Without protection. She was a virgin. That covers it."

"Yes, I'd say it does," Chrysander said.

There was another long silence and then Chrysander spoke again. "She was under our care. Our father agreed that the Anetakis family would always care for her should something happen to her father. You're going to have to marry her, Theron."

Adrenaline surged in Theron's veins. "I don't *have* to marry her, Chrysander. I'm *going* to marry her."

Fifteen

Isabella shoved aside the heavy curtains draped over the large window facing the street. Her apartment was on the top floor, larger by half than the apartments on the lower levels, and it had a wonderful view of a small park across the street.

There was no shortage of joggers, people out walking dogs, and children supervised by their nannies or mothers. It was a small mecca in the middle of a crowded city where someone could go and enjoy a short escape.

Could she live here knowing the man she loved was close by, married to someone else? On the surface it sounded absurd. In a city this size, she could go an entire lifetime without running into Theron. Except…except he controlled her inheritance and contact would be inevitable.

She sighed. She really did like the apartment, but she wasn't sure she could remain here.

The sound of her door opening didn't alarm her. Reynolds

had been left waiting when she'd only said she'd be a minute. He probably lost patience and was coming to collect her.

Footsteps sounded behind her, and yet she still couldn't tear her gaze away from the scene below. Maybe it was the normalcy of it all—the promise of an ordered existence where agonizing emotions such as love and jealousy or despair didn't dictate her every breath.

Firm hands took hold of her shoulders, skimming upward, eliciting a small gasp from her.

"Bella, *pethi mou,* are you all right? What are you doing here?"

She spun around in surprise and stared up at Theron's worried eyes.

"I went back to your suite and you were gone. I'm beginning to wonder if my life is going to be a study in never finding you where you're supposed to be."

There was a hint of amusement in his voice, but she was puzzled by his words. They made no sense.

"When I called Reynolds and he said you were here, I came right over. But Bella, there is no need of your apartment any longer," he said calmly.

She held up a hand to his chest, almost afraid to touch him. Her head was spinning a mile a minute, but she needed to understand what he was saying, or what he wasn't saying.

"I came to see if it was ready for me to move in," she said simply.

He captured her hand in his and held it in place over his heart. "You won't be needing this apartment, *pethi mou.*"

With his other hand, he dipped into his pocket and drew out a small square box. She stared suspiciously at it as he flipped the lid off and let it fall to the floor. Maneuvering still with the one hand, he turned it over and shook out the velvet jeweler's box. With a few more flips of his fingers, it came open, and a brilliant, sparkling diamond caught the light from the window and flashed in her eyes.

She watched in complete astonishment as he picked up her hand and slid the ring onto her third finger.

"We'll be married as soon as possible," he said matter-of-factly.

She shook her head, sure that she must still be in bed back in her suite—dreaming. "I don't understand," she stammered.

"We must marry," he said again, only this time the emphasis was on the *must*. "You were a virgin…and you could be pregnant," he finished softly. "I didn't think…that is I didn't use protection. For this I am sorry."

No, she wasn't dreaming. In her dreams, her marriage proposal had always been somewhat more romantic. But then she was getting precisely what she wanted. It was hard to argue with that, no matter the motivation behind the proposal.

"Okay," she said quietly.

Relief flashed in his eyes. Had he expected her to argue? Maybe play the martyr and give him a weeping, tragic refusal because he didn't love her?

He pulled her into his arms, but instead of kissing her, he hugged her tightly. "We should go back to your suite. We have arrangements to make. Unless you'd prefer my penthouse? I'm afraid I'm no more settled in this city than you are, but we'll remedy that. We can buy a house. Wherever you like."

She wedged an arm between them and levered herself away. "What about Alannis?"

There was quiet between them finally, and his expression sobered. "She and Sophia are flying back to Greece tomorrow."

Isabella tried to disguise the flinch. She didn't want to think of Alannis's heartbreak or her mother's disappointment. Neither woman had been anything but kind to her. And now she was the femme fatale. It wasn't a very good feeling.

She nodded, not wanting to delve too deeply into Alannis. She was a subject better left alone.

The sparkle of the diamond in the sun drew her gaze back to the gorgeous ring adorning her finger. And then she allowed some of the joy to shine on her like the sun beaming through the window.

With a tentative smile, she looked back up at Theron. "You really want to marry me? Okay, scratch that. Bad question. I'm sure you don't really want to marry me. But you don't have to. Just so you know. I mean the whole idea of putting a ring on my finger just because I was a virgin and we didn't use protection—well, it's archaic. Nobody does that anymore. I mean even if I turned out pregnant, there's nothing to say we'd have to be married—"

He silenced her with his mouth, pressing his lips to hers in a deep, lustful kiss. For several long seconds, all that she heard was the soft smooching sounds of their lips. She went positively boneless.

Finally he pulled away, his eyes glittering. He may not *want* to marry her, but she knew his eyes didn't lie. He wanted *her,* and he definitely desired her. It was a start.

"Now if we're through talking nonsense, let's return to the hotel," he said huskily.

He didn't look any different. Isabella watched Theron from across the sitting room of her suite as he went through a myriad of phone calls. First he'd talked to the person she'd rented the apartment from. Then a few business calls had interceded. Now he was back to talking to God-knew-who about flights and planes, and she wasn't sure what else. Her head was spinning.

Maybe she'd expected him to look…well, she didn't know. Engaged? But then he'd been engaged for several days. Just not to her.

A knock at the door interrupted her moody dissertation on Theron's phone calls. Reynolds, who had been going over plans with Theron, strode to the door and opened it.

Isabella couldn't see who it was with the way Reynolds held the door, but a moment after opening it, he stepped back and glanced over at her.

"Sadie Tilton to see you."

Isabella made a quick motion with her hand for him to let her in. Sadie popped her head around the door, her eyes filled with caution. They lightened as soon as she saw Isabella and she hurried over to where Isabella sat on the couch.

"What's going on?" Sadie hissed. "You sounded so weird when you called."

Isabella didn't say anything but she raised her hand so that Sadie could see. A quick glance around her told her that Theron wasn't paying either of them any attention, so involved was he on the phone.

"Oh my God!" Sadie exclaimed as she pounced on Isabella's hand. "He proposed?"

"Shh, he's on the phone," Isabella murmured. "And yes, well, sorta. He didn't exactly ask. He informed me we were getting married."

Sadie frowned. "Are you happy about it?"

Isabella smiled. "I will be. He's all I've ever wanted."

"What did he say then? And what about Alannis?"

"Not much. Just that he'd taken my virginity, I could be pregnant and we needed to marry."

Sadie winced. "Are you sure you want to marry a guy for those reasons? I mean what about love? Or at least a legitimate reason that doesn't predate this century."

Isabella looked at her friend and sighed. "I can't very well make him fall in love with me if we aren't together, Sadie. Yes, ideally he would love me now, and we'd marry for all the usual reasons, but I have to take what opportunities

I'm given. He feels something for me. That much I know. Something that goes beyond simple lust. He just needs time. But if I don't marry him, he'll marry Alannis, and where does that get me?"

"You're right, you're right," Sadie said in a low voice. "I was just hoping for something more. You've dreamed about this for so long. I wanted it to be perfect for you."

Isabella squeezed Sadie's hand. "It will be perfect. Maybe not yet, but it will be. The day he says *I love you* will make everything leading up to it worth it."

Sadie smiled. "Now that that's all settled, I have to say thank you. You didn't have to do it, but at the same time, I'm so grateful."

Isabella looked at her in puzzlement. "What on earth are you talking about?"

"The apartment, the rent, the account. You know, so I don't have to go back to work at the club."

Isabella shook her head.

Sadie frowned. "You didn't arrange for my apartment to be paid up for the next year?"

"No-o-o…."

The both turned and looked at Theron at the same time.

"Then I don't suppose you also arranged my meeting with Howard," Sadie murmured.

"No, I had no idea," Isabella said softly.

"You've got yourself a good man, Bella. Not that I'm fooling myself by thinking he did it for any other reason than he didn't want you ever going into that place," she said with a grin.

"He is a good man," Isabella agreed as she stared across the room at Theron.

As if sensing her perusal, he lifted his gaze, the phone still held to his ear and looked back at her. His eyes smoldered with quiet intensity. Suddenly all Isabella wanted was for everyone to be gone from her room and for it to be only the two of them.

In his arms, she could forget a lot. Including that she wasn't the one he would have chosen as his wife.

"How about I have Reynolds see you home?" Isabella murmured to Sadie.

For a moment Sadie looked startled but then she followed Isabella's gaze toward Theron and grinned. Sadie leaned forward and hugged Isabella tightly.

"Just don't leave town without letting me know what's going on, okay?"

Isabella hugged her back. "I won't."

Isabella got up and walked over to where Reynolds stood. "You'll see her home?" she asked, though it wasn't a request.

Reynolds looked quickly over at Theron, who evidently heard Isabella because he nodded at Reynolds and made a go gesture with his hand.

Moments later, Isabella closed the door, and for the first time since he'd put his ring on her finger, they were alone. Well, almost. There was still the phone.

Slowly, she walked over to where Theron sat at the desk in front of the window. He looked up, his eyes darkening when she placed her hands on his knees and then straddled him, sliding up against his chest.

He tensed and tried to ward her off as he continued talking, something about figures, finances, hotel plans, blah blah. None of that interested her as much as the possibility of getting Theron naked.

She took the hand he held between them and guided it to her chest, sliding it just inside the neckline of her shirt. He curled his fingers into a fist, as if denying her.

Isabella only smiled and began unbuttoning his shirt from the top down. His voice became noticeably more strained, and he even broke off twice as he seemed to lose his train of thought.

If she were a good fiancée, she'd leave him alone, become invisible while he conducted business and reappear later, but she'd already proven she wasn't the best at suppressing her own wants. Not when it came to Theron.

As she parted the lapels, she leaned forward and pressed her lips to his bare chest. She felt his quick intake of breath, heard his strangled response to whoever it was he was talking to.

She'd give him two more minutes tops. If he resisted beyond then, she'd have to give him credit for being very strong indeed.

Ignoring his disapproving look, she slipped from his lap and went seeking lower, unfastening the button of his pants. Every muscle in his thighs locked and went rigid when her hand caressed his equally rigid erection.

One minute left. Hmm.

She lowered her head as she gently freed him from constraint. When her mouth touched him, she heard his garbled response to whatever the other person on the phone had asked, and then she heard the unmistakable sound of a phone meeting the wall.

She smiled even as he lurched upward, grabbing her under the arms and hauling her into his arms.

A torrent of Greek flew from his mouth as he strode for the bedroom.

"English, Theron," she said with a laugh.

"*Theos,* but what are you trying to do to me?" he demanded as he tossed her onto the bed. "I'll have to ban you from my offices if this is the sort of thing you'll do when I'm trying to conduct business."

She tried to suppress the grin as he tore off his shirt and pants and sent them flying.

"Undress," he said seductively.

She raised an eyebrow. "Isn't that your job?"

He fell forward, landing his hands on either side of her shoulders as he stared down at her. Then he reached for her hands and pulled them over her head, transferring her wrists into one hand so the other was free.

Then he began to unbutton her shirt. His movements were jerky and impatient as he ridded her of every stitch of clothing.

When he was finished, he let go of her hands. "Turn over," he said.

She looked up in confusion.

His fingers roamed down her nakedness even as he urged her over.

"Do as I say, *pethi mou.*"

She shivered at the authority in his voice. Maybe she had started this whole thing, but it seemed he intended to finish it.

Carefully she rolled until her belly pressed against the mattress. She tucked her hands high, just over her head as she felt Theron lean down once more.

His fingers danced across the small of her back, and then she realized he was tracing her tattoo. She smiled.

"Do you like it?" she murmured.

"It's driven me crazy since the first day you walked into my office," he muttered. "I've had the most insane urge to throw you down and trace it with my tongue."

"There's nothing stopping you," she said lazily.

"Indeed not."

She jumped and closed her eyes when his warm tongue made contact with her skin. He emblazoned a damp trail over the small of her back and then he pressed a kiss right over her spine.

"The fairy is misleading. You should have had a devil tattooed on you."

She smiled again and rolled over, meeting his smoldering gaze. "And where do you propose this devil go?"

His lips curled into a half smile before he dipped his head and kissed the area right above the soft curls at the juncture of her legs. "Here," he murmured. "Where only I can enjoy it."

"Don't tease me, Theron," she whispered. "I want you so much."

"Then take me, Bella." He spread her legs and covered her

with his body. And suddenly he was inside her, deep and full. "Take all of me," he said hoarsely.

She wrapped arms and legs around him, holding him tight as he filled her again and again. His lips found hers, sweet and warm. She drank from him, took from him, and still she wanted more. She wanted everything he had to give.

This time they came together, an explosion she felt to her very depths. As his body settled comfortably over hers, she sighed in utter contentment.

After a moment he rolled to the side and gathered her in his arms.

"Where did you learn such wickedness, Bella *mou?*" he asked as she snuggled into the crook of his arm and he stroked his fingers over her shoulder.

She rose up, positioning her elbow underneath so she could look at him. "What do you mean?"

"You were a virgin and yet you seduced me as thoroughly as someone with much more experience."

She laughed. "Theron, tell me you aren't one of these men who thinks the presence of a hymen equals complete ignorance on the woman's part."

But then given his antiquated views on honor, and the fact that he was marrying her over that thing called a hymen, perhaps it wasn't such a stretch to believe he thought she should be ignorant of sex.

He looked uncomfortable as he grappled with his answer. "I suppose I thought it unlikely that someone with no experience would be so…"

"Good?" she asked cheekily.

He gave her a look that suggested he wasn't amused by her teasing.

"I never said I wasn't experienced," she said lightly.

He tensed and raised his head to stare at her. "What do you mean by this? Who do you have experience with?"

She laid a hand on his chest. "Now, Theron, stop with the testosterone surge. You're the only man I've ever made love with. Experience can be gained without participation you know."

"As long as you don't ever decide to participate with another man," he said gruffly. "I will teach you everything you need to know."

She grinned. "And maybe as we've previously discussed, there are things I'll teach you, as well."

He yanked her to him, and she landed with a soft thud, her lips a breath away from his.

"Is this so? Well then, Bella *mou,* by all means teach me. I think you'll find me a willing pupil."

Sixteen

Theron reached across the seat and buckled Isabella's belt. She roused sleepily and looked questioningly at him.

"We'll be landing soon," he said. "Then we'll take a helicopter to the island."

She yawned and nodded, trying to knock some of the sleep fog from her mind. "I'm looking forward to meeting Piers, well officially. I've seen him but just once and we didn't speak," she said as she shifted in her seat. "Though it's been so long since I've seen Chrysander, it will be like meeting him for the first time all over again. What's he like?" she asked.

He raised one eyebrow. "What's who like, *pethi mou?*"

"Piers," she said a little grumpily. "You know, the one I just said I hadn't met."

He smiled. "You're not at your best when you first awaken."

She yawned again and just frowned.

"To answer your question, Piers is...well, he's Piers,"

Theron said with a shrug. "He travels the most of any of us now that Chrysander has settled on the island. He's flying in from Rio de Janeiro right now where he's overseeing the building of our new hotel."

"Married or otherwise attached?"

Theron laughed. "Not Piers. He has an aversion to becoming entangled with any female for more than the length of a casual affair."

"Did your mother mistreat him?" Isabella asked dryly.

Theron shook his head. "You, Bella *mou,* have quite a smart wit about you. I'm going to have to think of ways to keep that mouth of yours occupied."

"And Marley?" she asked as the plane began its descent. Already she could see tiny twinkling lights from the ground. "What's she like? I admit, I find it hard to imagine a woman who could so easily subdue a man like Chrysander. He always seemed so…hard."

"It wasn't easy," Theron said, his expression growing serious. "They went through a lot together. Chrysander is lucky to have her."

"So you like her?" Isabella prompted.

Theron nodded. "I like her very much. She's good for him. Softens him just enough."

"She sounds…nice."

"You have nothing to worry about," he soothed. "You'll like them, and they'll like you."

She managed a stiff smile. What she really wanted to ask is whether they'd liked Alannis more. How would they feel about the fact he was marrying someone else? She didn't know how it worked in Theron's family, but would they have expected him to marry Alannis for business reasons?

Theron's hand found hers just a moment before the plane touched down. She was content to let her fingers remain entwined with his as they taxied. A few minutes later, they were disembarking the plane, and Theron was urging her toward a waiting helicopter.

"If I had thought, I would have arranged for us to stay on the mainland overnight so that you could see the beauty of the island from the air in daytime," Theron said as they boarded.

"I'll see it on the way back, right?" she said with a smile as Theron settled beside her.

He nodded as the engines whirred too loudly for conversation any longer.

The ride across the inky darkness was a little disconcerting, and then Theron pointed to a flash of light in the distance. She strained forward, leaning over him as they drew closer to the source of the light.

A few moments later, the helicopter lowered onto the well-lit helipad, and the pilot gestured to Theron when it was safe to get out.

Theron opened the door and ducked out, then reached back to help Isabella from the seat. His hand over her back, urging her low, he hurried across the concrete landing area toward the lighted gardens leading to the house.

As they approached the entryway, a man stepped from the door. Even from a distance, Isabella recognized him as Chrysander. He smiled, and she relaxed, even managing a smile in return.

"Isabella, how you've grown, even since your graduation," he said as he enfolded her in a hug.

"Thanks for making me feel like a girl who just shed braces and training bras," she said dryly as she pulled away.

Chrysander stared at her in obvious surprise and then burst into laughter. "My apologies. You're far from that as Theron has no doubt found out."

She couldn't prevent the flush that worked its way up her cheeks.

"Why don't you stop trying to find things to say and let us

through," Theron said balefully. "Before we have to extricate both feet from your mouth."

Chrysander chuckled and gestured for them to pass. "Marley is waiting in the living room. She's anxious to meet you, Isabella."

He moved past her and Theron to call out in Greek to the man collecting her and Theron's luggage from the helicopter.

Theron took her arm and they walked inside. The house was absolutely beautiful, and she couldn't wait to see it in full light. And the beach. She could smell the salt air and even hear the waves crashing in the distance, but she wanted to see it and dig her toes into the sand.

A small, dark-haired woman who was bouncing a blanket-wrapped bundle in her arms was standing in the living room next to the couch. Isabella offered a tentative smile when she looked up.

"Theron!" she exclaimed as she walked in their direction.

Theron smiled broadly and caught her and the baby up in his arms. "How are my favorite sister and my nephew?"

"I'm your only sister," she said.

"Marley, I'd like you to meet Isabella, my fiancée," he said as he turned to Isabella.

Marley smiled, her blue eyes flashing in welcome. "I'm very happy to meet you, Isabella."

"Please, call me Bella," she offered. "And I'm very glad to meet you, as well."

"Has Piers arrived?" Theron asked with a frown as he surveyed the room.

"He's coming," Marley said. "He left to go change when we heard the helicopter. We've held a late dinner for you and Isabella."

Just then a tall, dark-haired man entered the room. He was easily the tallest of the three brothers, a little slighter than Chrysander but a bit more broad in the shoulders than Theron.

Where Theron and Chrysander had golden-brown eyes, Piers's were dark, nearly black. His skin tone was darker as well, as though he spent a great deal of time in the sun.

His expression was bland as he looked at Theron. "There you are." He glanced over at Isabella. "And this must be the bride-to-be?"

"One of the many it would appear," Isabella said, refusing to dodge the inevitable awkwardness of the situation.

Piers's eyebrows drew together at her bluntness then he cocked one and offered what Isabella suspected was as close to a smile as he got. "I like her, Theron. She has spirit."

Theron didn't look disquieted by her outburst, but then he seemed resigned to her mouth, as he'd put it.

Chrysander moved to his wife's side and put an arm around her. "Want me to put him down so that we can eat?"

"If he'll go down," Marley said wearily. "Colic," she said with a grimace as she handed the baby to Chrysander. "We've been up with him for the last two weeks. I just hope you can sleep through it."

Chrysander brushed his lips across her forehead. "Don't worry, *agape mou.* I'll sit with him until he settles. You go eat and then I want you to get some rest."

Isabella's heart melted at the look of love in Chrysander's eyes. She wanted that. Wanted it badly. It was all she could do not to sigh as Marley smiled back at him, her eyes glowing. The look of a woman who knew she was loved.

Then Marley looked at Isabella, and she cocked her head to the side as if studying her. Isabella quickly looked away, hoping she hadn't betrayed herself in that moment. It was bad enough that she knew the truth about her engagement. She had no wish for anyone else to know she had schemed her way into Theron's life.

"Come, let's go into the dining room," Marley said.

Dinner was laid-back with casual conversation. Marley

asked general questions about Isabella, her likes and interests. Piers remained quiet, his eyes following the conversation as he ate, and more than once, Isabella found him staring at her as if he were peeling back the layers of her skin.

It was a relief when Chrysander rejoined them and the conversation shifted to business. Even Piers shed his reserve and entered the fray as they argued and debated.

Marley caught Isabella's gaze, rolled her eyes and then motioned for Isabella to follow her from the table. The men didn't even notice when both women slipped away.

"Would you like to take a walk down to the beach?" Marley asked. "It's so beautiful by moonlight, and it's been awhile since Dimitri has settled down before two in the morning."

Isabella smiled. "I'd love it. I can't wait to see everything in daylight. It's beautiful just from what I can see."

They stepped through the sliding glass doors, and Marley led her down a stone walkway. The sounds of the ocean grew louder and then the pathway gave way to sand. Marley stopped and shed her shoes and urged Isabella to do the same.

"Oh, it's gorgeous," Isabella breathed when they walked closer to the water.

The sky was clear and littered with stars, carelessly strewn across the sky like someone playing jacks. The moon was high overhead, shimmering and reflecting off the dark waters.

"This is my favorite place in the world," Marley said softly. "It's amazing, like my own little corner of paradise."

"I don't think I've ever seen anything so beautiful."

Isabella walked to the edge of the wet sand and waited for another wave to roll in. Then she stepped into the foaming surf, loving the tickle of water over her toes.

"I told you we would find them here," Chrysander said in an amused voice. "My wife is forever escaping to her beach."

Isabella turned to see Theron and Chrysander standing,

hands stuffed into their pants as they watched the two women. She couldn't discern their expressions in the darkness.

"Come, Bella," Theron said. "Let's leave the two love-birds. You must be tired from our long trip."

Marley smiled at Isabella as she walked past on her way to Theron. He held his hand out to her as she neared, and she slid her fingers into his.

He brought them to his lips and pressed a gentle kiss against her knuckles. Isabella relaxed for the first time. It would be easy if Theron acted as though he wanted to marry her, almost as though he felt something beyond lust and desire. And maybe he did. Did he? Could he love her?

She let him pull her back onto the stone walkway toward the house.

"They seem so in love," she said when she and Theron stepped inside the door.

Theron nodded. "They have quite a story. I'll tell it to you sometime. Right now, however, I'm only wanting a bed and a soft pillow."

She laughed softly and ran her hand up his arm. "There are parts of my anatomy that make for a good pillow."

His lips firmed for just a moment, and he glanced up at her, his expression indecipherable. "I think it would be best if we kept separate bedrooms here."

She recoiled, her head drawing away in confusion. "I don't understand. Why wouldn't we share a bedroom? We're engaged."

He pulled her into his arms. "Yes, we are, *pethi mou*. And as such, I'd show you the respect you're due by not flaunting our sexual relationship in front of my brother and his wife. It's enough that he knows I took your virginity, but I won't draw anymore undue attention to you."

Hurt and humiliation hit her hard in the chest. "He knows? You told him?"

Theron blinked in surprise. "It is my shame to bear, Isabella. Not yours."

She closed her eyes and looked away. So Chrysander, and by default, Marley, did know that Theron was only marrying her out of some outdated sense of honor.

"I'll go up to my room then," she said quietly. "I assume my stuff will be there. I can find my way."

"Bella," he called as she started for the stairs.

She turned and stared bravely at him, determined not to show any emotion.

"I didn't do this to hurt you."

She smiled. A tremulous, hesitant smile, but she pulled it off. "I know, Theron. I know."

Then she turned and headed up the stairs in search of her room.

Seventeen

Isabella stared up at the ceiling, her hands behind her head. Sleep had eluded her, as she'd slept for most of the flight over. She'd opened her window before going to bed, and the sounds of the waves lured her.

A look at the bedside clock told her she'd lain awake for hours. With a resigned sigh, she tossed aside the covers and swung her legs over the side of the bed. If she were quiet, she could walk down to the beach and watch the sun rise. It wasn't as if she was ever going to sleep. She was too tightly wound. Too restless.

The air was warm coming in the window, so she dressed in a pair of shorts and T-shirt. Not bothering with sandals, she slipped out of her room into the darkened hallway and crept down the stairs.

The house was quiet and cloaked in darkness as she made her way through the living room. She stepped onto the patio and breathed in the warm, salty air. Briefly closing her eyes, she let the breeze blow her hair from her face, and then she stepped onto the stone path leading to the sand.

The skies were already starting to lighten to the east, the horizon going pale lavender as the morning star shone bright, a single diamond against velvet.

The water was calm, lapping gently onto the shore, spreading foam in its wake. She walked down the beach, letting the waves rush over her feet as the world went gold around her.

A distance from the house, she saw a large piece of driftwood. Marley's seat, Chrysander had called it laughingly. She settled gingerly on the aged wood and stared at the beautiful scene before her. Truly she'd never experienced anything like it.

Unsure of just how long she sat there, basking in the dawn, she picked herself up and headed back toward the house. Sand covered her feet and she paused at the entryway to the stone path cutting through the garden to clean it off.

Voices carried from a short distance away, and she smiled. Theron was up. She could hear his soft laughter. Marley too and apparently Chrysander.

She started up the staggered steps when she heard her name. A surge of excitement hit her. Were they discussing the wedding? She took another step forward but faltered with Theron's next words.

He sounded…resigned. What was it he said? She glanced quickly over the hedge lining the walkway to the stone retaining wall surrounding the patio. There was a lattice wall that afforded the patio privacy and was covered with leafy greenery.

She strained to hear the conversation and then making a quick decision, she hiked her leg over the hedge and hurried to the retaining wall where she hunkered just below the breakfast area where the others were gathered.

As she listened to Theron's low voice explain the entire story to his brother and Marley, she turned so her back pressed against stone and slowly she slid until she sat with knees hunched to her chest.

Hearing her teasing and blatant flirtation from the mouth of someone else made it sound harsher, less earnest than it had been. She listened as he outlined his confusion over his desire for her and his desire to make Alannis his wife.

She put her head down on her arms. She wanted to close her ears, but she couldn't. This was the hard truth, and she'd done all that he said. Her only comfort was that he made it seem as though she hadn't done it purposely, as if she hadn't planned to seduce him. No, he still blamed himself for that.

And then the statement that hit her square in the gut, stealing her breath—and her hope.

"I wanted…I wanted what you and Marley have found," Theron admitted to Chrysander. "I wanted a wife and children—a family, a life with a woman I cared about. I had it all mapped out. Marriage to Alannis, a comfortable life. It all flew out the window so fast that my head is still spinning."

No longer able to stand the pain his words caused, she vaulted up, staggering down the slight incline. She landed on one of the smaller walkways that circled the gardens and nearly ran headlong into Piers.

He gripped her arms to steady her and stared down with piercing eyes.

"I'm reminded of the saying that eavesdroppers rarely hear good of themselves," Piers said.

"No," she said in a small voice. "It would appear they don't."

Something that might have been compassion softened his expression. She turned pleading eyes up to meet his gaze. "Don't tell him I heard. You already know everything. Everyone knows. There's no reason to make Theron feel any worse."

"And you?" Piers asked. "What about you, Bella?"

"It would appear I have a lot to fix," she said quietly.

She shook herself from his hands and hurried through the

garden around to the back entrance. She stopped at the door and stared for a long moment at the helipad. Then she walked inside, making sure she wasn't seen as she mounted the stairs.

When she got to her room, she closed the door and leaned heavily against it even as a tear slid down her cheek.

Theron didn't love her. He couldn't. Because he loved Alannis. And because of Isabella, his chance of finding the happiness he wanted was ruined. Taken away by her selfishness and single-minded pursuit of *her* wants and *her* needs.

She took a long hard look at herself, and she didn't like what she saw very much.

Loving someone shouldn't hurt so much, shouldn't be so destructive. Was she nothing more than a spoiled rich girl unwilling to accept that she couldn't have what she most wanted?

And then in a moment of sudden clarity, of anguish and realization, she knew that she had to let Theron go. She wasn't what he wanted. Alannis was. Isabella didn't even want to know the hurt and disappointment that the other girl had endured. What had Theron told her? That he'd been unfaithful?

Theron was bearing the brunt of Isabella's actions—the dishonor. When the blame was solely hers.

He isn't yours to keep.

The single thought echoed and simmered through her mind. And she knew it was true, no matter how much it hurt, how much it made her heart ache and pulse.

She bowed her head, allowing the tears to slither down her cheeks, falling to the floor beneath her. For a moment she let herself cry and then she raised her head, determined to regain her composure. She had to figure a way out of this mess.

First of all, she couldn't let Theron know that she'd overheard his conversation. He would feel hugely guilty. He'd want to do the right thing—according to him.

But this time—this time *she* was going to do the right thing. Wiping at her face with the back of her hand, she went to her bags and dug for her handbag. Sophia had given her a card with her address and telephone number, had invited her to visit her in Greece whenever she resumed her plans to travel to Europe. Never mind that those plans had revolved around Theron and had been abandoned when Theron had relocated to New York.

Next she needed to locate a helicopter service, preferably one that wasn't on Chrysander's payroll. Not exactly easy when she was on an island, in a country where she didn't speak the language.

Hopefully Chrysander had internet in his office, or a directory, or something….

And then she had to talk to Theron.

The worst part is that she had to pretend that she'd never heard what Theron said. She had to smile and act as if nothing was wrong. As if her heart weren't breaking.

Isabella checked her watch as Marley cleared the dishes away after the light lunch she'd served on the patio. Isabella deserved an Oscar award, surely, because she'd smiled and laughed, responded when appropriate. Even as she cracked and broke on the inside.

Piers had watched her, his gaze finding her often, probing and assessing. When the eating was finally finished, it was all Isabella could do not to sigh in relief. Now she had a little time to talk to Theron before the helicopter would arrive to pick her up.

"Theron," she said as he stood from the table. "Could I speak to you? Alone?" she added with an apologetic look in the others' direction.

Piers's brow furrowed, and he gave her an inquisitive look as he stood. She avoided his scrutiny.

"Of course, *pethi mou*. Why don't we go for a walk on the beach?" Theron suggested.

She avoided his hand when he extended it, and instead, she

brushed past him and to the walkway. He followed her down to the water, and this time, the water failed to soothe her. It mocked her with its false serenity.

The sheer beauty of the brilliant blue, stretching outward seeking the distant skyline, taunted her. Below the surface, there were ugly things. Things that never saw the light, that never disturbed the pristine surface that sparkled in the sun.

When she stopped, her feet sinking into the sand, Theron's hands closed over her shoulders.

"What's the matter, Bella *mou?*" he asked in his deep timbre. "You seem sad today."

She turned in his arms, finally finding the courage to face him. "There are things I need to tell you, Theron."

His expression sobered. "What things?"

She broke away and took a step down the beach before turning again. "The whole reason I planned to travel to London this summer was because I thought you would be there."

Confusion clouded his eyes, and he started to open his mouth. She silenced him quickly with an outstretched hand. "Please, don't say anything. Let me finish. There's a lot I need to say, and I won't be able to finish if you start asking questions."

He hesitated and then nodded.

"When I arrived in New York and learned that you would be remaining there permanently, I changed my plans on the fly, opting to rent an apartment I didn't really want and invented a host of other reasons to throw me into contact with you."

Her hands closed over her arms, and she rubbed up and down despite the heat that prickled over her skin.

"I knew you planned to propose to Alannis. I knew you'd planned your life with another woman. I was determined to try and seduce you away from her."

He sucked in his breath and opened his mouth again, but she stared at him so hauntingly that he quieted again. Only the glitter in his eyes gave the impression of what he must be thinking.

"I pursued you relentlessly. I'd even planned to crash your engagement party but arrived too late. That was the reason that Marcus was in my room. He'd followed me home in the rain when I took off on foot to try and stop your proposal."

His lips thinned, and he turned his face away to stare at the ocean.

"I thought I'd lost you, but then you came to the strip club, and then we made love in my suite. The next day you told me we had to be married, and I knew that you felt you'd dishonored me. I knew you didn't love me, but I was determined to have the chance to make you love me, so I said yes. I let you say all those things. Because in the end I'd have the one thing I wanted most. You."

She found his gaze again even as tears glided down her cheeks. "You see, Theron, I've loved you since I was a little girl. I thought it was infatuation, that it would go away, but each time I saw you, my love grew until I knew I had to try. I couldn't just live my life standing on the outside of my dream, never giving us a chance."

She took in a deep steadying breath, her quiet sobs shaking her shoulders. "But I was wrong. And I'm sorry. I ruined things for you and Alannis."

Quiet lay between them. Theron stood stock-still, his hands shoved into his pockets.

"You don't love me," she said in a remarkably steady voice.

She hadn't intended it to be a question, but felt like a plea from the depths of her soul. And then he turned to face her again and her hopes shriveled and died. There were a host of things reflected in those golden eyes. Confusion, anger, but not love. Never love.

Quickly, before he could react, she stepped forward and leaned up to kiss him on the cheek. "I hope someday you can forgive me."

She slid her ring off her finger then slipped her hand inside his. Without another word, she turned and ran back up the path to the house.

"Bella! Bella!" Theron shouted after her.

She brushed past Chrysander at the top of the pathway, ignoring his hands as they reached out to steady her.

"Isabella!" he called.

She swallowed the sob caught in her throat and ran inside. The helicopter would be here soon. Her bag was where she left it, at the doorway leading out the back of the house, past the pool and to the helipad.

She grabbed it and after a look back at the house, she hurried out to wait on the helicopter.

Eighteen

Theron stared at the ring resting in his palm then at Isabella's retreating back. He simply couldn't comprehend everything she'd admitted. It sounded too far-fetched.

Had she really loved him for so long? It didn't seem possible.

He watched as Chrysander slowly walked down the path toward him. He came to a stop a few feet in front of Theron.

"Trouble?" he asked.

"You could say that," Theron murmured, still trying to come to grips with all she'd told him.

"She seemed pretty upset," Chrysander said.

Theron closed his fist around the ring. "She gave me my ring back."

Chrysander arched an eyebrow in surprise. "Did she say why? It's easy for anyone with half a brain to see she's crazy about you."

Theron cocked his head then shook it. "She just told me the craziest story. I don't even know what to make of it."

"Care to share?"

Theron opened his hand to see the ring still lying there. It looked all wrong. It should be on Isabella's finger. She should be glowing with happiness, not staring at him with tearstained cheeks.

"She said she's been in love with me since she was a girl," Theron said slowly. "And that her trip to New York was because I was there." He looked up at his brother. "She said the entire reason she planned to go to London was because she thought I'd be there."

Chrysander smiled. "Sounds like a determined girl."

Theron nodded. "That's not all. She seduced *me*."

This time Chrysander laughed. "Now this I have to hear."

Theron quickly told Chrysander everything that had happened since the day Isabella had walked into his office, now armed with the knowledge of what she'd really been doing. It all seemed so much clearer now. The sultry teasing, the apartment hunting, the shopping.

Chrysander remained silent for a moment. "So, are you angry?" he finally asked.

Theron gave him a strange look. "Angry?"

"You wanted to marry Alannis. Isabella prevented that."

Theron shook his head. "Isabella didn't prevent that, Chrysander. I did. I didn't propose, and Isabella was nowhere near me when that happened."

"Okay, so what are you then?"

"Flattered? Overwhelmed? Completely and utterly gobsmacked?"

Chrysander grinned. "That about covers it."

"My God, Chrysander. She's so gorgeous. She lights up the entire room when she walks in. She makes me crazy. Absolutely and completely crazy. She could have any man she wanted. And she wants *me*."

"Enough to drive you to your knees, isn't it? Finding the love of a good woman. They can certainly tie you in knots."

"I love her," Theron whispered. "All this time, I've been so focused on wanting a wife and children, wanting to settle down with the picture-perfect family, and perfection has been staring me in the face all along."

Chrysander smiled. "Why are you telling me all this? It would seem you have a very upset young lady who seems determined to do what's best for you, whether you like it or not."

Theron frowned and clenched his fist around the ring. "Fool-headed, stubborn…" He shook his head and stalked up the pathway, Chrysander falling in behind him.

They were halfway to the house when Chrysander stopped. Theron turned around to see him frown.

"You hear that?" Chrysander asked.

Theron strained to hear. In the distance, he heard the unmistakable sound of an approaching helicopter. "Did you call for the helicopter?"

Chrysander shook his head. "One wasn't scheduled until Piers's departure tomorrow."

Both men hurried up the pathway then cut left to circle the gardens to take the shorter route to the helipad. Even before the helipad came into view, they saw the chopper descend.

"That's not one of ours," Chrysander said grimly.

Chrysander broke into a run, and Theron followed. If Chrysander was worried then so was Theron. But when they rounded the corner and he saw Isabella standing as the helicopter door opened, his blood froze.

"Isabella!" Theron shouted.

She didn't even turn around. She wouldn't have heard him over the roar of the blades.

Chrysander waved frantically to the pilot, and Theron raced ahead of him, trying to reach Isabella in time. He watched helplessly as the door closed behind her, and then, as he reached the edge of the concrete, the helicopter lifted off.

The draft blew his hair and clothing, but he stood, waving his arms in an effort to gain her attention. The helicopter rose higher and then headed in the direction of the mainland.

Chrysander cursed as Theron stood there frozen.

"I've got to find out where she's going," Theron said as he turned back to the house.

Ahead, Marley and Piers came out the back door, Marley in the protective arm of Piers.

"What's going on?" Piers shouted.

Theron strode past him and Marley while Chrysander hung back. He tore up the stairs and into Isabella's room only to find her things gone. There was no note, no hint of where she'd gone.

He ran back down, finding the others in the living room. Chrysander was on the phone trying to track down the pilot service and figure out a way to hold Isabella when she landed.

Piers approached him, a grim expression on his face.

"There's something you should know."

Theron looked sharply at him. "What?"

"This morning, Isabella was on the beach early. I found her on the other side of the patio, visibly upset by something she'd overheard in your conversation with Chrysander and Marley. She begged me not to say anything. She said she didn't want you to feel any worse."

Theron closed his eyes as he remembered waxing on about what he wanted. When what he wanted had been in front of his nose all along.

"I'm a damn fool," he muttered.

"No arguments here," Piers said with a wry smile. "The question is, what are you going to do to get her back?"

Isabella hadn't considered the repercussions of landing a helicopter on the estate of what appeared to be an extremely wealthy, Greek family. As soon as they settled on the ground, they were surrounded by a dozen security guards. All carrying guns.

So maybe this wasn't her best idea.

The door was wrenched open, and she found herself staring into the grim face of one of the gunmen. He barked out something in Greek, and Isabella stared helplessly back at him.

"I only speak English," she said.

"What do you want? Why are you here?" he asked in heavily accented English.

She took a deep breath and tried not to stare at the muzzle of the gun which was precariously close to her nose.

"I'm here to see Alannis Gianopolous. It's important."

"Your name," he demanded.

"Isabella Caplan."

He lifted a small wire and released a torrent of Greek into what she assumed was a microphone. A few moments later, he lowered the gun and took a step backward.

"This way please, Ms. Caplan."

He even reached a hand in to help her down. A few moments later, he escorted her inside the palatial estate that was situated on a cliff overlooking the ocean. In any other circumstance, she would have spared a moment of envy for such a gorgeous place.

"Isabella, my dear!" Sophia exclaimed as soon as Isabella was inside. She took hold of Isabella and kissed her on either cheek. "What on earth are you doing here? And where is Theron?"

Isabella looked down for a moment and then back up at the older woman. "I need to speak with Alannis. It's very important."

Sophia frowned slightly, concern filling her eyes. "Of course. Is everything all right?"

Isabella offered her a shaky smile. "No, but it will be."

"Wait here. I'll get Alannis for you," Sophia said.

Isabella walked to the huge glass window that overlooked the steep drop-off to the ocean. Alannis even lived in a perfect spot. Close to Chrysander and Marley. They could all be one big, happy family after Alannis married Theron.

"Isabella?" Alannis's soft voice filled the room.

Isabella turned to see the other girl staring at her, clear confusion written in her dark eyes.

"Mama said you wanted to see me."

Isabella gathered her courage and crossed the room to stand in front of Alannis.

"I came to apologize and to right a wrong."

Alannis frowned harder. "I don't understand."

Isabella took a deep breath. "I set out to break up you and Theron. I knew he wanted to marry you, but I've been in love with him forever, and I wanted him. I never stopped to think about what he wanted or that I was hurting two people in the process. You and him."

"But—" Alannis began.

"He wants to marry you," Isabella continued on, cutting her off. "You're who he wants. Go to him, Alannis. The helicopter is waiting to take you to the island. He'll be glad to see you. I've ended things with him. I gave him back his ring. Make sure he gives you a different one. You deserve a fresh start. One not tainted by me. Make him do it right, with all the romance and fuss you deserve."

Tears filled Isabella's eyes again. "I'm sorry I hurt you," she said. "I hope you'll be happy."

She turned to walk back out of the house.

"Isabella, wait," Alannis called. "You don't understand."

All Isabella understood is that if she didn't get out soon, she was going to come completely unraveled. She just prayed the taxi would be waiting as she'd arranged.

"Please show me out," she choked out to the security

guard who'd escorted her inside. "I have a taxi waiting out front."

As soon as the guard opened the front door, Isabella hurried down the drive toward the wrought iron gate. They opened automatically as she neared, and to her relief, a taxi waited outside on the street.

"The airport," she said as she climbed in. As she pulled away, she saw Alannis waving to her to stop. Isabella ignored her, turning away.

No one had ever told her doing the right thing would hurt so much.

"How long can it possibly take for the damn pilot to get out here?" Theron demanded as he ran his hand through his hair for the tenth time in an hour.

Frustration beat at him. He was stuck here on the island until Chrysander's pilot could come out. Now, finally, he was supposedly on his way.

Chrysander put down the phone and turned to Theron. "Isabella's pilot took her to the Gianopolous estate."

Theron stared at him in utter confusion. "Why on earth would she have gone to see Alannis? I had no idea she even knew where she lived."

"She's trying to make things right," Marley said softly. "First with you and now with Alannis."

He dug for his phone to retrieve Alannis's number. If he could reach Alannis before Isabella left then he could have her detained until he could go after her himself.

Chrysander handed Theron his phone, and Theron hastily punched in the numbers. A few seconds later, Sophia answered the phone.

"Sophia, thank goodness. Has Isabella been by there? What? She left in a taxi?" Sophia filled him in on where

Bella was headed then he hung up and turned to Chrysander.
"Now where is your damn pilot?"

It had been impossible for Isabella to purchase a ticket
leaving the country anytime soon. All the outgoing flights for
the next few hours were booked. In the end, she'd gone to the
charter service counter, plunked down her credit card, which
she hoped was as platinum as the name stated, and hired a
private jet to fly her to London.

At least she was on board now, waiting as the jet was
fueled and was placed in the queue for takeoff. Exhaustion
seeped into her bones. Not sleeping the night before
coupled with the emotionally draining day had taken it all
out of her.

She leaned her head back against the seat and closed her
eyes. She heard shuffling in the distance and assumed it was
the pilot, but then warm lips pressed gently to hers, and her
eyes flew open.

Theron drew away, cupping her face in his hands as she
stared at him in astonishment. He looked…well, he looked be-
draggled. His clothing was dusty and rumpled, his hair was in
disarray, and his golden eyes burned with feverish intensity.

Before she could say anything, he kissed her again, this
time foregoing the gentleness of before. He dragged her to
him, kissing her until she was left completely and utterly
breathless.

Then he pulled away and uttered a command in Greek
directed at the cockpit. To her increasing shock, the plane
began to move. With Theron in it.

"Theron, wait," she protested. "This plane is going to
London. You can't just leave here. What about Alannis? And
your family?"

He pulled her out of her seat, maneuvered to the couch,
then pulled her down onto his lap.

"Shouldn't we be in our seatbelts for takeoff?" she asked dumbly, still unable to comprehend that he was here.

"I'll catch you if there is any unexpected turbulence," he said silkily. "Now that you can't run anywhere and I have you all to myself, you'll have to listen to every word I'm about to say."

Her eyes rounded, and her mouth fell open. He traced her lips with his finger then pulled her down to replace his finger with his mouth.

"Foolish, impetuous, beautiful, frustrating woman," he murmured. "If you think you're going to get rid of me after you've hooked me and reeled me in, then you have another think coming, Bella *mou*."

Hope stuttered and made a soft pitter-patter in her chest. She stared at him unsure of what to say. So many things raced through her mind that she was absolutely speechless.

Then he rotated, sliding her off his lap and onto the seat next to him. He got to the floor on one knee and took her hand in his.

"I love you, my beautiful Isabella. I adore you. I can't imagine my life without you. Will you marry me and make me the happiest man alive?"

He slid the ring that she'd given him back on her finger. Then he leaned down and kissed her knuckle.

"This was never another woman's ring, *pethi mou*. I never gave Alannis a ring, and the one I intended for her was replaced by this one. I chose it for you. I never asked her to marry me. I was yours from the day you walked into my office. You turned my world upside down, and it's never been set to rights."

"You didn't propose?" she croaked around the swell of tears knotting her throat.

He looked back at her solemnly. "I would have never made love to you belonging to another woman. I intended to propose the night of the party. I had the ring. The moment was arranged. But all I could see was you. All I wanted was you. The morning after we made love, I went to see Alannis. I told her that I was going to marry you."

Isabella's face fell. Theron smiled and touched her cheek. "How tenderhearted you are, *agape mou.* Alannis isn't in love with me and is in fact, quite anxious for me to find you and put this ring back on your finger."

"She's not? You're not? In love with her, I mean?"

She closed her eyes and shook her head, sure she had to be dreaming.

"I'm in love with *you,*" he said softly. "Only you."

"But I heard what you told Chrysander, about you wanting what he and Marley had, a family, a wife. I don't fit into that anywhere," she said bitterly.

"What I want is you," he said simply. "Everything that I ever wanted, what I was so restless for and hoping to find was staring me in the face. I think I knew it that first day you came into my office. I saw that tattoo and it drove me crazy. I wanted to strip every piece of your clothing off so I could see more of it. But I had already started things rolling with Alannis. I fought my attraction to you because I was supposed to be acting as your guardian, not trying to think of ways to get you out of your clothing."

She raised a shaking hand to his face and cupped her palm to his cheek. He closed his eyes and leaned into her touch. Then he turned so he could press his lips to her fingers.

"Marry me, Bella."

"You want to marry me even if I don't want children right away?" she challenged.

"I have a feeling you'll keep me far too busy to think of children anytime soon," he said with an amused smile. He leaned in and kissed her again, his lips melting warm and sweet over hers. "We have all the time in the world, my precious love. Just promise me that we'll have it together."

She was sure that her smile lit up the entire universe as she stared back at him in awe.

"I love you, too," she whispered. "So much."

He sobered for a moment as he cupped her face lovingly. His expression serious, he said in a quiet voice, "You could already be pregnant. Will it upset you very much if you are?"

She grinned, her heart lightening with every breath. "I'm not pregnant."

"Oh, then you've already…it's that time of the…"

"No," she said with a slight laugh. "I'm on birth control."

His brows came together in confusion and then he glared at her, but there was no heat in his scowl. "You little minx."

"Are you angry that I didn't tell you when you informed me before that we were to be married?" she asked a little nervously.

"If you can forgive my dimwitted actions and the fact that I didn't give you the most romantic proposal before, then I can forgive you for effectively capturing me, hook, line and sinker."

"Yes," she said as she threw her arms around him.

He laughed. "Yes, what, *pethi mou?*"

"Yes, I'll marry you. I love you so much."

He stood and swept her into his arms. She blinked in surprise when she realized that she'd completely missed their takeoff.

"Now, if that's settled, why don't you and I go join the mile high club," he said wickedly.

She smiled as he carried her into the small bedroom in the back of the plane, her heart overflowing with sweet, unending joy.

And as they came together in body and soul, they whispered their love again and again.

Epilogue

The bride—and the groom—showed up to their wedding bare-footed. Theron stood on the beach of Anetakis Island waiting next to the priest as Chrysander escorted Isabella to him.

She was dressed in a bikini top, and a floral sarong floated delicately down her legs. Her toenails—which Theron had painted himself in a night full of decadence—shone a bright pink. An ankle bracelet caught the sun and shimmered above her foot, and Theron knew that it was his name engraved in the small silver band.

His gaze traveled upward to the diamond teardrop belly ring that he too had purchased and delighted in putting on her. But what took his breath away was her radiant smile. Just for him.

She was so beautiful she made his chest ache.

Piers stood to Theron's left, having flown in again for the wedding. Alannis and Sophia both were standing on the bride's side next to Marley.

There was a festive air, and everyone wore broad smiles. He could even detect the glimmer of tears in the women's eyes.

And then he reached out and took Isabella's hand, pulling her to him. It didn't matter that the vows weren't spoken, or that the priest cleared his throat cautiously. He simply had to kiss her.

Their lips met in a heated rush, soft against hard, sweet against salt. When he finally pulled away to allow the priest to officiate, tears shone in Isabella's eyes.

There was an odd catch in Theron's throat as he recited his vows. The words carried on the breeze, firm and clear.

Finally they were pronounced man and wife, and she became his.

There was much dancing on the beach, and later they moved to the gardens. Sophia and Alannis took great delight in teaching both Marley and Isabella traditional Greek dances while the men looked on, their smiles indulgent.

Later the helicopter came and whisked Theron and Isabella away to the bridal suite he'd arranged, a cottage on a cliff over-looking the sea.

He carried her to bed, where she whispered she had one last wedding gift for him.

Intrigued, he reared back as she untied the sarong and pulled it from underneath her.

"Do you remember telling me I should get another tattoo?" she asked with a mischievous glint.

His brow furrowed. "You didn't. Bella, tell me you didn't go to some tattoo parlor alone and undergo pain to get another tattoo."

"I didn't go alone. Marley went with me."

"And does Chrysander know this?" Theron asked incredulously.

Isabella laughed. "He might have had a thing or two to say when he barged in after us."

Theron muttered in Greek as he shook his head.

She hooked her thumbs in her bikini bottom and slowly, sensuously worked it down. There just above the juncture of her legs, right in the center, a straight line down from her belly ring, was an angel holding a pitchfork.

Theron couldn't contain his chuckle. Then he leaned down and brushed his lips across the design. "My own little demon angel," he said as he worked downward with his mouth.

* * * * *

Don't miss Piers's story in the last instalment of
THE ANETAKIS TYCOONS
available in November 2010 from Desire™.

THE BILLIONAIRE'S UNEXPECTED HEIR

BY
KATHIE DeNOSKY

Dear Reader,

In the past couple of months you've met the Garnier siblings, three more of Emerald Larson's ILLEGITIMATE HEIRS. You've watched her help Luke find his soulmate, Haley Rollins, and Arielle reconnect with the love of her life, Zach Forsythe. This month, Emerald turns her attention to Jake, the grandson she's worried might be as irresponsible as his philandering father.

After years of enjoying the blissful bachelor life in LA, Jake Garnier thinks that Emerald Larson has lost her mind when she gives him a thoroughbred farm in Kentucky's horse racing country. But when he comes face to face with the farm manager, Heather McGwire, and her six-month-old baby, he quickly realises that he's been sent to Hickory Hills for a reason. Learning that he's the little girl's father, Jake is determined to build a relationship with his daughter, as well as reconcile with her mother. Now all he has to do is convince Heather that's what she wants, too.

As I conclude THE ILLEGITIMATE HEIRS, I hope you enjoy *The Billionaire's Unexpected Heir.* I think you'll find a surprise or two along the way, and it is my fervent hope that you enjoy reading this series as much as I enjoyed writing it.

All the best,

Kathie DeNosky

Kathie DeNosky lives in her native southern Illinois with her big, lovable Bernese mountain dog, Nemo. Writing highly sensual stories with a generous amount of humour, Kathie's books have appeared on bestseller lists and received the Write Touch Readers Award and the National Readers' Choice Award. Kathie enjoys going to rodeos, travelling to research settings for her books and listening to country music. Readers may contact Kathie at PO Box 2064, Herrin, Illinois 62948-5264, USA or e-mail her at kathie@kathiedenosky.com. They can also visit her website at www.kathiedenosky.com.

This series is dedicated to Charlie, the love of my life.
And a special thank-you to my editor, Krista Stroever.
Here's to new beginnings.

One

"Hi, I'm Jake Garnier, the new owner of Hickory Hills."

From the corner of her eye, Heather McGwire saw the man stick out his hand in greeting, but she chose to ignore the gesture. She knew who he was and she'd just as soon have a snake crawl up beside her. Jake Garnier was the last person she wanted or needed to have to deal with this close to the big race. But now that he was the new owner of the thoroughbred farm she managed, there was no way of getting around it. She either had to get used to working for him or stick it out until after Stormy Dancer won the Southern Oaks Cup Classic, then look for employment elsewhere.

Besides, after what they'd shared, she took exception to the fact that he didn't even have the decency to remember her. The thought hurt more than she would have imagined or was comfortable with.

When she remained silent, he stared at her a moment as if trying to place her. "Heather?"

His smooth baritone caused her nerves to tingle and her heart to speed up, reminding her that a little over a year ago all it had taken was the rich sound of that voice to make her lose every ounce of sense she ever possessed. Now it only made her want to smack him for being the biggest jerk to ever draw a breath.

"Jake." She barely managed a short nod of acknowledgement.

Standing with her forearms resting on the white board rail surrounding the practice track, she concentrated on the stopwatch in her hand as Dancer passed the quarter-mile post and headed down the backstretch. The top contender for the prestigious Southern Oaks Cup Classic, the thoroughbred was on pace to break his own record.

"Come on, Dancer. You can do it." She glanced from the watch to the horse. "Just keep it up."

"I remember you mentioning that you worked at a thoroughbred farm, but I wasn't aware that it was

Hickory Hills," he said, sounding a lot happier to see her than she was to be seeing him.

"For the record, I'm the manager here." As Dancer headed for the home stretch, she added, "The name of the farm and where it was located never came up. Besides, you weren't that interested in hearing personal details, were you?" She glanced his way, and it was apparent her hostility didn't set well with him.

"Heather, I don't know what you think I've done, but—"

"It doesn't matter now," she interrupted. She didn't care to be reminded of how foolish she'd been.

He was silent for a moment. "At the risk of pissing you off further, how have you been?" he asked tightly.

Like you really want to know. If you had, you wouldn't have refused to take my phone calls.

She shrugged. "I've been all right." She didn't bothering asking how he'd been because she had a fair idea of what he'd been doing since they parted ways and didn't particularly care to hear the specifics.

"Is that our contender for the big race?" he asked, pointing toward Dancer.

Doing her best to ignore the man beside her, she urged the jockey, "Let him have his head, Miguel. Turn him loose." She glanced at the silver stop-watch again, and clicked the button on the side as the big bay sprinted past them. "Fantastic."

"I take it that was a good run?"

When Jake leaned close to see the time, his arm brushed hers and a tiny jolt of electricity shot straight through her. "It was excellent," she said, gritting her teeth and backing away. Turning to make her escape, she added, "Now, if you'll excuse me, I have work to do." She barely suppressed the urge to run when he fell into step beside her.

"I'd like for you to give me a tour of the farm if you have the time."

"I'm sure you need to unpack first," she said. Thanks to the mansion's housekeeper, Clara Buchanan, Heather had received a phone call the moment he passed through the security gates at the end of the half-mile-long driveway leading up to the mansion.

She desperately tried not to notice how his out-stretched arms caused his snug hunter green T-shirt to outline the muscles of his broad chest and empha-size his well-developed biceps when he stretched. "I've been cooped up in the car for the past four days on the drive from Los Angeles and it feels good to be out in the fresh air again."

"Mornings around here are pretty busy—we have our daily workouts and grooming," she hedged.

When they reached the stables, she grabbed a lead rope by one of the stalls, slid the half-door back, then eased inside to attach it to Silver Bullet's halter in an effort to escape Jake's disturbing presence.

"All right," he said, stepping back as she led the big dappled gray gelding out of the stall and down to the tack room. "This afternoon will be soon enough."

She shook her head as she tied the rope to an eye hook by the tack room door, attached another rope to the halter, then tied it to another hook on the opposite wall of the wide stable aisle. "That won't work. My schedule is pretty full today and to tell you the truth, tomorrow isn't looking all that good."

"Clear it for this afternoon." Jake's no-nonsense tone indicated that he was quickly running out of patience.

For the first time since he walked up beside her at the practice track, Heather met his irritated blue gaze full-on with a heated one of her own. "Will there be anything else, Mr. Garnier?"

Scowling, he stared at her for several long moments before he finally shook his head. "I'll be back after lunch." Turning to leave, he added, "And you might as well plan on working late this evening. After you show me around, I intend to meet with the other employees, then I want to go over the accounting records."

As she watched him walk away, a nudge against her leg had her glancing down at the big Bernese mountain dog that had sidled up beside her. "You could really use some work on your guard dog skills, Nemo. Instead of taking a nap in my office, you're supposed to keep varmints like him away."

The dog didn't act the least bit repentant when he looked up at her adoringly and wagged his thick black tail.

Returning her attention to the matter at hand, she released a frustrated breath as she picked up a brush and began grooming the gray. She had no idea how he'd managed to get his hands on Hickory Hills, but she'd told herself when she learned Jake was the new owner that she'd be able to handle seeing him again. That she could keep what happened between them all those months ago separate from their working relationship.

Unfortunately, that was going to be a whole lot easier said than done. The sound of his voice carried with it the memory of him calling her name as they made love.

Closing her eyes, Heather rested her forehead against the big thoroughbred's shoulder. Over the past year, she'd done everything she could to convince herself that Jake wasn't that good-looking, that her perception of their only night together had been clouded by loneliness and the haze of too much champagne. But she realized now that she'd been in deep denial.

Jake Garnier was well over six feet of pure male sex appeal and it was no wonder that he had an endless stream of women clamoring for his attention. With broad shoulders and narrow hips, he had the lean, muscular body of an athlete. When they'd met at the thoroughbred auction in Los Angeles, he'd been striking in a suit and tie, but today in jeans and a T-shirt, he was raw sensuality from his thick black hair to the soles of his outrageously expensive running shoes.

Sighing heavily, she went into the tack room, retrieved a saddle, then returned to place it on the horse's back. She tightened the saddle's girth, then bridling Silver, led him out of the stable toward the practice track.

As much as she'd like to forget what happened that night in L.A., she couldn't regret it. Jake was arguably the biggest player on the entire West Coast. But there was an earnestness to his charm that she'd found completely irresistible. And she was reminded of how captivating it was each and every time she gazed into her baby daughter's eyes. Eyes that were the same cobalt blue and held the same sparkle of mischief as Jake Garnier's.

Walking back up the path from the immaculately kept stables, Jake wondered what the hell had just taken place. He wasn't used to getting the cold shoulder from women and Heather's blatant snub didn't sit well.

There were only two things besides his siblings and highly successful law practice that caught and held his attention for any length of time and that was fast, flashy cars and shamelessly uninhibited women. And to his immense pleasure, the first frequently attracted plenty of the latter.

So why did one woman's obviously low opinion of him matter? He wasn't sure, but there had been a sparkle of hostility in Heather's eyes that had taken him completely by surprise.

Thinking back to the first time he'd seen her, he still couldn't believe how captivating she'd been. He'd attended a thoroughbred auction to personally see that the woman he'd represented in a bitter divorce sold the horses she and her husband had purchased as an investment. Jake had quickly lost interest in the parade of equine offerings and looking around spotted a pretty little filly of the human variety to divert his attention. And from the moment he introduced himself to her, he found Heather to be the most enchanting woman he'd ever had the pleasure of meeting.

They'd spent the rest of that day and one incredibly sensuous night together and over the course of the past year he'd come to the conclusion that he should have asked for her last name and a number where he could reach her. It was totally out of character for him and something he'd never contemplated before. Once he parted ways with a woman, he never looked back, never had the slightest regret about not contacting her again. At least he hadn't until Heather.

But surely she wasn't angry that he hadn't kept in touch over the fifteen months since. Besides the fact that he didn't know how to reach her, it was a well-known fact that he wasn't looking for a relationship of any kind and that none of his liaisons went any further than a good time.

He had no idea if that's what the problem was, but he had every intention of finding out and settling the animosity between them once and for all. If she was going to be running the horse farm that his newfound grandmother, Emerald Larson, had insisted he take over, it was essential that they get whatever had her panties in a twist straightened out so they could at least be civil.

In the meantime, he needed to unpack and put in a call to Emerald, Inc. headquarters to find out what the hell Emerald had up her sleeve this time. Given her track record of setting her grandchildren up to find their soul mate, he wasn't naive enough to think that she wasn't attempting to do the same thing with him. He wasn't sure how she'd done it, but she had to have discovered that, however brief it had been, that he and Heather had a bit of history.

But the old girl was in for a big disappointment if she thought her tactics were going to work with him. He wasn't looking to settle down with a wife, kids and the requisite canine. Nor was he inclined to trade his sleek little red Ferrari for a family-friendly minivan with car seats and clumps of dog hair.

With a plan of action to set down a few ground rules for both Emerald and his farm manager, Jake followed the path around the antebellum mansion to the circular drive in front where he'd parked his sports car. Just as he pressed the remote on his keychain to open the trunk, a teenage boy wearing stylishly ragged jeans, an oversize chartreuse T-shirt with It Is What It Is screen-printed on the front and a red baseball cap turned backward on his head came out of the house to greet him.

"Hi, Mr. Garnier," the kid said, crossing the veranda and bounding down the steps. He came to a sliding halt at the side of the car, then stood staring at it as if in awe. "Suh-weet."

"Thanks," Jake said, chuckling at the way the boy stretched the simple word into two syllables. "And you are?"

"Daily." He grinned. "My dad was a horse trainer before he died and talked my mom into naming me after the Daily Double at Churchill Downs." He reverently circled the car. "Dude, I have *got* to get me a ride like this when I get old."

Jake realized that the kid was talking to himself and meant no disrespect. But the comment reminded him that within a few short weeks he'd mark his thirty-seventh year and he supposed that in the eyes of a young teenager, he was probably considered a fossil.

Smiling, Jake reached into the trunk for the

suitcase he'd packed for his short stay at Hickory Hills. But Daily jumped forward to grab the handle.

"I'm sorry, Mr. Garnier. I didn't mean to get so carried away looking at your car." He hoisted the suitcase out of the trunk. "My grandma sent me out to get your luggage and take it upstairs for you."

"You're Mrs. Buchanan's grandson?" Jake asked, following Daily up the steps of the veranda.

The boy nodded. "Grandma's in charge of the house and Heather is in charge of everything else." Daily's youthful face suddenly split into a wide grin. "Wait until you meet Heather. For an older chick, she's way hot. Having her to look at every morning makes my chore of mucking out stalls a lot easier."

When Emerald and her stoic assistant, Luther Freemont, had met with him to turn over ownership of the farm, they'd informed him that Clara Buchanan was the live-in housekeeper. But they hadn't said a word about Heather being the farm manager. That just reinforced Jake's theory that Emerald was definitely up to something. Why else would she mention the name of the housekeeper and leave out all reference to the woman who ran the majority of the farm?

"I've met Heather." The kid couldn't be more than fourteen or fifteen years old, but it seemed he already had an appreciative eye for the ladies. "And I agree. She's very pretty."

When Daily opened the double doors and stood back, Jake entered the foyer and immediately felt as if he'd taken a step back in time. Decorated with furniture he had no doubt were period antiques, he half expected to see a woman in a wide hoop skirt descend the sweeping circular staircase. Or more likely a Kentucky colonel dressed in a white suit and holding a mint julep come strolling out of the study.

"Grandma told me to take your luggage up to the west wing," Daily said, walking toward the stairs. "If you want me to, I can show you where your room is, Mr. Garnier."

"Lead the way." When they reached the top of the staircase, Jake grinned. "I'll bet sliding down a banister like this one is as close to being on a roller coaster as you get without going to an amusement park."

"Oh, dude, talk about a rush," Daily said, his voice enthusiastic. He stopped suddenly, a concerned expression crossing his youthful face. "Uh, you probably don't want me doing that because of scratching the finish."

"It's water under the bridge now." Jake shook his head. "But I'm not as concerned with a few marks on the wood as I am about you taking a fall. That's a long way down and you could be badly injured."

"You won't tell my grandma, will you? She'll kill me if she finds out."

Jake took pity on the kid. "As long as you don't

do it again, I think we can keep it between the two of us."

Clearly relieved to hear Jake would be keeping his secret, the boy smiled. "Thanks. You're really cool, Mr. Garnier."

"I'll take that as a compliment." Every time Daily called him Mr. Garnier, he felt as old as dirt. "And while you're at it, why don't you call me Jake?"

After a delicious lunch, Jake strolled back down the path leading to the stables and couldn't help but wonder if he'd lost his touch with the opposite sex. He'd never had this much trouble with women in his entire life. If things didn't change, he just might end up developing a complex.

Emerald, for one, was purposely avoiding him and unless he missed his guess, she'd continue to do so for a while. She had to know he was on to her latest matchmaking scheme and no doubt wanted to avoid having him tell her to mind her own damned business.

But Mrs. Buchanan's sudden disappearance right after serving him lunch was a complete mystery. She'd been friendly enough when he first walked into the kitchen. But as soon as she put his plate in front of him, she'd apologized and rushed off to the housekeeper's quarters as if she thought he was contagious.

And then there was the chilly reception he'd

received from Heather that morning. Her body language and obvious contempt let him know in no uncertain terms exactly how she felt about his re-appearance in her life. But try as he might, he couldn't figure out why. He hoped for better luck with her during their meeting this afternoon, but he wasn't fool enough to count on that happening.

Entering the stable, he walked past several stalls to the opposite end of the structure where the manager's office was located. He wasn't the least bit surprised that Heather was nowhere in sight. Given her attitude toward him, he really expected no less. He wasn't, however, prepared for the very large black dog that got up from a blanket in the corner, walked over and stretched out on top of his feet.

"At least you're friendly," he said, reaching down to pet the dog's head.

Irritated that she'd obviously blown off his request to set up a meeting with the farm employees, he ex-tricated his feet from beneath the animal and covered the short distance to where the brood mares were kept. He found Heather bent over a horse lying on its side in one of the stalls, and his mouth went com-pletely dry. She was dressed in a pair of faded blue jeans and a pale pink T-shirt. With the denim hugging her shapely little bottom to perfection, he didn't think twice about taking in the delightful view.

As she straightened, an older man Jake assumed

to be one of the grooms brushed past him to enter the stall and hand her a pair of rubber gloves. When she pulled them on they extended up to her shoulders.

"What's going on?" he asked, venturing farther into the enclosure.

"The stork is going to make it before the vet." She knelt down behind the horse in the middle of the oversize stall. "Jake, I want you to hold her head to keep her from trying to get up, while Tony and I take care of things on this end," she instructed.

Jake wasn't used to anyone issuing him orders, but something in Heather's tone had him kneeling down to carry out the directive. As he watched, the man she'd called Tony held the horse's tail, while she helped guide the foal from the mare. She quickly lifted a membrane away from the colt's nose, then vigorously massaged the animal's small, wet body with a towel.

"Is that to make sure it starts breathing?" He found her skill and efficiency to be very impressive.

Nodding, she pulled off the gloves and stood up. "He was doing pretty good on his own, but it never hurts to have a little insurance when it comes to foals this valuable." She smiled down at the weak little creature. "We may be looking at the next Triple Crown winner."

Rising to his feet, he moved away from the mare's head as she started to get her legs under her. "Do you have to do this sort of thing very often?"

Before she could answer his question, the cell phone clipped to the waistband of her jeans rang, and she stepped out of the stall to take the call.

Jake turned to the groom. "By the way, I'm Jake Garnier, the new owner here."

Grinning, the man nodded. "I figured as much. Welcome to Hickory Hills."

"I have to go up to the main house for a few minutes," Heather interrupted, stepping back into the stall. "If you have any questions about the brood mares, training schedules or the farm's daily routine, Tony can fill you in."

Jake walked over to stand beside her. "I think I'll go with you, then you can show me around."

"There's really no need." Her long golden brown ponytail swayed back and forth as she shook her head. "I'll only be a few minutes and there's no sense in you walking all that way just to turn around and walk back."

Had that been a hint of panic he'd detected in her soft voice? Why didn't she want him going with her?

"I don't mind at all," he said, placing his hand to the small of her back to usher her along. There was no way she'd leave him behind now. "Afraid of a little exercise?"

Jake could tell she wanted to protest at his wise-crack, but clamping her lips together, she quickly stepped away from his touch and preceded him out of the stall. Neither spoke as they walked side by side up the path to the back entrance of the mansion and he couldn't help but wonder what she was trying to keep from him. And he had no doubt there was something. He hadn't been an attorney for the past twelve years without learning to recognize when someone was trying to conceal a secret.

When they entered the kitchen, Jake stopped short at the sight of Clara Buchanan with a crying baby in her arms. Never in a million years would he have thought the emergency calling Heather away from work would be a baby. But his astonishment was compounded tenfold when Heather hurried over to them and took the child from the housekeeper. The baby instantly calmed down and it was obvious that Heather was the child's mother.

"I think she might be running a little bit of a fever," Clara said, touching the baby's round little cheek.

Heather nodded. "I thought she felt warm when I got her up this morning." She tenderly pressed her lips to her daughter's forehead. "I think she might be trying to cut her first tooth."

"That's what the pediatrician said when I called her." The housekeeper smiled fondly at the tiny girl. "But I wanted to let you know and see what you thought about taking Mandy in to her office."

"It might not be a bad idea to have a doctor check her over," Jake said from behind her.

He knew even less about babies than he did about horses. But he and his twin brother, Luke, had raised their ten-year-old sister after their mother was killed in a car accident and remembered that when a child had an elevated temperature it was always better to err on the side of caution.

"Just to be on the safe side, I think I will take her to see Dr. Evans."

"I'll get the diaper bag," Clara said, disappearing down the hall toward her apartment.

As she and Jake stood in uncomfortable silence while she waited for Clara to return, Heather felt as if her nerves had been stretched to the breaking point. Was Jake aware that he was standing barely four feet away from his own daughter? Had he noticed that Mandy had his blue eyes and dark hair?

Ever since she'd learned that he was taking over Hickory Hills, she'd wondered how she was going to break the news to him about the baby. But she hadn't anticipated him meeting their daughter before she had a chance to tell him about her.

He hadn't said anything. Maybe he hadn't noticed how much Mandy looked like him. If that was the case, she'd be able to explain everything in a much less rushed fashion. She hoped.

"Needless to say, I won't be giving you that tour of the farm this afternoon or holding the meeting you wanted with your employees," she finally said as she cradled the baby close.

He nodded. "That's understandable. We can re-schedule for tomorrow morning or even the day after if she's still not feeling well."

When the housekeeper came back into the room, he reached out and took the diaper bag from her. "I'll help Heather and the baby get to the car."

"Call me when you get back to let me know what you find out from the doctor about our little angel," Clara called after them as they left the house.

"Would you mind letting Tony know that he's in charge until I get back?" Heather asked as they walked the short distance to the carriage house.

Jake shook his head as he watched her open the back door of the older-model sedan parked in front. "No problem. I'll take care of it. Is there anything else?"

"Not that I can think of."

When Heather turned to put the baby in the car seat, the little girl looked at him over her mother's shoulder for the first time and he felt as if he'd been flattened by a steam roller. He couldn't have gotten his vocal cords to work if his life depended on it and simply stood back as Heather got into the car and drove away.

As he watched the vehicle disappear around the corner of the mansion and head down the drive toward the main road, his heart pounded against his ribs and he found it extremely hard to draw air into his lungs. The baby had dark hair and big blue eyes.

Eyes the color of cobalt. The same color of cobalt that met his gaze when he looked into the mirror each morning to shave.

Two

That evening, when Heather answered the insistent knocking on her cottage door, she wasn't the least bit surprised to find Jake standing on the other side. In fact, she'd been expecting him. She'd known that once he saw Mandy it was just a matter of time before he put it all together.

"We need to talk." Instead of waiting for her to invite him in, he took hold of her elbow and propelled her back into the living room, kicking the door shut behind him. "I want answers and I'm not leaving here until I get them, Heather."

"It never crossed my mind that you would," she

said calmly. She wasn't going to allow him to upset or stress her out in any way.

"That baby belongs to me, doesn't she?" he demanded, cutting right to be heart of the matter.

"*That baby* has a name—Amanda Grace. I call her Mandy. She's almost seven months old." Heather walked across the room to pull the nursery door closed to keep their raised voices from disturbing her daughter. "And if by belong, you mean are you her biological father? The answer is yes."

"What happened? I used protection."

Was he actually questioning that he was the father of her child?

"I'm well aware of that. It obviously had a defect." She raised an eyebrow. "Surely you're aware that nothing is one hundred percent effective except abstention. And if we'd gone that route—"

"We wouldn't be having this conversation," he finished for her.

"Exactly." She looked him directly in the eye. "But let me assure you, Mandy is your daughter."

He shook his head. "I wasn't questioning that. She looks just like me."

Heather watched a muscle work along his lean jaw as Jake stared at her for what seemed like an eternity. She could tell his anger was bordering on outrage, but that was just too bad. As far she was concerned, not knowing he'd fathered a child was his own fault and she wasn't about to let him turn the blame back on her.

"Did you even think about getting in touch with me when you discovered you were pregnant?" he finally asked, his voice low and menacing.

Heather had told herself that she wasn't going to let him get to her, but his accusatory tone angered her as little else could. "I really don't think you want to go there, Jake. Believe me, you won't like hearing what I have to say."

"Go ahead. Try me." He took a step toward her. "I told you I'm here to get answers."

"Then I would suggest you drop the intimidation tactics as well as the idea of being the wounded party in all of this because you're not." When she turned to walk into the kitchen to put a little more distance between them and the nursery, she fully expected him to follow.

He didn't disappoint her. "Did you or did you not consider letting me know that you were expecting my child?"

Turning on him, she took a deep breath in an effort to calm down. She had a lot to say and she was going to savor every second of it. She'd wanted this conversation for over a year, but never thought she'd have the chance to have her say. She wasn't going to allow herself to lose momentum by becoming overly emotional. She refused to give Jake that kind of power over her.

"I not only considered letting you know, I spent my first trimester leaving messages that I needed to talk to you urgently." She met his angry gaze head on. "*You* never returned my calls, and I wasn't comfortable leaving that kind of information with your secretary."

"I—"

Holding up her hand to stop whatever lame excuse he came up with, she went on, "Then I spent the second trimester trying to convince myself that there had to be a reasonable explanation for you ignoring my requests to get back to me. It turns out I was wrong. There wasn't a good reason, other than you really are an insensitive, self-absorbed jerk who uses women, then casts them aside."

He opened his mouth to no doubt refute her assessment of his character, but she cut him off again.

"And somewhere during the course of my third trimester, I came to the conclusion that you really didn't deserve to know about our daughter and that we were both going to be a lot better off without you in our lives." She folded her arms beneath her breasts. "Any more questions?"

Heather could tell by the stunned look replacing the angry expression on his handsome face that she'd gotten through to him.

Rubbing the back of his neck as if to relieve tension, he shook his head. "I have my secretary—"

"Screen your calls so that you don't have to deal

with uncomfortable situations with the women you've bedded," she interrupted. When he remained silent, she knew that her comment had hit a little too close to home. "And you don't have to worry, Jake. Mandy and I are just fine on our own."

His eyes narrowed. "You're going to try to cut me out of her life?"

Heather shook her head. "That's not what I said. I'm telling you that you're off the hook. You're free to go back to Los Angeles and resume your life as if nothing happened. I don't want or need your help—financially or otherwise. I'm perfectly capable of taking care of and providing for my daughter. I just thought you had the right to know about her."

"She's mine, too."

Having had her say, she suddenly felt drained of energy. "I'm relieving you of that responsibility, Jake."

"I think we need to get this straight once and for all, Heather."

He stepped forward to place his hands on her shoulders. The heat from his touch seeping through her T-shirt and the determination she detected in his deep baritone sent tingles zinging straight up her spine. But when he used his thumb and forefinger to lift her chin until their gazes locked, the sensation danced across every nerve in her body.

"I accept that it was my own damned fault I

didn't know about the pregnancy. But it doesn't mean that now that I'm aware I have a child I don't intend to be a big part of her life. And that will be much easier for me to do when I move you and Mandy into the mansion with me."

"That's not going to happen, Jake. We're very happy right here in the carriage house."

"We'll see about that."

Before she could protest or step away, his mouth covered hers and the feel of his firm lips once again caressing hers with such care caused her head to spin. She tried with all of her might to remain unaffected, but her traitorous pulse took off and a delicious warmth began to flow through her veins.

Placing her hands on Jake's wide chest, instead of pushing away from him as she intended, she reveled in the feel of his strength beneath her palms and the steady beat of his heart. This was total insanity. He'd used her, then cast her aside with little or no regard for her feelings. But when he traced the seam of her mouth with his tongue, she parted her lips without so much as a second thought and allowed him to deepen the kiss.

As he wrapped his arms around her and pulled her more fully against his large frame, he teased her with a tenderness that caused every fiber in her being to quiver to life and her stomach to flutter wildly. The excitement she'd experienced in his arms fifteen long months ago began to fill her from head to toe and it scared her as little else could. Losing herself to Jake's kiss was the very reason they found themselves in their current set of circumstances.

"Please…stop," she said, leaning away from him.

Jake immediately put a bit of space between them, but continued to hold her loosely in his arms. "All things considered, I probably shouldn't have done that." He gave her the same seductive smile that had been her downfall that night in Los Angeles. "But I'll be damned if I'm sorry I did. You have the sweetest lips I've ever tasted."

She shook her head. "Forget my lips. It's not going to happen again."

He stared down at her for endless seconds and just when she thought he was going to argue the point, Nemo chose that moment to come lumbering in through the doggie door. Finding the two humans standing face-to-face, he apparently took it as an open invitation to push his way between them and plop his big, bulky body on top of their feet.

"What's his deal?" Jake asked, staring down at the dog. "Every time he sees me, he traps my feet beneath him."

Thankful for the distraction Heather stepped back then knelt down to scratch the big gentle dog behind his floppy ears. "It seems to be a trait of his breed. I think they realize that they're too big to sit on your lap, so they lay on your feet to be close to you."

Jake bent down to pet Nemo's thick, black coat. "So I guess this means he likes me, huh?"

"It looks that way." Only inches apart, they stared at each other for endless seconds before she straightened to walk back into the living room to peek inside the nursery door.

She should have named the dog Benedict Arnold. Nemo was supposed to be loyal to her, not cozy up to the enemy like they were long lost friends.

"What did the pediatrician say this afternoon?" Jake asked from behind her shoulder. "Is she cutting her first tooth or is something else wrong?"

Unaware that he'd followed her, Heather jumped as much from the unexpected sound of his voice as from his close proximity. "Uh…yes, she's teething. The doctor said she has two that should be through her lower gum by the end of the week."

"She'll start feeling better after that happens, right?"

Heather nodded as she pulled the door to and moved away from him. The concern in his voice touched her and that was something she didn't like one bit. It was much safer for her to think of him as the shallow, uncaring man who refused to take her phone calls, than a daddy worried about the welfare of his baby girl.

"I think it would be a good idea if you leave

now, Jake." She walked over to open the front door. "I have to be up by five in the morning and I really need to get some sleep."

Glancing at the gold watch on his left wrist, he nodded. "I have a lot to do tomorrow and need to be up early myself."

He walked over to her, then cupping her cheeks with both hands lightly pressed a kiss to her lips. As he raised his head, the determination she saw in his incredible blue eyes sent a shock wave all the way to her soul.

"If you and the baby need me before morning, don't hesitate to give me a call. You have my word that from this day forward, no matter what I'm doing or where I am, I'll always be available for you and our daughter."

Once the front door closed behind him, Heather squeezed her eyes shut against the tears of frustration threatening to spill down her cheeks. She'd known the former owner was looking to sell, but why did Jake Garnier have to be the new owner of Hickory Hills? What cruel quirk of fate had caused their paths to cross again? And why, after all that had happened, did she still find him to be the most handsome, irresistible man she'd ever met?

When he'd introduced himself at the annual thoroughbred auction in Los Angeles, he'd not only charmed his way past her defenses and swept her off her feet, he'd stolen her heart, as well. She'd always heard about love at first sight, but she'd never given it a lot of thought, never believed it would happen to her. Not until last year. Not until Jake.

Swallowing hard, she reminded herself of the disillusionment and emotional pain she'd suffered when he refused to return her calls and she'd realized she meant absolutely nothing to him. It had taken her a long time to move past that and no matter how drugging his kisses were or how wonderful it had felt to be in his arms, she wasn't about to put herself in that position again.

Besides, it wasn't just her emotions at stake anymore. She had Mandy's well-being to take into consideration, as well. And Heather wasn't going to stand back and watch her daughter bond with Jake, then be devastated when he moved on like the playboy he was.

As he walked down the long driveway toward the big wrought-iron entrance gates, Jake still couldn't quite wrap his mind around everything that had happened. In the span of a few hours, his life had changed in ways he could have never imagined. He had reconnected with the only woman he'd ever regretted not keeping in touch with, learned that by taking over Hickory Hills she'd become his employee and discovered that a little over six months ago she'd given birth to his baby.

Unbelievable.

But as he thought about Heather making several attempts to get in touch with him, his gut burned with anger. He deeply regretted that she'd been forced to go through the pregnancy alone. If his secretary hadn't become overly zealous about screening his calls, she wouldn't have. He'd have not only been there for Heather throughout the pregnancy and birth, he wouldn't have been cheated out of the first six months of his daughter's life.

His daughter.

Jake's heart slammed against his ribcage and he took several deep breaths. He had a tiny baby girl who looked just like him.

It blew his mind that he had a child. Fatherhood had been something he'd never expected to experience. And it wasn't because he didn't like little kids. He did. He'd just made a conscious decision years ago never to marry and have one of his own.

His own father had twice walked away after impregnating his mother, and even though Jake didn't think he was capable of doing something like that, he hadn't wanted to take the chance. What if he carried the same narcissistic gene that had caused his father to shirk his responsibilities to his children in favor of pursuing his next good time?

Jake shook his head. It was all a moot point now. He had a daughter. And even though it scared the living hell out of him to think that he might somehow let her down the way his father had his children, Jake was going to do everything he possibly could to be a good father.

Lost in his disturbing introspection, it took a moment for Jake to notice the shadowy figure climbing over the gates at the end of the drive. "Daily?"

The boy froze halfway over the gate. "Mr. Garnier, I…oh, dude, this probably doesn't look real good, does it?"

"No. It looks like I just busted you for sneaking out of the house." Stopping a few feet from where the boy was perched, Jake planted his feet and folded his arms across his chest. "You want to come down from there and tell me why you're out this late, as well as why you don't want to alert anyone up at the house that you're leaving by activating the gates?"

When Daily dropped to his feet in front of Jake, he seemed to take a great interest in the tops of his untied high-top tennis shoes. "It's kind of personal, Mr. Garnier."

Jake hid a smile. "Want to tell me what her name is?"

The boy's head snapped up so fast, Jake wouldn't have been surprised if Daily had suffered whiplash. "How did you know I was going to meet a girl?"

Jake did his best not to laugh out loud at the astonished look on the kid's face. "I know it's probably hard to believe, but I was fourteen once, Daily."

"I'll be fifteen in a couple of weeks," the boy said, straightening his skinny shoulders.

"That's still too young to be out this late. Not to mention the fact that you don't have your grand-mother's permission."

The boy's shoulders slumped. "Yes, sir."

"I think you'd better give your girlfriend a call and tell her that you won't be able to make it this evening," Jake suggested.

As he watched Daily whip out a cell phone and rapidly punch in a text message, a knot began to form in the pit of Jake's stomach. In about thirteen years some pubescent boy with more hormones than good sense could very easily try to set up a midnight meeting with his daughter.

He barely managed to suppress a groan. He'd already raised one girl through the teen years when he and his twin brother finished raising their younger sister, Arielle. And just thinking that he was going to have to do it all over again with his own daughter was enough to give him an ulcer. His only consolation was that this time he'd be sharing that responsibility with Heather, instead of his brother who had turned out to be as clueless as he'd been.

When the boy slipped his cell phone back into his jeans pocket, Jake motioned toward the tree-lined drive leading up to the mansion. "Come on, Daily. I think it's time we both called it a night."

They remained silent for some time before Daily asked, "Are you going to tell my grandma about me trying to sneak out tonight?"

Jake shook his head. "No, I'm not. But you are."

"Me?"

"Part of growing up is learning to accept responsibility for your actions," Jake said, reminding himself as much as Daily.

"I'm gonna be grounded for the rest of my life," the boy complained when they entered the mansion through the kitchen door.

"I doubt it will be that long," Jake said, chuckling. "But as long as you're going to be sticking close to home for the next week or so, there are a few things around here I'm going to need help with. Do you think you'd be interested in the job?"

"A real job? Really? Oh man, that would be awesome," Daily said, his voice suddenly filled with enthusiasm.

"You'll have to keep up with your other chores and check with your grandmother first, to make sure she has no objections." Jake gave the boy a pointed look. "Right after you tell her about what happened this evening and accept whatever punishment she deems necessary."

Daily nodded. "I will."

"Then you'd better get some sleep," Jake warned. "We have a big day ahead of us."

"Yes, sir."

As he watched the teenager hurry down the hall to his grandmother's apartment, Jake headed for the stairs. He'd made Heather a promise and he fully intended to keep it. While she oversaw Stormy Dancer's morning workout and attended to whatever else her job entailed, he and Daily were going to get her and the baby moved from the carriage house into the mansion. And once he accomplished that, he had every intention of spending the rest of his stay at Hickory Hills getting to know his daughter.

"Jake Garnier, how dare you?" Heather demanded when she found him sitting at the desk in the study. She was angry enough to bite nails in two and it was all his fault.

His unrepentant grin when he looked up made her want to throw something at him. "I assume you're referring to the moving of the baby's things and yours from the carriage house to the rooms upstairs?"

"You know good and well that's what I'm talking about. You had no right to do that."

He walked around the side of the desk to stand in front of her. "I don't know why you're so upset," he said calmly. "I told you last night that's what I intended to do."

She couldn't believe his arrogance. "And I told you it wasn't going to happen. Mandy and I are perfectly fine in the carriage house. It's all she's ever known."

"I'm sure you're happy." He took another step toward her. "But you'll be even happier here. There's a lot more room. And besides, it will be more convenient for all concerned."

"You've got to be joking." Where did he come up with that idea? "It might be more convenient for you, but it certainly isn't for me."

He was a lot closer than she was comfortable with. But there was no way she was going to back away. That would only give him the satisfaction of knowing he still had an effect on her.

"I fully intend to be a big part of my daughter's life," he said, sounding so darned reasonable it made her want to punch him.

"We live less than a hundred feet away. How is moving to the big house going to change anything?"

He gave her a smile that caused her heart to skip a beat. Just because he smiled at her it wasn't going to get him off the hook.

"I want to watch you put her to bed at night and get her up in the morning."

"You could do that at the carriage house."

"So you're telling me that you want me to move in with you and Mandy?" he asked, giving her that same charming smile.

"N-no. That wasn't what I said at all and you

know it." She should have known he'd twist her objections around to suit his purpose. After all, he was an attorney. "You knew what I meant. You could stop by around those times, then leave."

He took the last step separating them, then lightly touched her cheek. She suddenly had to remember why she was angry with him.

"If Mandy wakes up in the middle of the night, I want to be able to get up with her." He shook his head. "If I'm here and the two of you are in the carriage house, I can't do that."

"Take my word for it, being awakened from a sound sleep is highly overrated," she said before she could stop herself.

"I'm sure that taking care of her by yourself and trying to work has been very tiring at times. Wouldn't it be nice for a change to have someone sharing that responsibility?"

When he looked at her the way he was doing now, Heather was lucky to remember her own name, let alone what he'd asked. "No. I'm fine with the way things are."

"I could get up with her while you sleep," he pressed.

The heat from his touch branded her and the scent of his aftershave made her want him to hold her, kiss her and… She swallowed hard. She needed to escape his presence before her traitorous body had her agreeing to go along with what he wanted.

"I—I don't mind at all being solely responsible for Mandy," she insisted.

"But you don't have to be, honey. Not anymore." He moved his hands down to her waist, then pulled her into his arms. "I'm here now and you don't have to do everything alone."

"Please, Jake," she interrupted. "Don't." Pulling from his arms, she somehow found the strength to back away from him. "I won't try to stop you from being part of Mandy's life. But I want you to keep a couple of things in mind before you take that step. First and foremost, it's all or nothing. You're either her father for life or not at all. I don't want her becoming attached to you, then you walk away when you get tired of playing daddy. And second, count me out. I'm not part of the package."

He stared at her for several long moments before he slowly shook his head. "You have my word that I will never do anything that isn't in her best interest or yours."

"Good. Because hurt my daughter and you'll have me to deal with." She could tell from his expression that he meant what he said—now. The only problem was, whether they intended to or not, people sometimes broke their promises and others ended up getting hurt.

"Now that we have your main concern out in the open and settled, are you and the baby going to stay here in the mansion?" he asked, seating himself back behind the desk.

"Jake, I don't think—"

"I've missed out on a lot with her already, Heather." His chest rose and fell as he took a deep breath. "All I'm asking is that you give me a chance to get to know my daughter and build a relationship with her."

She knew if she and the baby did stay in the mansion with him, she would be taking a huge risk for both Mandy and herself. If she hadn't known that before he kissed her last night, she did now. No matter how much he'd hurt her or how hard she tried to resist his charm, she still found Jake to be six feet two inches of pure temptation. And that could very well prove to be disastrous for her if she didn't keep her wits about her.

But she'd told him she wouldn't stop him from trying to bond with Mandy and she couldn't, in good conscience, deny either of them the right to get acquainted. And while he was getting to know their daughter, she intended to learn more about him, his family and where he grew up. After all, she had the right to know about her daughter's father.

Heather sighed heavily. Unfortunately, now wasn't the time to put him through the third degree. Aside from the fact that she'd already put in a grueling day, she was still too angry. She wanted to be calm, rational and in complete control when she talked to him.

"We'll stay in the mansion as long as you're here at Hickory Hills. But only on one condition."

His eyes narrowed ever so slightly before he asked, "And what would that be?"

Walking to the door, she turned back. "I meant what I said about not being part of the equation, Jake. Don't count on me to be one of your…diversions when you get bored."

Three

Jake frowned as he watched Heather place their sleeping daughter into the small baby bed that he and Daily had set up earlier in the day. "Is that thing full size? It looks awfully small."

When she placed her finger to her lips, it was all he could do not to groan. He couldn't forget the kiss they'd shared the night before and wanted to once again taste her sweetness and feel the softness of her perfect mouth beneath his own. But he knew better than to push. She'd outlined her conditions and he had to admit it was probably for the best. It wouldn't be long before they had to address some very sensitive issues concerning shared custody and how they were going to raise Mandy. If they became involved, it could make doing that a lot more difficult. He just wished that the attraction between them wasn't as powerful now as it had been when they first met. That would certainly make things a lot easier.

"It's a mini crib," she whispered, drawing his attention back to his question.

He waited until she turned on the baby monitor, clipped one of the receivers to her belt and they'd both stepped out into the hall before he asked, "Why didn't you get a regular size bed for her?"

"The room I turned into the nursery at the carriage house is small and I wanted to save space," she answered as they started downstairs.

"What about when she gets a little older?" he asked, following her. He didn't like the idea of his child being in a room that was too small when she had every right to live in the mansion and enjoy the spaciousness of any one of the spare bedrooms. "How will you fit a regular size bed into that room and still have enough space for her to play?"

"When the time comes, I'll convert the room I use for a study into another bedroom." At the bottom of the steps, she turned to face him. "Why are you asking about this now? It won't be an issue for another year or two."

He smiled as the germ of an idea took root. "I

was thinking that the two of you could live here in the mansion even after I go back to L.A."

"No. That's not an option," she said, shaking her head until her ponytail swayed back and forth.

"Why not?"

She started toward the hall leading to the kitchen. "Because it's not *my* home."

Reaching out, he took hold of her arm and the feel of her soft skin beneath his palm sent heat straight to the pit of his belly. He did his best to ignore it. "This is my house now and Mandy is my daughter. She has every right to live here."

Heather gave him a look that stated in no uncertain terms that she didn't like his idea one damned bit. "But it's not mine, Jake."

He knew as surely as he knew his own name that there was a good deal of pride holding her back from accepting his offer. "I'm telling you it can be, Heather."

"I work for you and living in the carriage house is part of my contract."

"I'm offering you an amendment to that agreement." Barely resisting the urge to pull her into his arms, he hastened to add, "You don't have to make a decision about the move being permanent now. But I would like for you to give it some serious thought." Unable to stop himself, he reached up to brush a wayward strand of hair from her soft cheek. "It would make life for you and Mandy a lot more comfortable than being cooped up in a space where there's barely room for one."

Before she could come up with any more excuses why she and Mandy shouldn't live in the mansion permanently, he reluctantly dropped his hand to his side and crossed the foyer to enter the study. If he hadn't put some distance between them, there had been a very real possibility that he would have acted on his first impulse to grab her and kiss her until she agreed to his proposal. And that would have been a huge mistake.

It would take a fool not to see that just like a magnetic force, the attraction between them was too strong to fight and impossible to resist. But at this point, she didn't trust him anymore than she would a snake coiled to make a strike. And until he proved himself to her and they worked out an agreement to raise their daughter, he had no other choice but to bide his time and no doubt end up taking more than his share of cold showers.

He sighed heavily as he lowered himself into the chair behind the desk and reached for the phone. As he punched in his brother's number, he thought about the irony of it all. The only woman he hadn't been able to forget was back in his life, was the mother of his only child and thought him lower than the stuff she scraped off her boots after a trip through the stables.

"My life is just about as freaking wonderful as it can get right now," he muttered sourly.

"As a matter of fact, mine is going pretty good, as well," Luke said, laughing.

Wallowing in his own misery, Jake had missed hearing his brother answer the phone. "Good to hear, bro. How are things in Nashville?"

"We couldn't be better. Haley has passed the point where morning sickness is an issue and we're just waiting for the sonogram to see if we're having a boy or a girl." His twin sounded happier than Jake could ever remember.

"Glad to hear my favorite sister-in-law is feeling better," he said, wondering if Heather had experienced a lot of problems with morning sickness when she'd been pregnant with Mandy.

They were both silent a moment before Luke asked, "So what's wrong, Jake?"

"What makes you think there's a problem?"

He wasn't surprised by his brother's intuitiveness. As with many twins, he and Luke shared a sixth sense where the other was concerned and instinctively knew when things weren't going right. But Jake wasn't entirely certain how to deliver the news that upon his arrival at Hickory Hills he'd discovered he had a daughter and avoid having to listen to the I-told-you-so speech that was sure to follow. Luke had been warning him for years that his "love 'em and leave 'em" ways were going to catch up to him one day.

"You're talking to the only person who knows

you better than you probably know yourself." Luke paused. "So you want to tell me what's going on?"

"I have a daughter." Jake hadn't meant to deliver the news quite so bluntly, but once the words were out, he realized there wasn't any easier way to say it.

"Whoa! You want to back up and say that again?"

"You heard me," Jake said, wanting to reach through the phone and throttle his twin. "I have a six-and-a-half-month-old daughter named Mandy."

His brother was silent for so long, Jake wasn't sure they hadn't lost the connection. "And you found this out when you moved to the horse farm Emerald gave you?" Luke finally asked.

"Yeah." He took a deep breath. "Heather's the manager here at Hickory Hills. I'm betting when the old girl's investigators found us, they discovered that a woman I met at a thoroughbred auction last year had become pregnant from our one night together."

"That explains why you ended up in a place about as far removed from your life in Los Angeles as it's possible to get," Luke agreed. "Arielle and I wondered why you were given an enterprise that was totally out of your element when we were given businesses in our respective career fields."

"I don't know why Emerald didn't just tell me about Heather and Mandy instead of blindsiding me like this," Jake complained. "Didn't she think I would step up and do the right thing?"

His brother made a strangled sound. "You're getting married?"

It was Jake's turn to choke. "Hell, no. You know how I feel about marriage. It's not for me."

"Don't knock it until you've tried it," Luke advised. "I didn't think I was husband material, either, and look at me now."

"Whatever."

They were silent a moment before Luke asked, "Why didn't the baby's mother tell you about the pregnancy?"

"She tried, but my secretary didn't see fit to give me the messages." Jake made a mental note to call the woman the first thing in the morning and discuss her not bothering to give him a list of callers.

"Ah, if you'll remember, I told you—"

"Don't say it, bro."

Luke's laughter grated on Jake's nerves. "So when do we get to meet our niece and her mother?"

"That's the reason I called. How would you and Haley like to come up to Louisville for the Southern Oaks Cup Classic in a couple of weeks? The favorite to win the race came along with the farm."

"Sounds good," Luke said. "I assume you're inviting Arielle and Zach?"

"Of course, along with the rest of the clan."

A few months ago, when he and his siblings learned that the most successful woman in the corporate jungle was their paternal grandmother, they'd also been informed that they had three half brothers. After meeting them at one of Emerald's receptions and finding themselves in the unique position of being the unexpected heirs of one of the world's richest women, they'd become friends.

"And before you ask, I fully intend to invite our illustrious grandmother and her stiff-as-a-board assistant, too. She and I are going to have a little talk about her withholding information about my daughter," he added.

Luke snorted. "Good luck with that."

Making plans to talk again before the impromptu family reunion, Jake hung up, then called his other siblings to invite them to the gathering. With promises from all to attend, he walked into the foyer and ran right into Heather.

"Are you all right?" he asked, placing both hands on her waist to keep her from falling. A jolt of electric current as strong as a lightning strike shot through him and when she looked up, the awareness he detected in her aqua eyes let him know that she'd felt it, too.

"I—I'm fine."

"I'm sorry, I didn't see you," he said, filling his senses with her. The scent of her herbal shampoo and the feel of her softness beneath his hands sent heat coursing straight to the region south of his belt and his body's reaction was not only predictable, it was inevitable.

"I…was just…on my way upstairs." She sounded delightfully breathless and sent his blood pressure up a good ten points or so.

As if an invisible force held them captive they remained silent for so long, Jake finally forced himself to speak. "I…uh, was on my way to take a shower and call it an evening myself."

Still operating on West Coast time, he hadn't even entertained the idea of calling it a night. But he did need a shower. A cold one.

She nodded. "Well…I guess I'll see you in the morning."

"What time does Mandy wake up?" he asked, still holding her at the waist.

"Early."

Finally forcing himself to step back, he motioned toward the staircase. "Then it would probably be a good idea if we call it a night."

As if awakening from a trance, she blushed suddenly and ducking her head, started walking toward the steps. "Good night, Jake."

"Night."

He stood in the foyer long after Heather reached the second floor and disappeared down the hall. The sound of her voice and the realization that she would be sleeping just down the hall from him had him fully aroused in less than a heartbeat.

Taking the stairs two at a time, he made a beeline for the master bathroom. By the time he reached his bedroom, he'd already stripped off his shirt and left a trail of clothing on his way to the shower.

As he stood there punishing his body beneath the frigid spray, he couldn't help but wonder how long Heather was going to deny the chemistry that flowed between them. They could fight it, try to run from it and argue that it even existed, but it was just a matter of time before they made love again. He had no doubt about that. The only question was when.

With a record-breaking crop of goosebumps and his teeth chattering like the wind-up ones found in a novelty store, he turned off the water. He grabbed a thick towel and began to vigorously dry off. They were going to have to work out the agreement for Mandy, and Heather had to come to her senses and accept the inevitable. He didn't particularly like shivering his ass off in a shower so cold he could spit ice cubes.

"Heather, I'm sorry, but I'm not going to be able to watch Mandy for you this afternoon. I forgot that I have an appointment with the high school counselor to get Daily enrolled and set up his freshman schedule."

"I suppose I could take her with me," Heather said slowly, wondering how she was going to attend a meeting at Churchill Downs with a baby in tow.

"We can change that to another day, Grandma,"

Daily offered, sounding hopeful. "I don't care. I'm not all that into school anyway."

"Young man, you'd better get 'into it' real fast," Clara said sternly. "You're in enough hot water as it is after that stunt you pulled the other night."

"Listen to your grandmother, Daily. If you want a car like mine when you get 'old,' you're going to need a good job. And that takes education."

"Yes, sir," Daily answered, shoveling a fork full of scrambled eggs into his mouth.

Looking up, Heather's heart skipped a beat as she watched Jake stroll into the kitchen and seat himself at the head of the table. Dressed in a light blue polo shirt that emphasized the width of his broad shoulders and a pair of jeans that hugged his muscular thighs like a glove, he wasn't just his usual good-looking self. This morning, he was white-hot. Busying herself with Mandy's breakfast, she tried her best not to stare.

"What time is the meeting?" Clara asked. "Maybe we'll be back before you have to leave."

Heather shook her head. "It's a luncheon meeting and probably won't be over until late afternoon." She spooned a bit of baby cereal into Mandy's eager mouth. "I'll just take her with me and hope she has a good long nap during the speeches."

"I can watch her," Jake spoke up as he took a couple of strips of bacon from the platter in the center of the table.

"That's okay. I'm sure you have better things to do." She wasn't at all comfortable leaving her daughter with a man who she was almost positive had zero experience babysitting an infant.

Smiling, he shook his head as he took a sip of his coffee. "I don't have anything going on this after-noon. Besides, it will give Mandy and me a chance to get acquainted."

"Really, it's not a problem," she said firmly. "I'll take her with me."

An ominous silence suddenly reigned through-out the kitchen as Jake put down his coffee cup and their gazes locked. "Don't be ridiculous, Heather. She's my daughter, too. I have every right to watch her while you're busy."

"No way!" Daily said, his eyes wide. "You're Mandy's dad? I didn't know that."

"Come on, young man," Clara said, removing the boy's plate from the table. "You can finish your breakfast in our apartment before you go down to the stables to muck out the stalls."

"But, Grandma—"

"You heard me," the housekeeper said, cutting him off. "These two need to talk and they don't need you hanging on their every word. Now move."

Heather waited until Clara and a reluctant Daily left the kitchen before she turned her full attention back to Jake. "How many babies have you taken care of?"

"None."

"That's what I thought." When Mandy protested loudly, Heather spooned another bite of cereal into her mouth. "You don't have the slightest idea what to do with a baby."

His frown deepened. "I've got to start somewhere."

"My daughter isn't an experiment."

"She's *our* daughter." He placed his hand on top of hers. "I know you're worried I won't know what to do. But I promise, I'd never let anything hurt her."

She could tell from the sincerity in his voice and the look in his eyes that he meant every word he said. But he admittedly had zero experience with babies.

"I won't let her out of my sight the entire time you're away," he promised.

"Jake, I'm not at all comfortable with—"

"I'll even stay in the same room with her while she takes her nap," he interrupted.

"Have you ever changed a diaper?"

"No, but it can't be that hard to figure out. Besides, I'm a quick study," he said confidently. "You can show me how to put a new one on her before you leave."

She barely managed to hide a smile at his misguided self-assurance. He had no way of knowing that their daughter thought diaper changes were great fun and the perfect time to exercise her legs by kicking like a little karate champion.

"What about lunch?" she asked, beginning to realize she didn't have any other option. She couldn't get out of the meeting and it was no place for a baby. "Do you think you'll be able to feed her?"

"I watched you feed her breakfast and it didn't look all that difficult." He grinned. "Piece of cake."

Spooning the last bit of cereal into her daughter's mouth, Heather wiped the baby's face. "You'll call me if you have even the slightest problem?"

"Of course."

She lifted Mandy from the high chair and handed her to him. "Would you mind holding her while I wipe off the high chair and put it away?"

Jake had been too busy yesterday with the unauthorized moving of her things from the guesthouse to do more than watch her or Clara with the baby. It was time that father and daughter met officially. Besides, she needed to see how Jake was with Mandy before she agreed to him watching the baby.

He gently lifted Mandy to sit on his arm. "Hey there, Honey Bunny. I'm your daddy."

As Heather watched, the baby gazed at him intently for several seconds, then giggling, happily slapped her tiny hand against his cheek. But it was the look of awe and complete wonder that instantly came over Jake's handsome face that had her blinking back a wave of tears.

She wouldn't have believed it was possible to actually see it happen. But right before her eyes, Jake fell hopelessly in love with their daughter.

Four

When Heather returned from her meeting, she practically burst through the back door of the mansion. She'd tried several times on her drive from the Downs to call Jake on her cell phone, but he hadn't answered and with each passing second her concern increased. Searching the rooms downstairs, her heart began to pound hard against her ribs when she couldn't find either of them. Why had she let him talk her into allowing him to watch her baby?

But her anxiety turned to mind-numbing fear when she hurried up the staircase and entered the bedroom where Jake had set up the crib. The two were nowhere in sight.

In a near panic, she raced down the hall to the master suite. "If he's let something happen, I'll never forgive…"

Her voice trailed off as she came to a skidding halt just inside the suite door and a knee-weakening relief washed over her. There in the middle of the king-size bed her daughter lay curled up on top of Jake. Both were out like a couple of lights.

Leaning against the door facing, her panic began to recede and as she stood there catching her breath, she couldn't help but be touched by the moment. Heather knew for certain she'd never forget the poignant sight of her tiny baby girl sleeping so trustingly on her daddy's wide bare chest. For the second time in a matter of a few hours, she found herself blinking back tears.

Quietly, so as not to disturb either of them, she gently lifted Mandy into her arms and, walking back to the bedroom where the crib was, placed the baby in the small bed. Turning on the monitor, she clipped the receiving unit to the waistband of her khakis and turning to leave, came face-to-face with a wild-eyed Jake.

"Dear God, Heather, why didn't you wake me up to let me know you were taking Mandy?" he demanded. "When I opened my eyes and she wasn't there, I—"

Heather placed her index finger to his lips to silence him when the baby moved restlessly and let out a little whimper. "I'm sorry," she mouthed. She motioned for him to follow her out into the hall. "You looked like you might be a little tired from babysitting and I thought I'd—"

"Give me a heart attack," he finished for her.

That's when she realized that he'd been as terrified as she had when she'd been unable to find them. "I really am sorry. I didn't mean to frighten you."

Running a frustrated hand through his thick black hair, he took a deep breath. "I've never been that scared in my entire life."

As they stood there, she couldn't help but stare at his bare chest. Every muscle was well-defined and as her gaze drifted lower, she had an almost uncontrollable urge to reach out and trace her fingers over each one of the ridges on his abdomen.

"W-what happened to your shirt?" she asked instead.

"Oh, that." He frowned. "Do you know how disgusting baby food spinach looks? And dear God, it smells even worse. But when it gets on clothes, it's just plain nasty."

She laughed. "It is pretty gross, isn't it?"

"It's horrible." He made a face. "I thought I was going to lose it a couple of times when Mandy decided to take a handful and rub it in her hair."

Heather couldn't stop laughing. "Don't tell me. You set the dish too close to the high chair."

Nodding, he chuckled. "By the time lunch was

over, she had more food on her than in her. And I'm positive our daughter could hold her own in a frat house food fight."

"No doubt about it," she agreed, smiling. "Any other problems? How did the diaper changes go?"

"When I finally got her to hold still it went all right. Up until then, it was a little hazardous." He rubbed his flat stomach. "She's got a hell of a kick." His expression turned serious and he fell silent a moment before reaching up to touch her cheek. "Thank you, Heather."

The back of his knuckles stroking her skin sent a shaft of longing all the way to her toes. "W-what for?"

"For today." His voice took on a husky quality that stole her breath. "For giving me the chance to get to know my daughter."

Without a second thought, she closed her eyes and leaned into his tender touch. She might have been able to resist had it not been for the sincerity in his tone and the genuine gratefulness in his amazing blue eyes. But no matter how much she tried to fight it, he was the man who had stolen her heart all those months ago and given her a precious baby daughter.

"I want to kiss you, Heather."

His whisper made her feel warm all over. "T-that probably wouldn't be a good idea."

"Oh, I disagree, I think it's an excellent idea." His

firm lips lightly grazing the shell of her ear and his warm breath feathering over her skin caused excited little shivers to course throughout her entire body.

She was flirting with danger. This was Jake Garnier, player extraordinaire. But even as she tried to reason with herself, she swayed toward him.

Apparently, that was all the encouragement he needed because the next thing she knew he wrapped his arms around her and pulled her close. She opened her eyes just in time to watch him slowly, deliberately, lower his head and when his mouth covered hers in tender exploration, she thought she just might melt into a puddle at his feet.

As his tongue stroked her lips apart, her eyes drifted shut again and the intensity of his kiss caused her head to spin. But when he coaxed, demanded and persuaded her to respond, every cell in her body tingled to life and Heather found herself holding on to him for support.

She should stop him. It wasn't smart to kiss the man who obviously hadn't wanted anything more to do with her until he learned that she'd given birth to his daughter. But the thought evaporated when Jake crushed her to him and she felt his hard muscles against her tightening nipples and his insistent arousal pressed into her lower belly.

Her knees threatened to buckle and a swirling hunger began to flow through her when he moved his hand to cup her breast, then chafed the hardened tip through the layers of her clothing. She wanted him with a fierceness that frightened her more than she'd ever thought possible.

Jake must have sensed the change in her because he slowly eased away from the kiss, but continued to hold her close. "We've got plenty of time."

She could deny that having him kiss her, that being in his arms and having his body entangled with hers wasn't what she wanted, too. But they'd both know it was a total lie.

"No, it can't happen, Jake." It was hard to be convincing when his large hand still covered her breast. But she couldn't seem to find the strength to pull free of his arms.

"I'm not going to stand here and argue. Right now, I have to take a shower."

As she watched him retreat to the master suite, Heather couldn't help but wonder if she shouldn't take her daughter and run as fast as she could back to the safety of the carriage house. It was obvious that no matter what she said, he wasn't going to listen to her. And living in such close proximity was going to make resisting him extremely difficult.

But thankfully with the Southern Oaks Cup Classic only two weeks away and all of the activities that preceded it, they were both going to become very busy in a very short time. If she could just hold out a few more days, everything should be fine.

She was going to have to attend to Dancer seven days a week and make sure that he was ready to run the race of his life. And as the owner of the favorite to win the Cup, Jake would be away at the almost non-stop receptions and balls that were held to celebrate the annual event.

With her going to bed early in order to oversee the thoroughbred's dawn exercises and Jake sleeping in after being out late with Louisville's social elite, their paths probably wouldn't cross more than a handful of times. And the few times they did, it would most likely be in a public setting for pictures and publicity for the race.

Then, by the time the festivities came to a close, Jake would no doubt be bored with the comparatively slower pace of Hickory Hills and more than ready to head back to his exciting life in Los Angeles. She and Mandy would move back into the carriage house and once again settle into their comfortable, familiar routine.

As Jake sat in the study thumbing through a pile of invitations to teas, receptions and balls being held in honor of the big race, he frowned. How the hell was he supposed to work things out and reconnect with Heather when he was going to have to attend a string of social events?

But staring at the elaborate print on one of the invitations, a slow smile curved the corners of his mouth. The words "and guest" had him rising from his chair.

"Clara, could you watch Mandy for a few minutes while I walk down to the stables to talk to Heather?" he asked when he entered the kitchen.

"No problem." She smiled when he handed her the baby monitor. "How long has our little angel been down for her nap?"

"About a half hour." He checked his watch. "I'm not sure how long she sleeps, but I'll only be a few minutes."

"Take your time." Clara grinned as she motioned toward Daily seated at the kitchen table peeling a pile of potatoes. "We won't be going anywhere for at least the next two weeks."

"I keep telling you, Grandma. When somebody's grounded, it doesn't mean they have to do stuff like this," the boy complained. "It means they just can't go anywhere."

Jake hid a smile as he left the mansion and walking past the pool, started down the path toward the stables. Since his grandmother learned about his plan for a late night rendezvous, Daily had mucked out stalls, mopped floors, polished silver and performed any other menial task she could think to assign him.

In a few days, the kid would get a bit of a reprieve from doing household chores. Jake had already talked to Clara about having Daily help him with a few projects to improve the place. The housekeeper had readily agreed and expressed her gratitude for Jake's influence with the boy. It seemed that Daily was having a hard time adjusting to his mother re-marrying after the death of his father and she'd sent him to Hickory Hills in an effort to keep him out of trouble.

Shaking his head, Jake couldn't help but wonder what his friends in L.A. would think of that one. With his reputation for partying and entertaining a differ-ent woman every night, he was the last person most people would want influencing their teenage boy. But since his arrival at Hickory Hills, Jake had found that he was enjoying the slower, laid-back pace and had started thinking less and less about getting back to the hectic schedule he'd kept for the past several years.

Maybe it had something to do with finding out he'd fathered a child. Or it could be that it was just so vastly different from his usual lifestyle the novelty hadn't worn off yet.

He frowned. So why didn't going back to L.A. sound all that appealing?

As he entered the stable, another thought occurred to him, but he dismissed it. He refused to believe that he might finally be ready to settle down. That was just ludicrous. Of course, he wanted to return to his condo and highly successful law practice. He'd be a fool not to want that.

Greeting Tony and another groom as they attended

to one of the thoroughbreds, Jake relegated his self-analysis to the back of his mind. It was amusing to think that he owned over two dozen of the finest animals in the country and he'd never been on the back of horse in his entire life.

"What's up?" Heather asked when he walked into her office. "Is everything all right?"

Jake nodded. "Mandy is taking a nap and Clara is making Daily rue the day he even thought about sneaking out to see his girlfriend by making him peel potatoes for dinner."

Heather's smile sent a shockwave of heat straight to the pit of his belly. "Poor Daily. I doubt that he'll be eager to try that again."

Jake barely managed to suppress his frustrated groan. He seriously doubted she realized just how pretty she looked with soft curls escaping her ponytail and her creamy cheeks flushed from the early summer heat.

But it was her coral lips that fascinated the hell out of him. Since kissing her outside of Mandy's room two days ago, all he'd been able to think about was doing it again and a whole lot more. And it was the "whole lot more" that was about to drive him over the edge.

"Jake did you hear what I asked?"

"Uh…sorry." Lost in his own misery, he hadn't realized that she'd been talking to him. "What was that again?"

"I asked if you needed something," she said patiently.

Oh, yeah, he needed something all right. But she didn't want to hear what that was.

"As a matter of fact, there is something I need your help with." That was an understatement, he thought sardonically. Forcing himself to focus, he sat down in the chair in front of her desk. "I have a million receptions and a couple of balls over the next two weeks."

She nodded. "That's part of the Southern Oaks Cup celebration and as Dancer's owner, you're expected to make an appearance."

"From the number of invitations I've received, I'm beginning to realize just what a big deal this is," he said, choosing his words carefully. Over the course of the past several years, he'd gotten into the habit of attending parties without a date. Now, he couldn't believe how out of practice he had become at asking a woman out. "And I'd really like for you to go with me."

He watched her open and close her mouth several times before she found her voice. "You can't be serious."

He smiled. "I'm very serious. I wouldn't have asked you to be my date if I weren't."

"I…um, appreciate it, but I can't," she said, her eyes still wide with disbelief.

That wasn't the answer he wanted to hear. "Why not?"

"I'm going to be far too busy overseeing Dancer and preparing for the race to be able to attend." Her smile looked suspiciously relieved when she added, "I'm sorry, but you'll have to go without me."

It was perfectly clear to him why she was turning him down. The more time they spent together, the bigger the possibility she could no longer deny the pull between them. And that was the very reason he was going to insist that she go with him.

"But you would attend the various functions with me if not for your job, right?"

"Well…I…uh…since I'm not about to quit, it's not an issue," she hedged.

He knew he had her and if the look on her pretty face was any indication, she knew it, too.

Rising from the chair, he walked over and called for Tony to come to the office. When the man walked to the door, Jake smiled. "From now until the race is over, you're in charge of the stables. I want Heather free to concentrate on overseeing Dancer's training, preparations for the race and attending social functions."

The man looked as if he thought Jake might be joking. "Me?"

"Yes," Jake answered decisively. "Do you think you can handle the job?"

He watched the man's gaze cut to Heather, then back to him. "Sure. I can handle it, but—"

"Then it's settled." Jake shook Tony's hand. "If

anything comes up, you're still to consult with Heather."

When he turned to walk back and lower himself into the chair in front of Heather's desk, she looked as if she might blow a gasket. "What do you think you're doing?"

"I'm relieving you of your other duties until after the race is over." He smiled. "This way you'll be able to focus on Dancer and the race and attend the social side of this thing with me."

"You can't do that to me," she said, standing up to pace back and forth behind the desk.

"Sure I can."

She stopped to glare at him. "I have a signed contract that says otherwise. You may own this place, but I run it. I'm in charge and I call the shots."

"You're still in charge, Heather." He hadn't anticipated that she'd get this upset.

"At least running this farm will look good on my résumé," she muttered.

He narrowed his eyes. "You haven't been looking for a position elsewhere, have you?"

"Not yet," she admitted belligerently. "But you just made the decision to start the search a lot easier."

Rising to his feet, he walked around the desk and took her into his arms. "Look, you're still in charge. You're still overseeing Dancer's racing career. That hasn't changed. I'm just making it easier for you to concentrate your efforts on him."

"Get real, Jake. We both know the reason you relieved me of the majority of my responsibilities was purely self-serving. You want me to attend the social events with you. That's the only reason you did this."

He took a deep breath. "That's the way it started out. But the more I think about it, the more it makes sense for Dancer to be your top priority now."

"I can't argue that," she grudgingly agreed.

"And won't it make the next two weeks easier if you can turn your sole attention to that goal?"

She slowly nodded.

"I'm sorry I usurped your authority, but I'm used to being the one in charge." He kissed the top of her head. "From now on, I'll consult with you before I make a decision about the stables."

She leaned back to look him square in the eyes and he could tell she was only slightly less furious with him. "You'd better, because if you interfere again, I'm out of here."

If he'd doubted how seriously she took her job before, he didn't now. "Understood. Now, will you please consider attending events with me. It would be nice to have someone I know at my side."

"There isn't a shy bone in your body. You'll do just fine without me."

He smiled as he brushed an errant strand of golden brown hair from her soft cheek. "Yes, but I want you with me."

"I told you, I'm not one of your diversions while you're here," she stated flatly.

She wasn't going to give in easily. But then he wasn't, either. "Would you at least think about going with me?" he whispered close to her ear.

Staring at him for what seemed an eternity, she finally nodded. "I'll consider it, but I'm not promising anything."

Satisfied that his plan to spend more time with her had a chance, Jake lowered his mouth to hers to seal the deal with a kiss. His blood pressure skyrocketed as he slowly caressed her lips with his, and he decided he could easily become addicted to her sweetness as he savored the taste of her.

When he traced the seam of her mouth to deepen the kiss, he took advantage of her soft sigh and slipped inside to stroke her tongue with his. Teasing and coaxing, he encouraged her to explore him, as well, and when she tentatively acquainted herself with him, Jake felt as if a fire had been ignited in the pit of his belly.

But it was the feel of her breasts pressed to his chest, her nipples scoring his skin through the layers of their clothing, that caused his body to harden so fast it left him feeling lightheaded. He moved his hands down her back to the flare of her hips. Pulling her forward allowed her to feel the effect she had on him, how she made him want her. She whimpered softly and sagged against him, letting him know without words that she desired him as much as he did her.

Unfortunately, his timing was lousy. They were in her office in the stable with several people close by. And going back to the mansion was out of the question.

Reluctantly easing away from the kiss, Jake took a deep breath as he leaned back to stare down at her. He didn't think he'd ever seen a more beautiful sight. Heather's porcelain cheeks were flushed and her eyes were glazed with the haze of unfulfilled desire.

"I suppose I should let you get back to work now," he finally managed to get out through his dry throat. Before she could gather her thoughts and tear into him over kissing her again, he released her and, walking to the door, added, "Our first reception is this evening. You can fill me in on our host and hostess on the drive over to their place."

Five

Heather accepted the hand Jake offered as she got out of his Ferrari in front of the home of John and Martha Wainwright, then waited for him to hand his keys to the valet. She was still upset with him over his disregard for her authority at the farm, but the more she thought about it, the more she realized attending these social events with him could work to her advantage. If she did have to look for a position elsewhere, the contacts she made at receptions like this one could prove invaluable.

"So tell me about these people," he said as he cupped her elbow and they walked the short distance to the tall, carved oak front doors of the estate.

"John Wainwright is president of the Southern Oaks Bank and Trust and Martha is the treasurer of the local ladies' club," she said, quickly filling him in on their host and hostess. "Neither of them have the slightest interest in horses or the Classic. But they would both have a coronary before they passed up an opportunity to host a reception for it."

"In other words, they're all about showing off with a big party and getting a mention in the society column."

"Exactly."

When he handed the doorman their invitation, the man smiled broadly and swung one of the entry doors wide. "Welcome to Waincrest, Mr. Garnier." He nodded and gave her a wink. "And Miss Heather."

"Hi, Hank. How is Mae?" she asked, smiling.

The man's grin widened. "She's doing just fine, Miss Heather. Thank you for asking."

As they followed his directions past a sweeping staircase and out a set of French doors onto the terrace, she felt as if she'd stepped into a fairy tale. The place was decorated with a canopy of tiny white lights, white wrought-iron patio furniture and huge bouquets of red and white roses in marble urns. Clearly, the Wainwrights had spared no expense in transforming their lawn into a very elegant cocktail party.

"That's our host and hostess," she said, discreetly nodding toward a couple standing by the bar.

"This is why I needed you with me," Jake said,

leaning close. "You know who all these people are and what role they play in all of this hoopla."

She rolled her eyes. "Like you wouldn't have figured it out on your own."

When a waiter carrying a silver tray with glasses of champagne stopped in front of them, Jake removed two of the flutes, then handed one to her. "If I remember correctly, I think this is how we met."

She swallowed hard when his fingers lingered on hers a little longer than necessary and a feeling of déjà vu swept through her. He'd walked over to her, handed her a glass of champagne and the rest was history.

He leaned close. "Do you think the evening will end the same way it did that night?"

"With me pregnant?"

Jake's teasing smile faded. "I didn't mean *that*. But I'll be damned if I'm sorry it happened. We wouldn't have Mandy if it hadn't."

She could tell he was completely sincere, and she had to agree. "She's brought more joy into my life than I could have ever imagined."

Before either of them had a chance to say anything further, John Wainwright walked over to greet them. "You must be the owner of Stormy Dancer," the man said, turning up the wattage on his smile. Almost as an afterthought, he nodded at her. "Miss McGwire."

Wainwright wasn't interested in talking to her

and she knew why. His bank handled the accounts for Hickory Hills and he wasn't going to waste his time with a lowly farm manager when he could schmooze with the owner of one of the premier stables in the entire country.

As the man engaged Jake in a conversation about becoming a member of the local country club, Heather quietly excused herself and started to walk away.

Jake put his hand on her arm to stop her. "Where do you think you're going?"

Smiling, she pointed toward the buffet table. "I'll be over there."

She could tell he wasn't happy with the way John Wainwright had dismissed her as insignificant. But she really didn't mind being excluded from their conversation. She was far more comfortable talking to the Wainwrights' staff than she was mingling with people who thought they were better than everyone else.

"Dear, would you mind helping me?" a small, elderly woman asked politely. With a cane in one hand and a mint julep in the other, the poor woman had no way of carrying her plate of appetizers.

Smiling, Heather shook her head. "I don't mind at all. Where are you sitting?"

"As far away from these pompous asses as possible," she replied, her expression so sweet that Heather thought she might have misheard.

"Excuse me?"

"You heard right, dear. I called them pompous asses," the older woman repeated proudly. "I've finally reached the age where I speak my mind and don't give a fig what people think. Now, come. Let's find a place to sit and get acquainted."

When Heather followed the elderly lady to an empty table away from the majority of the crowd, she helped the woman get settled. "Is there anything else you need, Mrs…"

"Wainwright." The old lady shook her head disgustedly. "My son is the windbag who snubbed you in favor of kissing up to your young man." She patted the chair beside her. "Sit, dear. I need someone to talk to who doesn't act like they're something they're not." She gave a disgusted snort. "I just hate when John and Martha throw one of these receptions. They put on such airs, it's a downright disgrace."

Heather didn't know what to say. But she couldn't help but like the elderly woman and her candid observations.

"It's all right, dear." The old woman patted Heather's hand. "I have no illusions about how important most of these people *think* they are. And my son and daughter-in-law are the two biggest ducks in the puddle."

"Well, your son is the president of Southern Oaks Bank and Trust."

"Pish posh. It doesn't matter what job somebody ends up with, they should never forget where they came from." Mrs. Wainwright grinned. "I'll bet you didn't know that John grew up the son of a tobacco farmer who was land rich and dirt poor." She pointed an arthritic finger toward Jake. "But your young man seems to be different. You can tell he's got money, but he doesn't appear to act like he's better than everyone else. I'll bet he hasn't forgotten who he really is and where he came from."

Heather stared at Jake. She still knew very little about him. Busy getting ready for the race, she hadn't had the opportunity to ask where he grew up, about his childhood or his family.

Were his mother and father still alive? Did he have siblings? Could Mandy have family that Heather knew nothing about?

She didn't have a clue. But she had every intention of finding out.

As Heather continued to think about it, she had to admit that Mrs. Wainwright was correct in her assessment of him. Jake had never made her or anyone at the farm feel as if they were beneath him. Even Clara had commented that he went out of his way to make everyone feel comfortable.

Heather had watched him with the grooms and stable boys and he never failed to greet them by name or stop and talk to them for a few minutes. And he was probably the only billionaire she'd ever heard of who sat at the kitchen table to eat his meals with his housekeeper, her teenage grandson and his farm manager.

"Are you ready to thank our host and hostess for a nice evening and head home?"

Heather jumped. Lost in thought, she hadn't realized that Jake had ended his conversation with the bank president and crossed the lawn to join her and the man's mother.

Introducing him to the elderly Mrs. Wainwright, she smiled. "It was nice chatting with you."

"It was my pleasure, dear." Mrs. Wainwright placed a bony hand on Heather's arm and motioned for her to lean close. "You hang on to your young man," she said in confidence. "Mark my words, he's the real deal."

"Thank you, Mrs. Wainwright." She smiled. "I'll try to remember that."

After bidding the Wainwrights a good evening, Jake waited until he and Heather were seated in his car before he apologized. "I'm sorry, honey."

"What for?" She looked thoroughly bewildered and so damned beautiful it was all he could do to keep from stopping the car and taking into his arms.

"Wainwright had no right to ignore you the way he did." When the man dismissed Heather as if she didn't exist, a protectiveness he'd never known he possessed had consumed him and Jake had wanted to punch the bastard in his big pretentious nose.

They fell silent for some time before he felt Heather staring at him. "What?"

"Tell me more about yourself."

Glancing her way, he frowned. "What do you want to know?"

"Everything. Where did you grow up? Do you have siblings?" She laid her soft hand on his thigh and he had to concentrate to keep from steering the car into the ditch. "Does Mandy have an extended family?"

"What brought this on?" he asked, covering her hand with his to keep her from moving it. He liked when she touched him.

"Jake, we have a child together and beyond the fact that you're a successful divorce attorney in Los Angeles, I know very little else about you," she said quietly.

"There's no big mystery. My siblings and I were born and raised in San Francisco. I have an identical twin brother named Luke—"

"My God, there are two of you?" She sounded truly shocked.

Grinning he nodded. "But don't worry. He's always been the quiet, more serious one of us."

"In other words, your exact opposite." She looked thoughtful. "Is he married?"

"As a matter of fact, he just got married a few

months ago. He and his wife, Haley, are expecting their first child in about six and a half months." To his surprise, Jake found that he liked sharing details about his family with Heather. "And we have a sister, Arielle. She's ten years younger. She got married last month and is five months pregnant with twin boys."

Heather was silent so long, he thought she might have fallen asleep. "I'm so happy that Mandy is going to have aunts, uncles and cousins." She paused. "What about grandparents? Are your parents still alive?"

"No, our mother was killed in a car accident when Luke and I were twenty." He took a deep breath. No matter how long it had been, he still missed the woman who had give him and his siblings life.

"I'm so sorry. What about your father?"

He snorted. "We only met our father once. After he made our mother pregnant with me and Luke, he took off and she didn't see him again until we were almost ten. That's when he showed up, stuck around only long enough to make Mom pregnant with Arielle, then took off again." It was his turn to pause. "We recently got word that he was killed in a boating accident a couple of years ago."

"Who finished raising your sister after your mother died?" she asked, sounding genuinely concerned.

"Luke and I were in college and managed to work out a pretty good system. He would work one semester and take over most of Arielle's care while I went to school. Then I'd lay out the next semester, get a job and I'd be responsible for her while he attended classes."

"My God, Jake, that had to have been so hard for both of you." She turned her hand, palm up, to clasp his. "Did you try to get in touch with your father to see if he would send money to help out with your sister?"

Stopping the car at the entrance to Hickory Hills, he used the remote Clara had given him to open the wide iron gates. "We tried, but it proved to be impossible. We didn't even know his real name."

Her mouth dropped open. "He lied about who he was?"

Jake nodded. "We didn't find that out and who he really was until we were told he was dead."

When he drove the car through the gates, he pushed the button to swing them shut and as they traveled the long oak-lined drive, he decided to omit his newly discovered grandmother's name. Emerald Larson was Mandy's great-grandmother but he still wasn't comfortable with the fact or with the way she manipulated her grandchildren.

"Mandy does have a great-grandmother," he said, watching Heather from the corner of his eye.

"We learned about her at the same time we found out about our father's death."

She smiled. "It's nice that you finally found each other."

"More like she found us." He shrugged. "She knew how wild and unsettled her son was and after he died, she had a team of investigators search to see if he had any children so that she could set things right with all of us."

"That's when she got in touch with you and your siblings?" Heather asked, seemingly fascinated with what he was telling her.

"Among others."

He could tell from her expression that Heather was thoroughly shocked. "You mean…he fathered more children than just you and your siblings?"

"It turns out our father took the biblical passage where it says 'Be fruitful and multiply' to heart." He smiled as he parked the car in the circular drive in front of the mansion. "He also fathered three other sons by three different women in the ten years between fathering me and Luke and Arielle."

Her eyes grew even wider. "Wow! He certainly was…um, active."

"To say the least."

Jake got out of the car and as he walked around to open the passenger door for her, he couldn't help but see the parallel between the way he'd been living his life and the way his father had. And he wasn't overly proud of it. But he was different from his father in one very important way. Jake was going to be there for Mandy where his father had failed his children in every way possible.

When Heather got out of the car to stand in front of him, he didn't hesitate to put his arms around her. "I know it seems like I've been living my life a lot like my father did, and maybe to a certain extent, I have. But let me assure you, I'll always be there for Mandy…and for you."

"Jake—"

"I mean it, Heather. I'm not the irresponsible jerk my father was."

Deciding that enough had been said about his notorious father and atypical family, he let his gaze travel from her silky hair swept up into a stylish twist, down the length of her black strapless cocktail dress, to her impossibly high, black heels. In L.A. they had a colorful phrase for those kind of shoes and he seriously doubted that she realized some women wore them to send a message that they were open to a night of unbridled passion.

Groaning, he raised his head to rest his forehead against hers. "Do you have any idea how sexy you are? How beautiful?"

Before she had the chance to speak, Jake teased and coaxed her mouth with his own until she granted him the access he sought. But he was completely unprepared and not at all disappointed when

Heather took control of the kiss and touched her tongue to his.

At first tentative, her shy stroking sent electric sparks to every nerve in his being. As she gained confidence and engaged him in a game of advance and retreat, the sparks touched off a flame in the pit of his belly that quickly had him wondering if he was about to burn to a cinder.

The reaction of his body was instantaneous. He hadn't become aroused this fast since his teens.

With his knees threatening to buckle and his head swimming from a serious lack of blood to the brain, he reluctantly broke the caress. If he didn't put an end to the kiss, and right now, he was in real danger of making love to her right there on the steps of the veranda.

"Honey…I can't believe…I'm going to say this." He stopped long enough to draw some much needed air into his lungs. "Unless you're ready to go upstairs with me—to my room, my bed—we'd better call it a night."

He watched her passion-flushed cheeks turn a deep shade of rose a moment before she shook her head. "I'm sorry…I…not yet." She suddenly clamped her mouth shut, then took a step away from him, then another. "I mean…no. That's not going to happen."

When Heather turned and fled up the steps, across the veranda and disappeared into the house, Jake reached up to unknot his tie and unbutton the collar of his shirt. Then, stuffing his hands in his pants pockets, took off at a brisk walk back down the long drive toward the entrance gates.

He couldn't believe how the evening had turned out. He wasn't in the habit of divulging personal information to the women he dated. It kept things from becoming complicated when he went his way and they went theirs.

But Heather was different. For reasons he didn't care to contemplate, he wanted her to know all about him. And he wanted to learn everything about her. What had inspired her to choose her career? Did she have siblings? Were her parents still alive?

Shaking his head, he fell into a steady pace as he started back toward the house. He had no idea what had gotten into him. Yet as he got better acquainted with his only child, he had every intention of getting close to her mother, as well.

Checking on her daughter sleeping peacefully in her crib, Heather crossed the hall and, entering the bedroom she'd been using since Jake moved her and Mandy into the mansion, closed the door. What on earth had possessed her to take control of that kiss? And why had she the same as told him that at some point she would be ready to make love with him again? Had she lost her mind?

As she removed her heels and unzipped her dress, she thought about the details he'd shared with her about his family. There was a lot more to Jake Garnier than first met the eye or that he allowed people to see.

He was a self-made man who hadn't always had an easy life. He'd been there right along with his twin brother to step in and accept the responsibility of raising their younger sister, while still managing to complete his education. That had been a monumental undertaking and she could tell that he wouldn't have considered doing it any other way. He and his siblings had struggled to stay together and they'd made it. That certainly wasn't something a self-indulgent playboy would do.

She slipped out of her dress and hanging it in the closet, took down her hair and changed into her nightgown. When she climbed into bed, she closed her eyes and hugged one of the pillows tightly against her.

The more she learned about Jake, the more she admired him. Considering she was finding it almost impossible to resist him, that was extremely dangerous. She couldn't afford to let go of her pre-conceived notion that he cared little or nothing about anyone but himself. If she did, there was a very real possibility that she and her daughter would both end up getting hurt.

Lying there hugging the pillow, she must have drifted off to sleep because the next thing she knew, her daughter's cries coming through the baby monitor awakened her. She tossed the pillow aside and, getting out of bed, reached for her robe. But the sound of Jake's voice stopped her.

"What's wrong, Mandy? Did my little honey bunny have a bad dream?" He must have taken the spare receiver to his room before he turned in for the night.

As she listened to him comfort their daughter, tears filled her eyes and spilled down her cheeks. It was clear from the tone of his voice that he loved Mandy, and Heather knew as surely as she knew her own name that he would be just as committed and protective of their daughter as any father could possibly be.

Without a second thought, she quietly opened her door and tiptoeing across the hall, watched Jake gently cradle Mandy to his bare chest. She waited until he put their sleeping daughter back in the crib, then walked out into the hall. "I appreciate your trying to let me sleep."

Running his hand through his thick hair, he shook his head. "Too bad it didn't work out."

When they both fell silent, Heather found it hard not to stare. Dressed in nothing but a pair of navy silk pajama bottoms, he looked absolutely... yummy. She suddenly felt warm all over.

"Heather, are you all right?"

"I...um, yes." She needed to make her escape while she still had the presence of mind to do it.

His slow smile said that he knew exactly what she'd been thinking. "I like the way you look, too." Reaching out, he traced one of the thin spaghetti straps of her gown with his index finger. "You make turquoise look real good, honey."

"I thought that was supposed to be…the other way around," she said, realizing that she'd forgotten all about her robe when she'd heard Jake talking to the baby. "Isn't the color supposed to compliment the person wearing it?"

"Not in your case, Heather." He trailed his finger down the strap to the gown's rounded neckline. "You make everything you wear sexy."

A shiver flowed through her when the tip of his finger lightly grazed the slope of her breast. "I'm… going back to…my room."

He took her into his arms. "I'd rather you stay with me."

"Out here in the hall?"

Staring up at him, she knew she was playing with fire. The feel of him holding her and the rich sound of his voice lowered to an intimate timbre caused an ache that she knew for certain only he could ease.

"I was thinking more like my room." His seductive smile sent her pulse into overdrive.

What she wanted was to go with him. What she needed was peace of mind. And that would be in serious jeopardy if she let her heart overrule her head.

She took a deep breath as she summoned every ounce of strength she possessed. "I want you to go to your room and...I'll go to mine."

"Are you certain that's what you really want, Heather?"

They both knew she was telling a huge lie. The last thing she wanted was to go back alone to the big empty bed across the hall. But making love with Jake would only add another wrinkle to their already complicated situation, not to mention pose a serious risk to her heart.

"Y-yes." Turning to go across the hall to her room, she wished she'd sounded more convincing. "Good night, Jake."

When he placed his hand on her shoulder to stop her, the look in his amazing blue gaze caused her heart to beat double time. "You can only run from this—from us—for so long." He leaned forward to kiss her with such tenderness she thought she might do something stupid like give in. "Sleep well, sweet Heather."

As she watched him stroll down the hall toward the master suite, she had to lean against the door frame to keep her knees from folding beneath her. How on earth was she ever going to be able to resist such blatant sexuality?

She somehow managed to walk into the bedroom and close the door. If it was just a matter of physical attraction, she was pretty sure she'd be successful.

But the more she learned about Jake and the more she saw how much he cared for their daughter, the closer she came to listening to her heart. And that was something she couldn't let happen again.

She climbed into bed and hugged the pillow close again. There was no doubt about it. If she intended to survive Jake's visit to Hickory Hills, she was going to have to keep her emotions in check. She was in danger of losing a lot more than her heart if she didn't. They still had yet to discuss how they were going to raise Mandy, and considering the high-handed way he'd relieved her of most of her duties, she might end up losing her job.

But as she lay there thinking about how it felt when he touched her, held her, she knew that keeping her wits about her was going to be all but impossible to do. She was falling for him all over again and there didn't seem to be anything she could do to stop it.

Six

"Where's Heather?" Jake asked when he walked into the kitchen and found Clara feeding the baby breakfast.

"Tony called. There was a problem down at the stables with one of the horses and he wanted her to come down to assess the situation." The housekeeper shook her head. "He knows Heather would never forgive him if he hadn't let her know about it."

Jake frowned. He'd put Tony in charge to free Heather from having to deal with this sort of thing until after the race. "Is there something wrong with Dancer?"

"No. I think she said one of the other studs has a really nasty cut on its pastern." She spooned a mouthful of cereal into Mandy's open mouth. "Heather's almost as good as a vet when it comes to taking care of horses and I'm pretty sure Tony wanted her to take a look at the injury to see how bad it is."

Clara might as well have been speaking a foreign language for all he understood about where the horse was injured. "How did she learn so much about horses?" he asked as he grabbed a mug from the cabinet, then poured himself a cup of coffee.

"Bless her heart, she learned from the best," the housekeeper said, smiling fondly. "Before he died five years ago, her dad, George, was the manager here. From the time she was old enough to walk, she followed him around like a shadow and soaked up everything he knew about horses."

Fascinated by the details he was learning about Heather, Jake leaned against the kitchen counter. "What about her mother? Is she still around?"

Clara snorted. "No, and I say good riddance. She was a wild one, always looking for a good time. She took off when Heather was six and they never heard from her again."

It sounded to him like Heather's mother and his father were a lot alike—narcissistic and completely irresponsible. "I think I'll walk down to the stable and see what's going on. Would you mind watching Mandy until Heather and I get back?"

"Not at all." Clara grinned as she wiped the baby's face. "Take all the time you need. The only thing I have to do this morning is come up with another list of chores to keep Daily busy after he finishes mucking out the stalls."

Chuckling, Jake wondered how much longer the woman was going to make the boy suffer for his lapse of judgment. "I have another project that I'd like his help with. Do you think you could pencil that in on the schedule for tomorrow?"

Clara nodded. "Will you need him all day?"

"Probably several days. Will that be a problem?"

"Not at all." She smiled. "What have you got up your sleeve this time?"

"When we moved Heather and the baby, I noticed the carriage house could use a fresh coat of paint and some new carpet."

As Jake left the house and walked the distance to the stables, his thoughts returned to Heather and he couldn't help but wonder how she'd slept the night before. If he was taking bets, he'd wager that she hadn't gotten any more sleep than he had.

Entering the stable, he followed the sound of a loud commotion. What had been so important that Tony felt the need to call Heather?

"Hold him while I get him tranquilized."

Jake automatically turned at the sound of Heather's voice inside one of the stalls and it felt as if his heart came up into his throat. As he watched, she, Tony and another groom jumped back just in time to keep from being kicked by a very large, extremely agitated horse.

"Heather, get out of there." He tossed the coffee cup onto a pile of straw and reached to open the stall's half door.

"Don't you dare open that door," she warned. "Just stay back. We've got this under control."

It didn't appear that they had everything in hand. It looked as if someone was about to get seriously hurt. The thought that it might be Heather had his heart hammering so hard that he thought he'd surely end up with a few cracked ribs.

When Tony and the other man finally caught hold of the thoroughbred's halter, Heather moved swiftly to jab a long needle into the animal's shoulder. The horse lurched to one side, then kicked the back of the stall with a blow that Jake knew for certain would have killed someone had it connected with one of the humans inside the enclosure. But just when he thought all hell was going to break loose, Heather and the grooms managed to open the half-door and escape.

Fear ignited an anger in him that quickly flared out of control and he was itching for a confrontation. "What the hell do you think you were doing in there?" he demanded when she stood safely in front of him.

"The job you pay me to do."

He stubbornly shook his head. "I pay a veterinarian to attend injured horses. And if the size of his bills are any indication, I pay him quite well."

As he and Heather glared at each other, Jake noticed Tony and the other man hurrying toward the far end of the barn. They apparently decided that retreat was the better part of valor.

"For your information, the vet *is* on the way." Her aqua eyes sparkled with anger and he didn't think he'd ever seen her look prettier.

"Then why were you in the stall? Why didn't you wait for Dr. Pennington to get here?"

"Because Magic needed a sedative immediately," she shot back. "We couldn't run the risk of him making the injury worse."

"I don't care," he said angrily. "You could have gotten yourself killed."

"I've been around horses all my life and I know what I'm doing," she insisted. "Besides, that horse is a full brother to Dancer and almost as valuable as he is. His stud fees alone are going to make you a fortune once he's retired from racing."

Reaching out, Jake took her by the shoulders. "Don't you understand? It's not about the money, Heather. Your safety is far more important to me than any money I could make off of a damned horse."

She stared at him for several long seconds before her stormy expression began to ease a bit. "Honestly, I really wasn't in as much danger as it might have seemed, Jake."

He crushed her to him. "Even the slightest chance of you being hurt in any way is one chance too many, honey."

As his heart slowly returned to a more normal beat, he couldn't get over the fear that had coursed through him when he saw the horse come so close to kicking her. It had rivaled the feeling he'd experienced a few days ago when he'd awakened to find his napping daughter missing from where she'd fallen asleep on his chest.

Before he could analyze what that might mean, he lowered his head to cover Heather's mouth with his. He told himself that he needed to reassure himself that she was indeed all right. Yet the truth of the matter was he'd become quite good at looking for reasons to kiss her.

Soft and pliant, her lips immediately fused with his as she wrapped her arms around his neck. But when she used the tip of her tongue to invite him to deepen the kiss, her eager response to the caress sent blood surging through his veins and his body hardened so fast it made him dizzy.

As he slipped inside and teased, he slid his hands from her back to her delightful little blue jeans-clad bottom and tried to pull her even closer. But an insistent nudge against his legs had him breaking the kiss to look down at the big dog trying to work his way between them.

"Thank God Nemo came along when he did."

Heather's cheeks colored a pretty pink as she glanced down the wide aisle to see if anyone had been watching.

"I thought you were supposed to be man's best friend," Jake groused when he bent to pick up his discarded coffee cup. He scratched behind the big dog's ears. "How would you like it if I interrupted you and one of your female friends?"

"Since he's been neutered, I doubt he'd care," she said dryly.

"Nemo, buddy, I'm so sorry to hear that," Jake said sympathetically.

She looked confused. "Why are you sorry he's been neutered?"

"It's a guy thing." Jake shook his head. "You wouldn't understand."

"The vet just arrived," Tony called from the opposite end of the stable, drawing their attention back to the matter at hand.

"Heather and I are going back up to the house," Jake said before she could answer or find an excuse to stick around. "You assist him with whatever he needs."

"No problem, boss."

"I'm not going anywhere," she stated. "My job is to stay right here and see to Stormy Magic's welfare."

"Dr. Pennington has arrived and Tony will see that he takes good care of whatever treatment the animal needs." Turning her, Jake put his arm around her shoulders and started walking them from the stable. "Besides, if you'll remember, we have a dinner meeting with a couple of the other owners and then the Southern Oaks Ball to attend this evening."

"You could go without me."

"Nope. You agreed to be my date for these things. It's too late to back out now."

She shook her head. "It was more like you pulled rank and told me I was going."

He chuckled. "Whatever. You'll need to start getting ready early."

"Why? We're not meeting the other owners until seven this evening."

"I was contacted this morning by the television network carrying the race. They want to interview us before dinner and get some footage for their *Meet the Owners* pre-race segment."

"I don't own Dancer. You do. There's no reason for me to be included in that." She shrugged from beneath his arm and stopping, glared at him. "Right after he was named the favorite to win the Classic, they showed up here to tape his daily exercises and grooming. They interviewed me then and I told them everything there is to know about Dancer." She shook her head. "This particular fifteen minutes of fame is all yours."

* * *

When Jake helped her out of the back of the limousine, Heather felt as if she'd stepped right into the middle of a three-ring circus. Cameras whirred and reporters called out questions as they walked along the carpeted runway toward the entrance of one of the oldest and most prestigious hotels in Louisville.

"This is just like a Hollywood premiere," Jake said, placing his hand to her back to guide her.

"And the very reason I would have preferred staying at home," she muttered. They'd spent an hour and a half before dinner being interviewed by the television network as well as a couple of reporters from the print media. She was more than ready to escape the spotlight.

"What was that, honey?" he asked, leaning close.

"It's not important." She wasn't surprised he hadn't been able to hear her. The noise was almost deafening.

Thankfully they left most of the chaos behind as they crossed the lobby to enter the Grand Ballroom. She waited while Jake presented the doorman with his invitation, then walking into the ornate room, looked around. The light from the massive crystal chandeliers caused the gold accents on the pristine white walls to take on a rich glow and complemented the heavy floor-to-ceiling red velvet drapes. As she continued to scan the room, she spotted a few of the same guests that had attended the Wainwrights' reception along with several well-known celebrities and foreign dignitaries.

"Is that who I think it is?" Jake asked as a sheikh and his entourage strolled past them.

She nodded. "That's Sheikh Kalid Al-Kahra. He owns Dancer's biggest competition."

"Do you think we have anything to worry about?" Jake asked.

"Not a chance." She couldn't stop her smug smile. "The sheikh's jockey has a tendency to take the horses he's riding to the lead right out of the gate and doesn't let up. By the time they reach the home stretch, the horse has nothing left for the sprint to the finish."

"I'm glad that jockey is riding the sheikh's horse and not ours," Jake said, grinning.

"The previous owner of Hickory Hills demanded the best. That's why we have Miguel Santana wearing our silks." She nodded toward a group standing off to the side of the orchestra. "See that distinguished-looking gentleman over there with all the medals and ribbons? He's the Crown Prince of Marunda. He owns the long shot."

"The Wainwright affair was small potatoes compared to the company we're keeping this evening," Jake said, accepting champagne for both of them from a passing waiter. "There are some very impressive pedigrees here this evening."

"I suppose you could say that." She accepted the

sparkling wine he handed her and took a sip. "But I'm more impressed by the horses than I am with the people owning them."

He looked thoughtful. "You really mean that, don't you?"

She nodded. "Owners like the sheikh and the prince were born into their positions in life. They didn't have to work to get where they are. But every horse starts out the same. They may have impressive bloodlines, but they still have to work and prove themselves on the track. That's something to be admired."

They fell silent for several moments before she felt him watching her.

"Is something wrong?"

"Not at all." His smile caused her pulse to speed up. "Do you realize you're the most beautiful woman here tonight?"

"I really hadn't given it much thought," she said truthfully.

She had, however, thought a lot about how handsome *he* was. Dressed in a tuxedo she knew for certain hadn't come off of a rack, he looked absolutely amazing.

When a beautiful young woman stepped up to the microphone in front of the orchestra and began to sing the song "At Last," Jake set both of their glasses on a nearby table. "Let's dance."

He took her hand and leading her out onto the dance floor, took her into his arms. The awareness suddenly arcing between them was spellbinding. Gazing into the other's eyes, neither spoke as the orchestra played and the young woman sang about finally finding love. Jake held her close, and swaying in time to the music, Heather knew that she'd remember the moment for the rest of her life.

When the song ended, the orchestra immediately played the beginning notes of another slow, dreamy love song and he pulled her more fully to him. Resting her head against his broad chest, she closed her eyes. She'd never felt more cherished, more secure than she did at that very moment in Jake's arms.

"Honey, I want you more right now than I've ever wanted anything in my entire life," he whispered close to her ear.

His warm breath caused a shiver to course through her. She could deny that she didn't want him just as much, but she was tired of lying. From the moment he arrived at the farm, she'd fought what she knew now to be the inevitable. Jake's touch, his drugging kisses and being held in his arms had worn down her defenses, and she'd lost the battle she'd waged with herself. She wanted him just as much now as she had the night they'd conceived Mandy.

Leaning back to stare up at him, the heat in his cobalt gaze stole her breath.

"How long are we expected to stay at this thing?" he asked.

Her heart sped up. "We've put in an appearance. That's all that's expected."

"Then what do you say we call it an evening and go home?" The promising look he gave her sent excitement coursing through her veins.

Before she could answer, he led her off the dance floor and out of the ballroom straight to the concierge desk. Requesting that their limousine be sent to the front entrance, Jake helped her into the backseat. He raised the window between them and the driver, then gathered her into his arms.

Touching her chin with his index finger, he smiled when their gazes met. "You do know what's going to happen when we get back to the farm?"

Her smile robbed him of breath. "Yes."

Crushing her to him, he covered her mouth with his and it suddenly felt as if the temperature in the car went up a good ten degrees. As she put her arms around his neck, she parted her lips and he didn't hesitate to deepen the kiss.

Her eager response sent blood surging through his veins and he didn't think twice about slipping his hand inside the low cut neckline of her evening gown. Caressing her breast, he touched the beaded tip with his thumb. Her moan fueled the fire building in his belly, but when she moved her hand upward from where it rested on his thigh, the rush of heat tightening his groin made him feel as if the top of his head might just come off. He would have liked nothing more than to strip her of the sexy dress and make love to her right then and there. But he hadn't made out in the backseat of car since he was in his teens and he'd forgotten just how uncomfortable it could be.

Breaking the kiss, Jake breathed in some much needed oxygen as he removed his hand, rearranged her dress, then tucked her to his side. As much as he needed her at that moment, he didn't want their lovemaking to be rushed. He wanted their first time together again to be special.

When she snuggled against him and rested her palm on his chest, he covered her hand with his. The ride to Hickory Hills seemed to take twice as long as it should have and by the time the chauffeur stopped the limo in the circular drive in front of the mansion, Jake felt as if he had enough adrenaline running through his veins to run a marathon. Without waiting for the driver, he opened the door and helped Heather out of the car.

Neither spoke as they walked the short distance to the veranda and climbed the steps. Opening the door, Jake stood back for Heather to enter and once they stood inside the foyer, he put his arms around her.

"Is Clara babysitting Mandy in her quarters for the night?"

She nodded. "She volunteered and since I wasn't

sure how long we would be out this evening, I took her up on the offer."

Kissing her until they both gasped for breath, he slipped his arm around her waist. "Let's go upstairs, honey."

When they climbed the stairs and started down the hall toward the master suite, he forced himself not to pick her up and sprint the short distance. He wanted her with a driving urgency. But he focused his entire attention on taking things slowly and refreshing her memory of how good they'd been together in Los Angeles.

Entering his bedroom, he guided her over to the side of the bed, then turning on the bedside lamp, gathered her into his arms. He kissed her forehead, her eyes and the tip of her nose.

"I'm going to kiss you all over and by the time we're finished there won't be a single inch I haven't loved."

As he nibbled his way from the hollow behind her ear down her delicate throat to her collarbone, he reached behind her to unzip her cream-colored sequined gown. When the garment lay in a glittering pool at her feet, his heart stalled at the sight of her white lacy garter belt, sheer nylons and spike heels. He didn't know a man alive who didn't have some sort of fantasy about a woman wearing one of those little scraps of lace and a pair of impossibly high heels.

"If I'd known you were wearing this, we'd have left after that first dance," he said, meaning it.

Her sultry smile sent his blood pressure off the charts as she stepped away from the gown. "When I get dressed to go out, I like feeling feminine."

He grinned. "We'll have to start going out more often."

Releasing the garters, Jake bent to slowly slide his hands down one of her thighs, taking the sheer hose past her knee and down her slender calf. He lifted her foot to remove her shoe, then pulled the nylon off and tossed it to the side. He did the same thing with her other leg and as he straightened, he leisurely ran his hands up along her thighs, enjoying the feel of her smooth skin beneath his palms.

As he raised his head to capture her mouth with his, he unfastened the garter belt and added it to the growing pile of clothing. Her soft, moist lips clung to his and he knew he'd never tasted anything quite as enticing.

He broke the kiss and holding her gaze with his, made quick work of unhooking her strapless bra. When it fell to the floor, his breath lodged in his lungs at the sight of her perfect breasts. Taking the weight of them in his palms, he watched her close her eyes and a blissful look come over her as he chafed the tips with his thumbs.

"You're so beautiful, so perfect."

"So are you," she said, bringing her hands up to

slip them beneath the shoulders of his tuxedo jacket. Sliding them down his arms, she took his coat with her and it soon joined her clothing on the floor.

His heart hammered hard against his ribs as she toyed with the studs on the front of his shirt, then slowly released them one by one. When she parted the linen to place her hands on his chest, her delicate touch caused him to harden to an almost painful state.

"I've wanted to do this since returning from my meeting at Churchill Downs the other day," she admitted as she explored him.

"Not as much as I've wanted you to, honey."

He closed his eyes and enjoyed her fingers tracing the pads of his pectoral muscles and the ridges of his belly. But when she traced the line of hair from his navel all the way down to the waistband of his slacks, his eyes snapped open as a shaft of heat shot straight through him.

Quickly reaching to stop her, he shook his head. "I love the way your hands feel on my body, but I'd rather not start this party without you."

She raised her gaze to meet his and the need he detected in the aqua depths robbed him of breath. "It's been so long," she said breathlessly.

"I know, honey."

He kissed each one of her fingertips before he placed her hands on his shoulders, then brought his to rest at her waist. Staring down at her, he ran his index finger along the waistband of her panties and watched her eyes darken with desire.

Without a word, he slipped his fingers beneath the elastic and sliding his hands down, bent to remove the scrap of satin. When she stepped out of them and he straightened to face her, his heart stalled at the look she gave him just before she reached out to unfasten the waistband of his trousers.

Before she caused him to have a coronary, he stepped back and made quick work of removing his shirt and pants. But when he reached to remove his boxers, she stopped him.

"Do you mind?" The sound of her voice slid over him like a fine piece of silk.

"Not at all, honey," he said, grinning. "You're doing just fine."

Their gazes remained locked as she slid them from his hips and down his legs. Kicking them aside, he stepped forward and took her into his arms. The feel of her soft breasts crushed to his chest, her hardened nipples pressing into his skin, had his body feeling as if he'd go up in flames.

A shaft of need knifed through him when she skimmed her hands over his back and down his flanks, but when her slender fingers found him, Jake felt as if the intensity of pleasure would knock his knees right out from under him. As she gently measured his length and girth, he leaned down to capture one of her puckered nipples between his lips and worried it with butterfly flicks of his tongue.

Her soft moan was his reward and raising his head, he kissed her smooth cheek. "I think we'd better get into bed, honey. Otherwise, I'm not sure I'll have enough strength left to get there."

When she turned toward the bed, he reached into the night stand drawer to remove a small foil packet, then placing it under his pillow, stretched out beside her. Gathering her to him, he covered her mouth with his and let his kiss tell her how much the moment meant to him, how much he wanted her.

He'd never wanted to please a woman as much as he wanted to please Heather. "Honey, I'd like to take this slow, but I'm not entirely certain that's an option," he said hoarsely.

Heather gave him a look that sent liquid fire rushing through his veins as she wrapped her arms around his neck. "And I've wanted you just as much, Jake."

He'd been positive that she was experiencing the same desire, but having her confirm his assumption caused a fever within him that threatened to send him up in a blaze. Kissing her parted lips, he brought his hand up to cup her breast and tease the beaded tip.

When he took her nipple into his mouth, then sucked on it gently, a tiny moan escaped her lips and running her fingers through his hair, she held him to her. "That feels so…good."

Kissing his way down her smooth, flat stomach, Jake slid his hand along her side to her hip, then down her slender thigh to her knee. She shivered against him and he knew her excitement was building. He wanted to bring her to even greater heights and, trailing his fingers along the inner part of her thigh, teased the sensitive skin as he went.

"Jake, you're driving…me crazy," she softly gasped.

When he parted her and found her hot, wet and ready for him, he was the one feeling as if he might go insane. Just knowing that she needed him as much as he needed her sent blood racing through his veins and he had to use every ounce of his concentration to keep from losing the slender thread he still held on his control.

He wanted nothing more than to bury himself deep inside of her, to bring them both the completion they desired. He took a deep breath and forced himself to slow down. He was an accomplished lover and never failed to satisfy his partner. But it was more important to him than ever that he ensure Heather's pleasure above his own.

"P-please…Jake."

Apparently, she was feeling the same urgency because she suddenly moved to find his arousal, then taking him into her delicate hand stroked him intimately. A white-hot haze began to build deep within him and he had to fight with everything that was in him to keep from plunging over the edge.

"Just a moment, honey," he said, reaching for the packet beneath his pillow. Quickly rolling their protection into place, he nudged her knees apart and settling himself in the cradle of her hips, entered her with one smooth stroke.

Gritting his teeth at the mind-blowing tightness surrounding him, he leaned down to capture her lips with his as he slowly began to move within her. But the tension building between them was like a wildfire, untamed and out of control. Each movement, each kiss, fanned the flame and drove them ever closer to being consumed by the passion.

When Heather suddenly arched up to meet him and he felt the immediate tightening around him, felt her feminine muscles cling to him, he deepened his strokes. He held her close and watched in awe as the ecstasy overtook her and she let go.

With his own release close, he moved into her again. He felt Heather suddenly tighten around him one more time and cry out his name. The mind-numbing realization that he'd brought her to a second release sent him over the edge. As he surged into her one final time, shock waves so strong they reverberated throughout his entire being shook him.

Easing to her side before he collapsed on top of

her, he gathered Heather close and held her to him as they both tried to catch their breath. Shaken by the intensity of what they'd shared, Jake knew for certain that he'd never experienced anything as meaningful as their lovemaking. But even though he wasn't at all ready to try to put a name to what he was feeling, he wasn't fool enough to try to deny that it existed, either. And that should have made him nervous enough to jump out of his own skin. It was a mystery to him why it didn't.

"Are you all right?" he asked, kissing the top of her head where it rested on his shoulder.

"Mmm. That was incredible."

"I couldn't agree more." When she yawned and snuggled against him, he smiled and tightened his arms around her. "Why don't you get some sleep, honey? It's been a long day and the week has just started. We have about half a dozen more parties and receptions to attend before all of this is over."

"That many?"

"Unfortunately."

When she started to get up, he tightened his arms around her. "Where do you think you're going?"

She tilted her head up to look at him. "My room."

"I don't think so." He reached over to turn off the bedside lamp. "I want you right here."

"But—"

"I want to wake up with you tomorrow morning and make love again." He brushed her lips with his.

"I can't do that if you're in one room and I'm in another."

She nibbled on her lower lip and he could tell she was waging an internal debate with herself. "Jake, I'm not sure this is such a good idea."

He knew she was afraid of getting in over her head. Hell, he was in uncharted waters himself.

"Please spend the night with me, honey," he pressed. "Then we'll take this one day at a time and see where it goes."

She stared at him for what seemed like forever before she finally nodded. "I'll stay tonight, but that's it. And when your family arrives in a few days, Mandy and I are going to move back into the carriage house."

"Why?"

"Because by my calculations, you're going to need our bedrooms to accommodate everyone."

"This suite is huge," he said, thinking fast. "We can move Mandy's crib in the sitting room and you can sleep with me."

She stubbornly shook her head. "I told you, I'll only stay with you tonight. And we will move back to the carriage house in a few days."

He could tell she wasn't going to concede the issue. But he didn't like the idea of not having her with him, in his house, in his bed.

"All right," he finally agreed.

Apparently satisfied that he'd given up, she laid

her head on his shoulder and in no time he could tell that she'd drifted off to sleep.

As he lay there holding her and staring at the ceiling, determination filled him. Hickory Hills was her and Mandy's home and they belonged right where they were. And he was certain he could come up with some reason for them to stay in the house. All he had to do was find it.

Seven

"Heather isn't gonna like this," Daily said, looking uncertain.

Jake gave the boy an encouraging smile as they carried the sofa from the carriage house and loaded it onto a truck. "You let me worry about Heather. Just make sure you don't drop your end of this thing."

After she, Clara and the baby had left to go into Louisville for lunch and shopping, Emerald had called, prompting him to enlist Daily's help in emptying out the carriage house. Heather was probably going to throw a fit about it, but once he explained everything, she'd surely understand. The place needed to be repainted and recarpeted, and it wouldn't hurt to have some of the furniture replaced. He'd intended to make some of the renovations for her anyway, just not quite this soon.

But when Emerald finally returned his call to tell him she was accepting his invitation to attend the race, she'd asked for downstairs rooms for herself and her assistant, and in doing so handed him the perfect excuse to keep Heather and Mandy in the house with him when the family descended upon them in a few days. Due to Emerald being somewhere in her mid-seventies and her assistant, Luther, being every bit as old, she'd reminded him that climbing the staircase in the mansion might not be a good idea for them. That's when he'd come to the conclusion that the one-level carriage house was the perfect solution.

"How long before the painters get here?" Daily asked, interrupting his thoughts.

As they turned to go back inside for the last pieces of furniture, Jake checked his watch. "They should be here any time. We'd better get the rest of this stuff loaded on the truck and take it to the storage unit, so the men can get started." He was having to pay double the normal rate to get everything done in time. But in the end, it was going to be well worth it.

Daily looked almost as nervous as the night he'd tried to sneak out to see his girlfriend. "Have you figured out how you're going to keep Heather from finding out what's going on until everything's finished?"

"I'm not." Jake laughed at the boy's horrified expression.

"She's gonna kill both of us when she finds out," Daily said, shaking his head. "It's been nice knowing you."

"Don't worry. I'll take the heat with Heather," Jake assured. "You're just doing what I asked you to do."

An hour later, he and Daily had the carriage house emptied and the furniture unloaded into the storage unit. The painting crew had just finished taping the woodwork and were laying down drop cloths when Heather, Clara and the baby drove up in Heather's old sedan. "Jake, what's going on?" she asked when she got out of the car.

"I'm having the place renovated," he answered, hoping her reaction wasn't going to be as dire as Daily had predicted.

"What do you mean by that?" she demanded, her voice reflecting her displeasure.

"I'm having it painted and recarpted."

She propped both fists on her shapely hips. "What did you do with my furniture and all of my things?"

"I stored the furniture until the work is finished and put all of your personal effects in your room in the mansion." He'd contemplated moving them to his room, but abandoned that idea after some careful thought. He'd reasoned that she'd be irritated enough that her plans to move back into the carriage house had to be changed, and there was no sense adding more fuel to that particular fire.

"You can't do this, Jake." Her voice shook with anger as she walked up to stand toe to toe with him. "I liked everything the way it was."

"You're on your own, dude," Daily said, taking off down the path toward the stables like the hounds of hell chased him.

"I'll go ahead and take Mandy into the house," Clara offered as she quickly moved to get the baby out of the car seat.

Jake waited until Clara crossed the patio and entered the house with Mandy, before he turned his full attention on Heather. If he was going to get himself out of the hole he'd dug with her, he figured he'd better do some fast talking.

"Before you become too upset, let me explain."

She folded her arms beneath her breasts. If looks could kill, he figured he'd be a dead man in nothing flat. "This had better be good."

"I received a call from my paternal grandmother this morning. She's going to join the rest of the family here for the race this weekend."

"And?"

"She and her assistant are both elderly." He

wasn't about to tell her that Emerald and Luther were two of the spryest septuagenarians he'd ever met and that he strongly suspected Emerald's request was another ploy to control the situation. "There isn't an elevator in the mansion and I don't think it's a good idea for them to climb the stairs to get to their rooms. At their ages, a fall could be disastrous."

He could tell by her sudden frown that she was giving his reasoning consideration. "I can understand your concerns, but you should have discussed this with me first, instead of taking it upon yourself to start changing things." She pointed to the front door of the carriage house. "That's my home and I should have something to say about what goes on with it. You had no right to get rid of my furniture."

Reaching out, he pulled her into his arms. "Honey, this whole farm is your home. And your furniture will be moved back in as soon as the work is done. I promise the only thing different will be the color of the walls and carpet."

He lowered his head and kissed her until they both gasped for air. "If you decide later to move back into the carriage house, won't it be nice to have those things already done?"

"There's still a problem of not having enough bedrooms in the house when your family arrives."

"I'll have it all worked out by the time they get here." He was just glad she wasn't still glaring daggers at him. "Now, let's go into the house so you can show me the hat you bought for the race and explain to me why all of the women wear them."

After dinner, Heather sorted through the boxes Jake had moved from the carriage house. She should have anticipated him finding a way to get her to stay in the mansion while his family visited. But she had to admit he did have a valid reason. There was no way she'd subject two elderly people to the perils of climbing all of those steps. She'd never forgive herself if one of them fell and was seriously injured.

"What are you doing in here, honey?" Jake asked from the door.

"I'm trying to organize and find a place to put everything until after your family leaves and Mandy and I can move back into the carriage house," she answered without looking up.

He walked over to sit on the bed beside her. "I meant it when I told you that I want you and Mandy to feel free to live in the mansion whether I'm here or not."

She sighed heavily. "Do we have to go over this again? It doesn't belong to me and I wouldn't feel right—"

"We'll cross that bridge when the time comes," he interrupted. "Right now, I have something I want you to see."

"This is the only free evening we've had in the past few days and I'd really like to relax." When she'd discovered they didn't have a reception to attend, she'd looked forward to a quiet, uneventful night.

Taking her hand, he pulled her to her feet. "Trust me, you're going to like this."

She allowed him to lead her down the hallway to the stairs. "Let's get this over. I have a date with the Jacuzzi a little later."

His grin caused her to feel warm all over. "Want company? I'll wash your back if you'll wash mine."

The thought of being in the bubbling water with him caused a delightful fluttering in the pit of her stomach.

"We'll talk about it later." She stopped as he led her toward the front door. "I forgot the baby monitor."

"Don't worry about Mandy," he said, opening the door. "I asked Clara to watch her." He covered her eyes with his hand. "Now, follow me."

"But she has been babysitting so much the past few days." She let him lead her out onto the veranda. "I hate to take advantage of her."

"Clara volunteered." She could hear the smile in his voice as he helped her down the steps. "I think she knows we both need some down time. Besides, she told me the other day that it's a lot easier to grandmother a baby than a teenager."

Nodding, Heather laughed. "I've seen Daily turn as red as a beet when she kisses his cheek, whereas Mandy loves it."

"Are you ready for the surprise?"

"I suppose so." She couldn't imagine why he was being so secretive.

He removed his hand. A shiny royal-blue minivan with the farm logo sat in the driveway. "What do you think?"

"Who does that belong to?" she asked cautiously.

"The farm. But it's primarily for your use."

She turned to stare at him. "Why?"

He pulled her along as he circled the car and opened the sliding side door. "I saw how cramped the backseat of your car is with Mandy's car seat and you can definitely use the room. Besides, it's not fair for you to drive your car for the farm business."

He handed her a set of keys. "Try it out."

She bit her lower lip. It was such a pretty car and would save her from having to put a lot more miles on her aging Taurus. "I'll only use it to go to meetings and to pick up things for the farm."

"Honey, I want you to feel free to use it whenever you like. I'd feel better if you and Mandy were in this than a car that could break down and strand you somewhere." He urged her to get behind the wheel, then walked around to close the side door. But before he slid it shut, Nemo jumped in and sat down on the bench seat in the back. "What the hell?"

"He likes to go for rides," she said, laughing.

Jake patted the big dog's head, then closing the door, got into the passenger seat. "I guess we'll take Nemo for a ride."

By the time they drove several miles down the road and back to the mansion, Heather had fallen in love with the new car. "This is wonderful," she said when she parked it and they coaxed Nemo out of the backseat.

"I'm glad you like it," he said, smiling warmly as he picked up a clump of dog hair from the leather seat, then tossing it to the ground, closed the door. "I'll install a car seat tomorrow and you'll be good to go."

As they walked hand in hand into the house, she started to go back upstairs, but he stopped her. "Where do you think you're going? The evening has just started."

"What do you have up your sleeve this time?" she asked, smiling.

Leading her into the den, he motioned for her to sit on the sectional couch in front of a large flat-panel television. As she sank into the plush cushions, she noticed a bowl of popcorn and a couple of soft drinks on the coffee table.

"I thought we could watch a movie together," he said, sitting beside her. He picked up a remote control, pushed a button to start the movie, then put his arms around her shoulder and pulled her close.

"We've been on the go so much lately, I figured it might be a good way to relax."

Settling back into his embrace, Heather munched on popcorn and watched the comedy he'd selected for them. She briefly wondered if Jake felt as happy and content as she did. This was her idea of the perfect evening, but she wasn't sure about him. He seemed to be enjoying the quiet evening at home. But he could very well just be marking time until he could get back to the fast-paced lifestyle he led in Los Angeles. After all, he was used to going out every night and partying until the wee hours of the morning.

"What's running through that head of yours?" he asked, startling her. He switched off the television.

"Why do you ask?"

"Because you look pensive and you're not paying attention to the movie." He used his index finger to brush a strand of hair from her cheek. "Otherwise, you would have laughed. Especially at that last part."

She stared at him for several seconds before she voiced her thoughts. "I was just wondering if you're bored yet."

He frowned. "Where did that come from?"

Shrugging one shoulder, she met his confused gaze. "You've been here a week and other than the sedate receptions and the ball last night, you haven't gone out to any of the clubs. And you've had more than enough time after you brought me home to go back out. But you didn't. I would have thought by now you'd be climbing the walls."

"Honey, I haven't missed that scene one time since I've been here." He looked thoughtful as if he couldn't quite believe it himself. "In fact, I don't find the idea of going clubbing the least bit appealing."

"Are you feeling all right?" she asked before she could stop herself.

He unbuttoned his shirt, then taking her hand in his, placed it on his bare chest. "You tell me."

Her pulse sped up. "I think you feel pretty good. Wonderful actually."

Pulling her onto his lap, he cradled her to him as he tugged her shirt from her jeans and slipped his hand under the hem. When he cupped her breast, he rested his forehead against hers. "You feel pretty awesome yourself."

A delicious warmth began to flow through her veins and she closed her eyes as she lost herself to the sensation of his hand on her sensitive skin. Was it possible that he really didn't miss his old lifestyle? Or when the first opportunity presented itself, would he revert to his old ways?

Jake covered her mouth with his and she gave up all speculation. She didn't want to think about what tomorrow would bring. At the moment, she was in his arms and that was all that mattered.

"Let's go upstairs, honey," he said, ending the

kiss. "I think your suggestion about our having a date with the Jacuzzi is an excellent idea."

Putting her arms around his shoulders, she smiled. "I thought that was *my* date."

His mischievous grin caused her heart to skip a beat. "Do you mind if I make it *ours?*"

"Not at all."

When he set her on her feet and stood, she didn't think twice about placing her hand in his and walking out of the den and up the stairs. As they entered the master bedroom, he ushered her into the sitting area and over to one of the chairs.

"Stay right here," he said a moment before he disappeared into the bathroom. A couple of minutes later, he walked back into the room and smiling, leaned down to kiss the tip of her nose. "Come with me, Heather. I have a surprise for you."

Doing as he requested, when he led her into the bathroom, she couldn't believe her eyes. The flicker of white candles in all shapes and sizes lit the otherwise dark room and the filled bathtub was already bubbling.

"When did you do this? There wasn't enough time—"

"I set the candles out and filled the tub earlier. The thermostat kept it warm for us." He took her into his arms. "I just lit the candles."

She wrapped her arms around him and laid her head against his chest. "This is perfect. Thank you."

"Let's get undressed and see if it's as relaxing as it looks," he suggested.

Taking turns removing each others clothes, Jake stepped into the Jacuzzi and eased her between his thighs. The feel of his body against hers when he pulled her back to lay against him sent electricity skipping over every cell in her being.

"This feels so good," he said as he tightened his arms around her.

"Yes, it does." She blissfully closed her eyes. "The water is just right."

His low chuckle caused goose bumps to shimmer over her. "I wasn't talking about the water." A shiver of excitement coursed through her when he kissed her shoulder at the same time his hands covered her breasts. "Tonight is all for you, honey. I'm going to love you so well that there won't be a doubt left in your mind how much I desire you."

The sound of his deep baritone promising a night of passion and the feel of his rapidly hardening body against her backside caused her to feel as if she never wanted to be anywhere else but in his arms. And that's when it hit her. She'd told herself that it wasn't happening and tried her best not to do it, but she'd fallen hopelessly in love with him.

If she'd had the chance, she might have been frightened beyond words. There was a very real possibility that she would get hurt again. But Jake didn't give her the opportunity. His hands were moving over her body with precision care and robbed her of all thought.

When he slid his palm down her abdomen to the apex of her thighs, then gently parted her to stroke the tiny nub nestled within, Heather felt as if a spark ignited in her soul. The intensity of the sensations coursing through her caused her body to hum with a need stronger than anything she had ever known.

"Jake, please."

"What do you want, Heather?"

"Y-you."

She turned her head to look over her shoulder at him. "Please make love to me."

His deep groan vibrated against her back. "Turn around, honey."

When she did as he commanded and straddled his thighs, he lifted up to meet her and entered her in one smooth motion. The feel of his hard body nestled inside of her and the hunger darkening his blue eyes stole her breath.

She watched him tightly close his eyes as he struggled for control and she knew his need was as great as hers. Without hesitation she wrapped her arms around his neck and slowly moved against him. His eyes immediately snapped open and placing his hands on her hips, he helped her set a steady pace.

Feeling more cherished than she had in her entire

life, she bit her lower lip to keep from crying out at the intensity of emotions swirling through her. She loved Jake with all of her heart and soul.

As the knowledge filled her, an undeniable tension built inside of her and she rapidly began to climb toward the peak. Jake must have sensed her readiness and deepening his thrusts, sent her over the edge. As her body clung to his, waves of pleasure flowed through her and almost immediately, she felt him tense, then give into the force of his own climax. His tremors rocked them both and she held him close as they rode out the storm together.

When they slowly drifted back to reality, Jake's heart suddenly pounded so hard against his ribs, he wasn't entirely certain it wouldn't jump out of his chest. "Dammit all to hell."

"What's wrong?" Heather asked, clearly startled by his outburst.

He set her away from him and moved to get out of the Jacuzzi. "I wanted you so much, I didn't even consider protection."

She smiled. "Oh, that."

Why was she taking it so lightly? They already had one baby they hadn't planned. And although he loved Mandy more than life itself, he didn't think having another was going to help an already complicated situation.

"Let's get out of here and dry off," he said, won-

dering if he'd lost his mind. As he got out of the
bathtub, he handed her a plush towel, then dried
himself off with another.

There was no question about it. He didn't want
to make her pregnant again. Hell, he didn't know if
he was a good father to one child yet, let alone two.

He shook his head in an attempt to clear it. There
hadn't been one time in his life that he'd failed to
use protection. Even as a teenager, he'd been conscious of the implications and responsibilities
attached to an unplanned pregnancy.

"Jake, are you listening to me?" she asked,
wrapping the towel around her.

He'd been so distracted, he hadn't realized she
was trying to talk to him. Securing the towel at his
waist, he motioned toward the door. "Let's go into
the bedroom, honey. We need to talk."

"But I'm trying to tell you—"

He placed his index finger to her lips. "Not until
I've had my say."

She looked thoughtful for a moment before she
nodded and walking into the bedroom, sat down on
the side of the bed. "I'm listening."

Unable to stand still, he paced back and forth in
front of her. "There's no excuse for my forgetting
to protect you." He stopped and ran his hand over
the tension building at the base of his neck. "But I
want you to know that if you do get pregnant
because of my carelessness, I'll be there this time."

He knelt in front of her and took her hands in his. "I promise you won't have to go through everything alone like you did when you were pregnant with Mandy. This time I'll know, and I give you my word that I'll be there for you, Heather."

"Are you finished?"

He couldn't believe her lack of concern. Did she want to become pregnant again?

Nodding, he drew in a deep breath. "Yes, I think that about covers it."

"You can stop worrying. I'm not going to get pregnant." She shrugged one bare shoulder. "There was an issue of my being regular after Mandy was born, so the doctor put me on the Pill."

Instead of the relief he should have felt, disappointment settled in the pit of his belly. Had he really wanted to make her pregnant again? Had he lost what little sense he had left?

Of course not. The thought was ludicrous. But he couldn't seem to chase away the let-down feeling that accompanied her announcement.

"Why didn't you tell me?" he asked.

"The subject never came up. And besides, it really wasn't any of your business."

She was right, of course. But what he couldn't understand was why he wanted it to be.

Reaching out, she touched his cheeks with her soft hand, then leaned forward and gave him a kiss so sweet it robbed him of breath. "You wouldn't have gotten so worked up if you'd only let me explain. You really could use some work on your listening skills, Mr. Garnier."

Two hours later, after making love to Heather again, Jake held her close as she slept and thought about his uncharacteristic emotions. Not quite two weeks ago, he'd been a carefree, commitment-shy bachelor with nothing more on his mind than paying a visit to his newly acquired horse farm, sticking around for the big race and then he was supposed to be back on the road to L.A. But all that had changed with the discovery that he'd not only found the one woman he'd regretted not staying in touch with but also that she'd had his baby.

Why did he all of a sudden want all of the things he'd spent most of his adult life trying to avoid?

Tightening his arms around her, he pulled her close and tried to relax. But as sleep began to overtake him, Jake couldn't help but feel that he was walking a fine line. And once crossed there would be no going back.

"How's my little angel?" Heather asked as she picked the baby up from the crib. "Did you have a good nap?"

Mandy's happy grin as Heather changed her diaper revealed a small white place on her lower gum.

"Your tooth has broken through." Kissing her

daughter's soft cheek, Heather picked her up from the changing table and walked out of her bedroom toward the stairs. "We'll have to find your daddy and show him. He's been worried about when it was finally going to stop bothering you."

Shortly after awakening to find herself alone in Jake's bed that morning, she'd gone in search of him and found that he had moved the crib into the room she'd been using. He'd explained that with his grandmother and her assistant staying in the newly decorated carriage house there would be plenty of rooms for everyone when they descended on them later in the day.

Hearing voices when she reached the bottom of the steps, she crossed the foyer and entering the den, found several people taking their turns hugging Jake. It appeared that his family had arrived.

"Heather, I'd like you to meet the clan," Jake said when he noticed her standing just inside the door. Walking over he lifted Mandy onto his arm and put his other arm around her shoulders. "This is my daughter, Mandy, and her mother Heather."

"Please let me hold her," his sister, Arielle, said reaching for Mandy. Almost six months pregnant, she and her husband, Zach, had just learned they were expecting twin boys. "She's absolutely adorable. And she looks just like you, Jake."

As everyone greeted her and made a fuss over the baby, a bittersweet feeling filled her chest at the pride in Jake's voice. She only wished he could love her half as much as he did their baby.

When he finished making the introductions, Heather couldn't help but notice how much Jake and his half brothers were alike. All of them were quite tall, had the same athletic build and bore a strong facial resemblance. They even shared some of the same mannerisms. When his brother Hunter O'Banyon talked about the stress of being an air medevac pilot, he ran his hand over the back of his neck, which Jake had a habit of doing, too.

"Where's your twin and his wife?" she asked, noticing their absence.

"Haley had a doctor's appointment," Jake answered. "Luke said they'd meet us at Churchill Downs before the race tomorrow."

"Heather, I hear you're the one in charge of the winning horse," Nick Daniels said. "Jake told us you raised him from a colt."

Smiling, she nodded at the rancher from Wyoming. "Actually, I was responsible for choosing his bloodlines as well as helping the mare foal when the vet couldn't get here in time."

"Hang on to her, Jake," Nick advised. He put his arm around his pretty wife, Cheyenne. "Take it from me. You can't go wrong with a woman who knows her horses."

"I'll remember that," Jake said, smiling.

"Heather, do you have time to go shopping with

us?" Caleb Walker's wife, Alyssa, asked. "I've heard that it's a tradition for all of the women to wear a hat to the race."

"I got a new one a couple of days ago and I'd be more than happy to take all of you to the shop where I bought it," Heather offered. "They have a great selection, in all colors and styles."

Callie O'Banyon sighed. "A shopping trip without little ones in tow sounds like heaven."

"By the way, where are your children?" Jake asked.

Caleb chuckled as he pointed to his brothers. "We all decided to leave them with the babysitters and enjoy spending a little alone time with our wives."

"If everyone's agreeable on the shopping, we could go right after I take a nap," Arielle suggested, yawning. She handed Mandy to Alyssa, then with her husband's help, rose to her feet. "Could you tell me where our room is, Jake?"

"I'll be happy to show you where you'll be staying," Heather spoke up, earning a warm smile from Jake.

When they climbed the stairs and Heather showed the pretty young woman where she and her husband, Zach, would be sleeping during their stay at Hickory Hills, Arielle motioned for Heather to follow her into the room. "Are you up for some girl talk before I crash?"

Heather liked all of Jake's brothers and sisters-in-law, but there was something about Arielle that told Heather if given the chance they would become very good friends. "Of course."

Lowering herself to the side of the bed, Arielle smiled. "I just wanted you to know how thrilled I am that someone has finally tamed Jake. I couldn't be happier for both of you."

Heather frowned. "I think you must have gotten the wrong impression. Jake and I are just—"

"Don't tell me you're just friends," Arielle interrupted. "I've seen the way my brother looks at you and there's a lot more to the way he feels about you than friendship."

Heather wasn't quite sure what to say. She wasn't going to lie to the woman. But she wasn't certain there was anything more going on for Jake than a strong attraction and undeniable desire.

"It's…complicated," she finally said, settling on the truth. Whatever was going on between them was going to take some time to sort out. They still hadn't discussed how they were going to handle raising Mandy together with so much distance between their residences. Jake had talked about going back to Los Angeles and leaving her and Mandy the run of the farm, but that didn't mean the custody issue was settled. He could still come up with demands for equal time.

Arielle placed her hand over Heather's. "You love him, don't you?"

She didn't even think to hesitate. "Yes."

"Trust me, Jake may not realize it yet, but he's in love with you, too," Arielle said, smiling. "I've never seen him like this. He can't keep his eyes off of you."

"It's not like he has much to choose from here," Heather said dryly. "Besides the housekeeper, Clara Buchanan, who's sixty if she's a day, I'm the only other woman here at Hickory Hills."

Arielle laughed. "How many times has he been out since he's been here?"

"Other than the receptions and ball we've had to attend, he hasn't," she admitted.

"I rest my case." Arielle hid a yawn behind her hand. "I know my brother. If he didn't have some very strong feelings for you, he would have been out every night."

"I wish you were right, but—"

"I am." The young woman yawned again. "Now, why don't you go downstairs and get to know the others while I take my nap. When I get up we'll all go shopping and buy some wildly expensive hats we'll probably never wear after the race tomorrow."

Heather gave Arielle a hug, then walked out into the hall and quietly pulled the door shut behind her. She'd give almost anything for Jake's sister to be right. But she couldn't trust that Jake had changed for good. Before coming to Kentucky, he'd been perfectly content being the irresponsible bachelor with no children and no commitments. And once he was back in his element in Los Angeles, around friends who enjoyed partying all the time, he just might find that he'd missed that nonstop excitement and revert to his old ways.

Eight

"Heather, I'd like for you to meet my paternal grandmother, Emerald Larson," Jake said, wondering how she'd take the news that he was the grandson of one of the richest women in the world.

The one thing that Emerald had respected and taken great pains to protect was her grandchildren's right to privacy. She left it entirely up to them when and to whom they revealed the relationship. And as if by unspoken agreement, all six of them had been discreet and managed to keep the news fairly quiet.

As he watched, Heather's aqua eyes widened a moment before she recovered and shook Emerald's hand. "It's nice to meet you, Mrs. Larson."

"I see Jake has taken his cue from the rest of my grandchildren," Emerald said, patting Heather's cheek. "Don't worry, dear. None of the others revealed my identity until they had to, either."

"If you'll excuse me, I was just on my way to the paddock to see if Tony has everything under control," Heather said, rising from her seat.

As she started past him, Jake caught her hand in his. "Will you be back in time for the race?"

Her smile lit the darkest corners of his soul. "Absolutely. I wouldn't miss this for anything."

"Where's your assistant?" he asked Emerald as he watched Heather disappear into the crowd.

Since Emerald never went anywhere without the distinguished-looking gentleman, Jake knew he couldn't be too far away. He just hoped he didn't have to go looking for Luther in the sea of people. Churchill Downs had a record crowd and he'd probably never find the poor old guy.

"Luther is placing a small wager for me on your horse, Jake," Emerald said as she found a seat in the box section he'd reserved for the family to watch the race.

Unless she'd changed her ways, Emerald never did anything on a small scale. No telling how much she'd had Luther put down on Stormy Dancer. But it wasn't as if she couldn't afford it. She could probably buy the entire race track with all of the horses and not even scratch the surface of her bank account.

"This is such a festive atmosphere," she said, looking genuinely excited. "And I love that all of the ladies have such decorative hats." She touched the brim of her own elaborate headwear. "I think it's sad that these aren't called for on more occasions. I can remember a time when all the women wore hats for every occasion."

Jake paid little attention to what she was saying as he scanned the crowd for Emerald's assistant, Luther Freemont. When he finally spotted him, Jake breathed a sigh of relief. The man was slowly making his way through the crowd to the box section with a mint julep in each hand and a bet slip sticking out of the breast pocket of his suit.

"Mr. Garnier." Luther nodded a greeting in his usually stiff manner, then handed one of the glasses to Emerald. "Your julep, madam."

"Thank you, Luther." Emerald patted the seat beside her and the man lowered himself into it. "I'm so glad we're right here in front of the finish line. We'll be able to see Jake's horse win."

As the bugler played the call to race, his brothers and their wives began to file into the box. Jake checked his watch. Where the hell was Heather? She should have been back from checking on Dancer down at the paddock by now.

Just as the horses began their parade past the grandstand on their way to the starting gate, he saw her hurrying up the steps. "Was everything all right?" he asked, when she reached him.

"Dancer was a little more skittish than usual," she said, sitting down beside him. "Thoroughbreds are high-strung by nature—he can sense this is the race of his life."

"Which one is Stormy Dancer?" Caleb asked from behind them.

"That's Dancer," Heather spoke up, pointing to one of the bays. "Our silks are red and blue with a white stripe cutting diagonally across the jockey's chest. When they're running along the back stretch or packed up, look for the colors and you'll be able to keep track of him during the race."

"Thanks for the tip," Caleb said, picking up a set of binoculars.

"There's a lot to remember in this business," Luke said, laughing as he sat down on the other side of Jake.

"Tell me about it, bro." Glancing at his twin, he felt as if he looked into a mirror. Lowering his voice, he admitted, "I couldn't have gotten through these past couple of weeks without Heather. Every time a question was asked about Dancer or his training, she'd tell the reporters and sportscasters what they needed to know."

Luke looked thoughtful. "When's the wedding?"

"How many mint juleps have you had?" Irritated, Jake shook his head. "If I were you, I'd lay off for a while."

Luke shrugged. "Still in denial, huh?"

Before he could tell his brother to mind his own damned business, they started loading the horses into the starting gate and everyone jumped to their feet. As soon as the last horse was guided into place, the front of the chutes flew open at the same time the announcer shouted, "They're off."

The roar of the crowd made it impossible to be heard, and when the horses raced past the grandstand, Heather grabbed his hand and squeezed it until his fingers went numb. He barely noticed. He was too busy watching her. Her cheeks had colored a pretty pink and he didn't think he'd ever seen her look more breathtaking. With sudden insight, he realized that he'd underestimated how much it would mean to her if the horse she'd raised won. She'd chosen his bloodlines, overseen his development and this race was her validation—the culmination of her work.

The horses entered the backstretch and Jake noticed that the sheikh's horse was way out in front, just as Heather said he would be. Picking up the binoculars he'd brought with him, Jake searched for Dancer and found him in the middle of the pack. As they rounded the turn and headed for the home stretch, their jockey must have turned Dancer loose because he suddenly shot to the outside and made his way to the front. And as Heather predicted, the sheikh's horse started slipping back into the pack and Dancer took over the lead. By the time he sprinted across the finish line he was five or six lengths ahead of his nearest challenger and there was no doubt he'd won the race.

"We won!"

With enough adrenaline flowing through his veins to lift a freight train, Jake caught Heather up in his arms and kissed her like a soldier returning from war. He knew his level of elation had nothing to do with the their horse winning and everything to do with the relief that she hadn't been disappointed with the results of the race.

When he set her on her feet, she grabbed his hand. "We need to get down to the track. After Miguel weighs in with the saddle, they'll want you in the winner's circle."

Jake shook his head. "They want *us* in the winner's circle, honey. I may be the owner on paper, but Dancer has always been your horse and always will be."

Tears filled her eyes and she raised up on tiptoes to lightly kiss his cheek. "Thank you, Jake. That means a lot to me."

After posing for endless pictures and helping Jake get through the required interviews with the media, Heather called Clara to check on Mandy. Then, leaving orders with Tony to give Dancer an extra scoop of oats to celebrate, she joined Jake and his family for an elaborate dinner at the hotel where the Southern Oaks Ball had been held.

Once their waiter had popped the cork on a bottle of outrageously expensive champagne, Jake stood up and raised his glass. "To Heather, her excellent instincts and expertise. Today was the culmination of your hard work and the realization of a dream. May Dancer be the first on many winners under your expert management."

As everyone added their congratulations, Jake sat back down beside her. "Thank you," she whispered, blinking back tears. His recognition of her accomplishment meant more to her than he'd probably ever know.

"You deserve all of the credit and accolades for the outcome of today's race, honey." His hand found hers beneath the table and he gave it a gentle squeeze. "And I couldn't be happier for you."

When the waiter served the main course, conversation turned to catching up on what was going on in the various lives of Jake's siblings, and Heather found it heartwarming that in spite of their unconventional relationship, they'd all become good friends.

"What's up next for you, Jake?" Hunter asked. "Any more big races on the horizon?"

"I'm leaving that up to Heather," he answered. "I called a Realtor yesterday to put my condo on the market and have her find a house along the beach in Malibu for me."

As the group left the private dining room and entered the Grand Ballroom for the victory party, Heather didn't have time to dwell on what Jake might have planned as she noticed several celebrities milling around the bar. All of them had notorious reputations for partying and she couldn't help but wonder if some of them were Jake's friends.

When a singer started singing the song they'd danced to at the ball, Jake turned to her, smiling. "I think they're playing our song, Heather." Leading her out onto the dance floor, he wrapped his arms around her. "Are you happy, honey?"

She stared up at the man she loved with all of her heart. "And you?"

"Let's see. Our horse won the Classic. The family all made it for the big race. I have a sweet baby daughter with a new tooth who loves to throw baby food at me. And you're in my arms," he brushed his lips over hers. "What more could a man ask for?"

She wanted to believe that all of that would be enough for him. Unfortunately, she knew it wasn't. If he'd already started looking for a house along the beach in Malibu, where she was certain several of his acquaintances had property, he wasn't considering leaving the wilder side of life behind.

The song ended and the orchestra immediately began to play the other tune they'd danced to. Looking up into his cobalt eyes, she blinked back tears. "You arranged for those songs to be played back to back, didn't you?"

His smile made her feel warm all over in spite of the disappointment filling her. "They will always remind me of you and a very special night we spent together." He tenderly kissed her forehead. "You're so beautiful and I want you so much right now."

She loved the way his body felt against hers. "I want you, too. But—"

"I know. You don't have to say it." He shook his head. "Do you think I can charter a jet to take my family all back to their homes tonight?"

She shook her head. "I don't think that would be a good idea."

"I do."

When the music stopped and he led her off the dance floor, her earlier speculation was answered about the celebrities in attendance being his friends when a tall, dark-haired man she recognized as one of Hollywood's baddest bad boys walked toward them. "Jake Garnier, I heard you owned the horse that won today. I hoped you'd stop by this evening." The man grinned from ear to ear, showing off a mouthful of capped teeth. "Now I know this little bash is going to rock."

"What are you doing here, Cameron?" Jake asked, smiling at his friend.

"One of the actresses in my latest film is part owner in one of the nags that ran in the big race and she asked me to come along with her to watch." The conspiratorial wink he gave Jake set Heather's teeth on edge. "You know me. If a woman asks, I'm always up to the challenge." Turning his attention her way, the man's grin evolved into an outright leer. "And who do we have here?"

She felt the arm Jake had draped around her waist, stiffen. "Heather McGwire, this is the infamous Cameron Strombeck."

"Jake!" a tall willowy redhead called as she made her way across the dance floor toward them. "Congratulations. I'll bet you'll be out all night. Be sure and save a dance for me, darling."

As the celebrities continued to gravitate toward them, Heather felt increasingly more uncomfortable. It appeared that instead of having to go back home to pick up his life where it left off, Los Angeles had come to him.

"I think I'll join your family," she said, slipping from his arm before he could stop her.

She walked over to the table where the women were gathered as they waited for their husbands to return with their drinks and sank into an empty chair beside Arielle. "I hope you don't mind my joining you."

"Not at all," Callie O'Banyon said, smiling warmly.

"You and Jake looked amazing out there on the dance floor." Arielle reached over to hug her. "Congratulations, I'm so happy for you."

"Thank you. Dancer's win was definitely exciting." She knew that wasn't what the woman meant, but it was easier to change the subject than to accept good wishes for something that was never going to happen.

When the orchestra started playing again, the volume made conversation impossible and they all fell silent. Heather glanced at Jake several times and her heart broke a little more each time. He looked as if he was having the time of his life with his friends from Tinseltown. As she watched, the redhead melted against him on the dance floor. He didn't seem to mind in the least.

"I hope you don't mind but I think I'll call it a night," she said, rising to her feet.

"Heather, wait," Arielle said, placing a hand on her arm to stop her.

"I'm…um, really pretty tired. I'll see you all in the morning." She had to get out of there before she humiliated herself by dissolving into a torrent of tears. She'd done the very thing that she'd told herself she couldn't let happen. She'd started to believe that Jake might be content staying with her and Mandy. But she knew now that wasn't going to happen. He would soon be leaving Hickory Hills to return to his life in L.A. and the sooner she accepted that, the better off she'd be.

Hurrying across the hotel lobby, when she stepped out onto the sidewalk, she found Mrs.

Larson and her assistant waiting on their limousine. "What's wrong, dear?" Mrs. Larson asked, clearly concerned.

Heather forced a smile. "It's been a full day and I'm going back to Hickory Hills before I collapse."

"Would you like to ride with us?" Mrs. Larson offered. "It's past our bedtime and we'd like to get a good night's sleep before we fly back to Wichita tomorrow."

"I would appreciate it. Thank you."

She'd intended to get a cab, but she was going to have to watch her money for a while. There was no way she could continue working for Jake after what she'd just witnessed. Effective the first thing tomorrow morning she was going to resign her position as farm manager and find employment elsewhere.

"Back off, Lila," Jake demanded, setting the woman away from him. Aside from the fact that he wanted nothing to do with the woman, he didn't want Heather getting the wrong idea.

"I thought you'd be open to having a little fun for old times." Her expression turned to a pout that he was certain she'd practiced for years. He couldn't for the life of him remember why he'd ever found her attractive.

"I'm with someone else. Besides, if you'll remember, that ship sailed a long time ago. We went out a total of three times. You've got to move on."

Her lips curled into what could only be described as a snarl. "You don't know what you're missing."

"Oh, I think I do." He started to walk away, then turned back. "And don't worry. I'm sure you'll find someone to help you have a *good time* this evening. Have a nice life, Lila."

He glanced over at the table where his sister sat and breathed a sigh of relief. At least Heather hadn't been around to witness Lila's brazen move.

"Hey, Jake, would you like to go see what the clubs around here have to offer?" Cameron asked, stopping him half way across the room. "This is dull. We want a lot more action than what this horse crowd has to offer."

As he stared at the man, Jake couldn't believe he'd ever considered him a friend. A pleasure-seeker from the word go, Cameron Strombeck was about as shallow and self-absorbed as a human could possibly be. His disdain for the fine people of the racing industry—for people like Heather—grated on Jake's nerves as little else could.

"No, I'm fine right where I'm at. But you might want to check with Lila Dixon. I happen to know she's looking for a little excitement."

"Really? That could be interesting. I'll catch you when you get back to L.A., then," Cameron said, turning to find Lila. "Give me a call."

"Don't hold your breath on that happening," Jake muttered. Continuing on to the table where Arielle sat, he noticed that she looked ready to tear him in two. "What's wrong?"

"Sit."

"Where's Heather?"

"I said sit!" He didn't think he'd ever seen his sister look as determined as she did at that very moment.

"Where's Heather?" he repeated, desperately searching the ballroom for her. He saw his brothers and their wives on the dance floor and his brother-in-law, Zach, over by the bar. But Heather was nowhere in sight.

"She left." Arielle shook her head. "And I don't blame her. How could you do that to her, Jake? What were you thinking?"

"What the hell are you talking about? I didn't do anything."

When he started to get up, Arielle stopped him. "Stay right where you're at, big brother. I have something to ask you."

"It's going to have to wait, Arielle. I need to find Heather."

"You and Luke have made me listen to both of you all of my life, now you're going to hear what I have to say." He'd never known his sister to be this upset with him.

"Could you make it quick?" he asked impatiently. "I've got to get to Heather and find out why she left."

Arielle looked thoughtful a moment. "She's ex-tremely important to you, isn't she, Jake?"

"Yes."

"You love her, don't you?" Arielle pressed.

"I wouldn't go that far," he said stubbornly. He knew he had deep feelings for Heather, but he wasn't comfortable with the word *love.*

"Oh, Jake." Arielle's voice softened as she reached out to put her arms around him. "You're frightened, aren't you?"

"That's ridiculous, Arielle." He hugged her back. "I can't think of one single thing I need to be scared of."

Leaning back, she smiled sadly. "How about losing Heather? Aren't you afraid of that?"

His chest tightened painfully at the thought of never holding her, loving her, again. "You don't under-stand, I…"

When his voice trailed off, his sister nodded. "That's exactly what's going to happen if you don't take the chance, Jake. I don't know what's holding you back, but whatever it is, you've got to let it go."

As he stared at his younger sister, he knew that she was right. He'd avoided making a commitment for fear of turning out to be as irresponsible as his father. But he was nothing like Owen Larsen and never would be.

No other woman incited the degree of passion in

him or made him want her the way Heather did. And he'd never met any other woman who made him want to be a better person. Not until Heather.

Taking a deep breath, he rose to his feet and kissed Arielle's cheek. "For a kid, you're pretty damned smart."

"What's going on?" Zach asked when he walked up to the table.

"I have to go find Heather and do some serious explaining," Jake answered, turning to leave.

"Stop by a sporting goods store first and get a set of knee pads," Zach called after him. "If Heather is anything like Arielle, you're going to need them when you're on your knees begging her to give you another chance."

After checking with Clara to see if she could watch Mandy for the rest of the evening, Heather barely managed to make it to her room upstairs and close the door before the tears she'd been holding in check spilled down her cheeks. How could she have let herself think there was a chance that Jake was different now than he'd been over a year ago? How could she have been so stupid?

Collapsing on the bed, she hugged one of the pillows. She should have known better than to think that he had changed. Jake was Jake. He couldn't be someone he wasn't, couldn't be the man she wanted him to be. Seeing him with his friends tonight and hearing his plans to buy a house in Malibu had been all the proof she needed to see that she and their daughter weren't enough for him.

She wasn't certain how long she lay there sobbing against the pillow, but when she finally managed to stop crying, she gathered the scraps of her broken heart and got up. There were things she needed to do before she faced Jake tomorrow morning.

Going into the bathroom, she washed her face, then took off the evening gown she'd changed into for dinner and put on a pair of jeans and a T-shirt. She needed to pack her and her daughter's things and take them down to her old car, then draft her resignation.

As she opened the dresser drawers and started pulling out clothes, the sound of a car coming to a screeching halt in front of the mansion caused her to jump. Almost immediately she heard the front door bang back against the woodwork.

Hurrying to the top of the stairs to see what was going on, she stopped short at the sight of Jake, standing in the open doorway staring up at her.

"Heather, honey, we have to talk."

Nine

"I don't *have* to do anything," Heather stated flatly.

She watched him release a frustrated breath. "Would you please come down here? I need to tell you something."

"Where are your friends?" she asked as she slowly descended the steps.

"Damned if I know and damned if I care." He closed the front door, then walked over to stand at the bottom of the staircase.

"I would have thought you'd be out celebrating with them," she said, drawing on every bit of strength and pride she could muster.

"That's one of the things we need to discuss."

When she descended the last step, he started to take her by the hand, but she sidestepped him. He stared at her for a moment before he motioned toward the study. "Please follow me."

"I don't really want to discuss anything right now, Jake." Did he think hearing that he was leaving her and Mandy would make everything all right?

She walked over to the fireplace and traced her finger along the frame of a snapshot that he'd had Clara or Daily take of himself holding their daughter. Just like the photograph, she was never going to be a part of the picture. The thought caused an ache so deep inside, she had to look away to keep from crying out.

When Jake put his hands on her shoulders to turn her to face him, she backed away from his touch. "Please don't."

"Heather, honey, you have to listen to me."

"You don't have to make excuses or explain," she said, surprised that her voice remained steady. "You're an adult. You can do as you please."

"But I'm going to tell you anyway," he interrupted. "Now, will you stop arguing with me and start listening?"

Sighing heavily, she walked over to sit in one of the chairs. "Let's get this over with. I have things to do."

He stared at her for several long seconds. "What do you have to do at this time of night?"

"I need to pack."

He folded his arms across his broad chest. "Are you going somewhere?"

"I suppose now is as good a time as any to tell you that I quit effective immediately." She had to pause before she could finish. "You'll have to find someone else to manage Hickory Hills and oversee your horses."

A dark scowl wrinkled his forehead. "You can't do that."

"Watch me." A sudden anger swept through her and she started to get up.

He quickly stepped forward to block her. "I won't let you quit and I don't want you leaving."

"You can't stop me," she said, settling back in the chair.

"Dammit, Heather, Hickory Hills is your and Mandy's home." He pulled another armchair over to sit in front of her. "You belong here."

"Not anymore, I don't." She glared at him. It was much easier to let her anger build than to give into the misery of a broken heart. "You're going back to your life in L.A. and I'm staying here. But do you honestly think I want to be here when you bring a woman with you for your next visit? Or wait for you to return so that I can be a diversion while you're here?"

He shook his head. "That's not going to happen."

She watched him close his eyes as if garnering

his patience. When he opened them, there was a determined spark in the cobalt depths.

"If you'd stuck around long enough you'd have seen me decline Cameron's invitation to go barhopping with him and a few others I know from L.A."

"Didn't you want to reconnect with your friends?" she asked.

"Those people wouldn't know how to be a friend if their lives depended on it. They're too self-centered, too shallow." He sat back in his chair. "You probably won't believe this, and I wouldn't blame you if you didn't, considering my track record. But I've been tired of the party crowd for quite some time. I just didn't realize it."

"That is pretty hard to believe," she said, tamping down a tiny bubble of hope.

Sitting forward, he reached out to take her hands in his. "Honey, I'm not going to pretend that I've been a saint since you and I were together in Los Angeles. But I can tell you that after you left, I realized that something was different about me. I suddenly felt like I wanted more out of life than being part of that scene."

"So you're telling me that I caused you to have some grand revelation about yourself?" she snorted.

He laughed. "I'm a little more thickheaded than that." His expression turned serious as he stared down at their entwined hands, then looked up to capture her gaze with his. "It's not an easy thing for me to admit, but all of my adult life I've been afraid to risk my heart, afraid to love. Deep down I was afraid I'd turn out to disappoint a woman the way my father had my mother. So I ran from it. I went out to clubs and dated more than my share of women to keep from becoming too involved."

Was he telling her he was incapable of loving?

Without warning, he reached over to lift her onto his lap. "But then I met you and all that changed."

"In what way?" It felt so wonderful to be in his arms, but she couldn't let herself believe that everything was going to work out between them. When she tried to get to her feet, to escape the temptation he posed, he tightened his arms around her.

"I couldn't forget your laughter, your smile. I couldn't forget you." He nuzzled her hair with his cheek. "I found myself lying in bed at night regretting that I hadn't learned your last name, where you were from and how I could keep in touch with you. And that's something that had never happened to me before."

"Never?" She had a hard time believing that he'd been able to forget every other woman he'd ever gone out with, but her.

"It's the truth, honey." He kissed her cheek. "I never thought I'd ever say this to a woman, but I think I've loved you ever since I spotted you standing there at that horse auction."

Tears welled up in her eyes as the hope within

her burst free and spread throughout her being. "You love me?"

"With all of my heart, Heather." He cupped her cheek with his palm. "And I'm tired of running, honey. If you can find it in your heart to forgive me for being so thick-headed, I want it all. You, marriage, brothers and sisters for Mandy. I even want the minivan filled with car seats and clumps of dog hair."

"Are you sure?" she asked cautiously.

"I've never been more certain of anything in my entire life." His smile caused her heart to skip a beat. "I love you, Heather McGwire. Will you marry me?"

"Oh, Jake, I love you, too." The tears spilled down her cheeks. "But—"

"That's all I need to hear," he said, capturing her mouth with his.

Tracing her lips with his tongue, he deepened the kiss and she knew she had to take the chance. She loved being held by him, kissed by him. And knowing that he wanted to spend a lifetime showing her how much he cared for her caused her heart to swell with more love than she'd ever thought possible.

When he finally broke the kiss, he leaned back to gaze at her and the love she saw in his eyes stole her breath. "There's something else we need to talk about," he said, smiling.

"What would that be?"

"Where we're going to live."

She worried her lower lip for a moment. She'd never imagined herself living anywhere but in the heart of Kentucky's horse-racing country. But as long as she, Mandy and Jake were together, she could live anywhere.

"I've never lived in a huge city." She took a deep breath. "But they have horses in California, too."

Giving her a smile that made her feel warm all over, he shook his head. "Don't get me wrong, I love California. It's one of the most beautiful places on earth. But I think I'd like to live right here."

"Really? Why?" She couldn't have been more surprised. "You told Hunter you were looking for a house in Malibu."

"That will be our vacation home. I want you to be able to continue making a name for yourself in the racing industry," he said. "You have a real knack for choosing bloodlines and producing champions. I want you to have the opportunity to build your reputation as the best in the business."

"I could do that in California."

He nodded. "That's true. But you've already made Hickory Hills a force to reckon with. Why not continue to build it into a racing empire?"

Loving him more with each passing second, she laid her head on his shoulder. "What about your law office? It's in Los Angeles and quite successful. Are you sure you want to give all of that up?"

"Honey, I can practice law anywhere." He shrugged. "But to tell you the truth, I'm tired of helping people end their marriages." He paused a moment. "I think I'd like to give being a gentleman farmer a try and help my wife raise her champion thoroughbreds." He laughed. "Besides, having me around all of the time is going to save you and Clara a lot of grief."

She sat up to stare at him. "I don't understand."

"Mandy can practice her food-fighting skills on me, instead of you." He smiled. "And Daily's a good kid, but he's a lot like I was at that age."

"Heaven help us," Heather said, rolling her eyes.

His low chuckle sent a shiver coursing through her. "No kidding. I think Clara is going to have her hands full when he gets a little older and could use the help."

"I know she'll appreciate it."

Content with being in each other's arms, they remained silent for some time before he spoke again. "You never did give me an answer, honey."

"About getting married?"

He nodded. "You said you love me, but you haven't officially accepted my proposal. Will you marry me, Heather McGwire?"

"Yes."

"How soon?" His grin was bright enough to light a small city. "We've already wasted a year being apart and I'd like to make you mine as soon as possible."

Before she could tell him that she wanted that, too, the sound of the front door opening and several people entering the house intruded.

"It appears that your family has made it back from the victory party."

"Good." He set her on her feet, then rose to take her by the hand. "Let's go share our news with them."

When they walked out of the study arm in arm, everyone fell silent and turned to look at them expectantly.

His eyes never leaving hers, he announced, "I've asked Heather to marry me and she said yes."

Apparently shocked by the news, silence reigned, then everyone seemed to start talking at once.

"I'm so happy for you both," Arielle said, rushing over to give both of them a hug.

Luke laughed. "I told you so, Jake."

"Have you set a date?" Hunter wanted to know.

Smiling, Heather shook her head. "We haven't gotten that far."

Jake kissed the top of her head. "It can't be soon enough for me. If I had my way, we'd be standing in front of a minister right now."

"Me, too," Heather said, gazing up at the only man she'd ever love.

"Do you mean that?" Alyssa asked, stepping forward.

When they both nodded, Heather watched the

women exchange a brief look a moment before Arielle spoke up, "We can do this, girls."

"Absolutely," Callie agreed. "Would tomorrow evening work for both of you?"

"Yes, but we can't possibly get ready in time," Heather said, disappointed. "Tomorrow is Sunday. We can't even get a marriage license until Monday."

"Don't underestimate this bunch," Haley said, laughing.

"Let's make a list." Cheyenne reached into her purse for a notepad and pen. "Nick, go get Emerald and Luther. We're going to need their help with this."

"Yes, ma'am," Nick said, his grin wide as he left the house.

When he returned with the elderly pair, Emerald breezed into the room in her satin and chiffon robe to hug Jake and Heather. "This is wonderful. I can't tell you how happy I am for you." Then, before Heather's eyes, the woman turned from a doting grandmother into a decisive, corporate giant on a mission. "Luther, find out who we know in the Louisville city government and get them to open the clerk's office first thing tomorrow morning so the kids can get their license."

Distinguished-looking even in his slippers and robe, the older gentleman gave a stiff nod. "Consider it done, madam."

Turning back to the group, Emerald continued, "Caleb, Hunter and Nick, call your nannies and babysitters and tell them my corporate jet will pick them and the children up by noon tomorrow. I want the entire family to be here for this. Luke, you and Zach are assigned to helping the girls with whatever they need to pull all of this together."

"Wow!" Heather could understand why Emerald Larson was the highly successful businesswoman she was. Seeing her in action was like watching a battlefield general direct his troops.

"Heather, dear, would you prefer the ceremony be performed here or do you have somewhere else in mind?" Emerald asked, smiling.

There was no question in Heather's mind. "Right here."

"Excellent. Indoors or outside?"

"I've always dreamed of coming down that staircase to meet my groom at the bottom of the steps," Heather answered, pointing toward the sweeping structure.

Jake gave her a tender smile. "And I'll be there waiting for you."

"Another excellent choice," Emerald approved. Turning to Heather's soon-to-be sisters-in-law, the woman grinned. "Divide up the list and get started first thing in the morning, girls. We have a wedding to get ready for tomorrow evening."

When Jake walked out of the master suite the next evening, Luke was waiting for him. "Are you ready to take the plunge?"

"I never thought I'd ever hear myself say this, but it can't be too soon," Jake admitted as they descended the stairs.

Taking his place at the bottom of the steps, he looked around. He'd never loved or appreciated his family more. They'd all worked hard to pull a wedding together on the spur of the moment and everything was picture-perfect. Heather was going to love it.

When the string quartet began to play, Jake's attention was drawn to the top of the stairs and the sight of his bride robbed him of breath. Heather was absolutely stunning. Her golden brown hair lay in soft curls around her bare shoulders and the white lace and antique satin wedding gown emphasized her enticing figure. But it was her radiant smile that he knew he'd never forget as long as he lived.

As she came down the circular staircase, he heard the baby start fussing, and walking over to Clara, took Mandy from her. Then, with his daughter in one arm, he extended his other to her beautiful mother and together they walked over to stand in front of the minister to exchange their vows and become the family he wanted with all of his heart and soul.

"Oh, Luther, I was so afraid this day might never happen," Emerald said as she dabbed her eyes with her linen handkerchief. "I was worried that Jake would turn out to be like his father and remain an irresponsible philanderer for the rest of his life."

"There was that possibility, madam," Luther agreed, nodding.

As she watched the minister pronounce Jake and Heather husband and wife, Emerald couldn't help but feel a bit sad. The investigative team she'd hired to find all of her grandchildren had concluded their search and they'd reported back that there were no more heirs to be found. Her family was finally complete.

When the group gathered in the foyer for pictures, Emerald motioned for Luther to join her. "You need to be in the picture, too, Luther. You've been instrumental in helping me find my heirs."

"It was my pleasure, madam," he said, walking over to stand at her side.

"You know, I'm going to miss helping my grand-children find their soul mates," she whispered wistfully as the photographer tried to get the children to stand still for the picture.

"You've done a fine job with that task, madam," Luther said, keeping his voice low as he patted her hand. "They've all made good matches."

"After all of the unhappiness that my son caused, I'm pleased that we were able to make everything right and give them all their rightful place in Emerald, Inc." Clasping his hand with hers, she gave it a little squeeze. "Now, I can concentrate on trying to find my own bliss."

He squeezed her hand back. "I don't think you'll have far to look, madam," he said gruffly.

Turning, she gave him a happy smile. "Neither do I, Luther. Neither do I."

Epilogue

One year later

"Do any of you have the slightest idea why we've been summoned to Wichita?" Jake looked at his brothers and brother-in-law expectantly as they sat in the family room at Emerald's Wichita mansion. When they all shook their heads, he shrugged. "Me neither."

"All she told me was our presence was mandatory," Luke said, setting the baby bottle down and shifting his six-month-old son to his shoulder to be burped.

"Yeah, I told her I had plans to go to a cattle

auction in Denver and she told me to cancel it," Nick added.

"Arielle has become pretty close to Emerald," Hunter said, looking thoughtful. "Does she know anything, Zach?"

"If she does, she didn't tell me," he said, glancing over to check on his eight-month-old twin boys sleeping peacefully in their baby carriers beside his chair.

"When are she and our wives supposed to return from their shopping trip?" Caleb asked. "All of the kids will be waking up from their naps pretty soon and it'll turn into a three-ring circus again."

Hunter grinned. "Yeah, with ten kids between us, it does get a little hairy sometimes."

"This time next year, there'll be eleven," Jake said proudly. "We just found out Heather is pregnant."

"Make that an even dozen," Nick said, laughing. "Cheyenne is pregnant again, too."

"More like a baker's dozen," Caleb added, grinning like a fool. "Alyssa is close to entering her second trimester."

As they all congratulated each other, Emerald, Luther and their wives walked into the room. "I would imagine you're all wondering why I've asked you here for the weekend," Emerald said, smiling.

"It's crossed our minds a time or two," Luke said dryly.

When Heather walked over to sit on the arm of the chair beside him, Jake put his arm around her waist and gazed up at her. He couldn't believe how happy he'd been in the past year. Marrying her was the best thing he'd ever done. He loved her more with each passing day.

"I have a couple of announcements to make that will have a direct impact on all of you," she said, seating herself in an empty armchair.

"You have our attention," Jake said, watching Luther move to stand beside Emerald. Something was definitely up. Normally as stiff as a board, Jake had never seen the old gent look so relaxed.

"I'm retiring," Emerald said without preamble.

Jake was certain he could have heard a pin drop in the suddenly silent room. The first to find his voice, he asked, "When?"

"Next month." She paused to let the information sink in, then added, "And I'm appointing all of you to the Emerald, Inc. board of directors. I'll maintain ten percent of my stock, but the other ninety percent will be divided equally between my six grandchildren."

"Are you sure you want to do this?" Arielle asked, clearly concerned. "You started out with a home business fifty years ago and built Emerald, Inc. into a corporate empire. It's been your life."

Emerald smiled serenely. "I'm getting ready to enter a new chapter in my life."

"What are you up to this time?" Hunter asked, grinning.

Jake watched her glance at Luther and for the first time since he met the older man, Luther grinned.

"Your grandmother is going to do me the honor of becoming my bride," Luther said, placing his hand on her shoulder.

"We'll be getting married right after we both retire," Emerald said, placing her hand on Luther's. "Then we intend to take an extended honeymoon and travel the world. So I'm counting on all of you to see that Emerald, Inc. remains solid and the gold standard for corporate excellence."

After everyone expressed their surprise and promised not to let their grandmother down, Jake spoke up. "I think I speak for all of us when I say we wish you every happiness. If not for you and Luther, I might never have found Heather and Mandy."

Each of his siblings agreed that if not for Emerald and her matchmaking they might not have found their spouses and true happiness.

"Is there anything we can do to help get ready for your wedding?" Haley asked.

Jake didn't think he'd ever seen a brighter smile on his grandmother's face. "As a matter of fact, there is, dear. You all did such a wonderful job with Jake and Heather's wedding that Luther and I were wondering if you'd all like to plan ours."

"I think that's our cue to retire to the media room, boys," Hunter said, rising to his feet. "The Astros are playing the Cardinals this afternoon."

"If you don't mind, I'd quite like to join you," Luther said, surprising all of them. He kissed Emerald's cheek. "If you'll excuse me, my dear. I think I'll attempt to 'bond,' as the younger generation are so fond of saying, with my future grandsons."

"There just might be hope for you yet, Luther," Jake said, standing to shake the older man's hand.

To his surprise, Luther actually winked. "I have twenty that says the Cardinals win. Anyone want to place a little wager?"

As Emerald watched her grandsons and the man who had stood by her side for over forty years leave to watch the ball game together, she smiled contentedly. In her day, children born out of wedlock had been considered illegitimate and in some cases went unclaimed by their families. But she'd never considered her grandchildren illegitimate. She'd searched high and low to find them and now her life was filled with more happiness than she'd ever thought possible.

She'd done everything in her power to help each one of them discover their own happiness, and to her immense satisfaction they had.

* * * * *

&Desire™

WEDDING AT KING'S CONVENIENCE by Maureen Child

When a night of passion leads to pregnancy, film exec Jefferson proposes a marriage of convenience. But Maura, his bride-to-be, refuses to settle for anything less than love.

BEDDING THE SECRET HEIRESS by Emilie Rose

When Gage hires a female private pilot, he's looking for proof Lauren's after his friend's money. Neither expects the sparks that fly between them at thirty thousand feet!

THE MAVERICK'S VIRGIN MISTRESS by Jennifer Lewis

Tycoon Rick has met the perfect woman. But when he offers her protection in his posh penthouse, will Alicia discover their relationship is built on a lie?

LONE STAR SEDUCTION by Day Leclaire

Alex Montoya can't allow himself to fall for the one woman who nearly destroyed his empire…no matter how much he still wants Rebecca.

THE MAGNATE'S BABY PROMISE by Paula Roe

This eligible bachelor must marry and produce an heir. So when Cal discovers his one-night affair with Ava left her pregnant, he claims mum and baby as his own.

HAVING THE BILLIONAIRE'S BABY by Sandra Hyatt

After one hot night with his sister's enemy, Nick's stunned when Callie reveals she's carrying his baby!

On sale from 17th September 2010
Don't miss out!

*Available at WHSmith, Tesco, ASDA, Eason
and all good bookshops*

www.millsandboon.co.uk

0910/51

2 FREE BOOKS
AND A SURPRISE GIFT

We would like to take this opportunity to thank you for reading this Mills & Boon® book by offering you the chance to take TWO more specially selected books from the Desire™ 2-in-1 series absolutely FREE! We're also making this offer to introduce you to the benefits of the Mills & Boon® Book Club™—

- **FREE home delivery**
- **FREE gifts and competitions**
- **FREE monthly Newsletter**
- **Exclusive Mills & Boon Book Club offers**
- **Books available before they're in the shops**

Accepting these FREE books and gift places you under no obligation to buy, you may cancel at any time, even after receiving your free books. Simply complete your details below and return the entire page to the address below. You don't even need a stamp!

YES Please send me 2 free Desire stories in a 2-in-1 volume and a surprise gift. I understand that unless you hear from me, I will receive 2 superb new 2-in-1 books every month for just £5.25 each, postage and packing free. I am under no obligation to purchase any books and may cancel my subscription at any time. The free books and gift will be mine to keep in any case.

Ms/Mrs/Miss/Mr _____ Initials _____

_____

Surname _____

Address _____

_____

_____ Postcode _____

E-mail_____

Send this whole page to: Mills & Boon Book Club, Free Book Offer, FREEPOST NAT 10298, Richmond, TW9 1BR